BIKER

OTHER BOOKS BY JERRY LANGTON

BIKER

INSIDE THE NOTORIOUS WORLD
OF AN OUTLAW MOTORCYCLE GANG

JERRY LANGTON

HARPERCOLLINS PUBLISHERS LTD

Published by HarperCollins Publishers Ltd

Originally published by John Wiley & Sons Canada, Ltd.: 2009

First published by HarperCollins Publishers Ltd in this
trade paperback edition and an EPub edition: 2013

HarperCollins Publishers Ltd
2 Bloor Street East, 20th Floor
Toronto, Ontario, Canada
M4W 1A8

www.harpercollins.ca

Library and Archives Canada Cataloguing in Publication
information is available upon request

ISBN 978-1-44342-809-5

Printed and bound in the United States of America
RRD 9 8 7 6 5 4

To my own little gang: Tonia, Damian, and Hewitt

CHAPTER 1

Even though his girlfriend was gyrating on stage completely nude, Steve Schultz wasn't paying any attention. The former Miss Nude Springfield—who went by the name of Lexus onstage and Connie Horvath away from it—was doing her best to be seductive, but Steve was busy with something he considered far more pressing. He was in the middle of a meeting with his two most trusted confidantes—Warren "Lizard" Lessard and Daniel "Bamm Bamm" Johansson—and one of his most promising young newcomers, Ned Aiken.

The subject was a phone card scam. Steve had fake long-distance phone cards printed in Thailand and he marketed them through convenience stores in Toronto, across the border. The immigrants who bought them were desperate for a bargain, and too scared of the authorities to raise a fuss when they discovered that Steve's cards didn't actually connect to anything.

Unlike Steve, the rest of the patrons of Foxes Gentlemen's Club (known throughout town as "the Strip") were eating up Connie's act. Connie was exactly what they had come for. She was tall and blonde. But under the harsh light at Foxes, her natural blonde hair darkened and appeared light brown, so she dyed it nearly white. Away from the stage, it looked harsh and unnatural, but that's not where she made her money. She was painfully thin. You could easily count her ribs from behind. The view from the front was a different story. A former boyfriend, intent on advancing her career, had sprung for radical breast augmentation surgery. Distinct lines ran down from her sternum and they ended a few inches below her ribcage. The implants in no way resembled actual breasts—and the crowd adored them.

Calling the collected patrons at Foxes a crowd might be too ambitious. There was seventy-one-year-old Hank, who sat silently in the back of the bar, three shy Chinese teenagers who popped up the collars of their golf shirts and sipped long-necked Buds, and Buddy, a morbidly obese kid with a learning disability who cleaned the place and worked the dishwasher in exchange for not having to pay a cover charge or order drinks.

Steve didn't own Foxes. The actual owner was a wealthy man named Myron Fishman whose luck was in decline. Myron had made his considerable fortune manufacturing cardboard boxes. He had retired to Florida not long after Steve made his first appearance at Foxes in the company of Lessard and Johansson, who were decked out in full Death Dealer colours—complete with club patches that featured a skull in a top hat with four aces and a joker tucked into the brim. Now Steve had the run of the place.

A full-patch member of America's largest bike gang, the Sons of Satan, Schultz had been hand picked by the gang's national president, Ivan Mehelnechuk, to bring the ragtag assembly of Springfield's bikers under the Sons' control. The larger goal was to wrest the city's drug and prostitution rackets out of the hands of their biggest rival, the Lawbreakers, who had adopted the Satan's Own, a proudly independent local club, as their Springfield chapter.

Many of the disenfranchised and disillusioned local bikers approached the Death Dealers when word spread that they were now headed by a bona fide Son of Satan. Steve had earned his nickname "Hollywood." He was handsome, he was larger than life, and he never, ever stopped talking about himself. Steve wasn't from Springfield and he never let the other guys forget it. He had moved there when he was fifteen, then left to enjoy a successful career with the Sons of Satan in Mehelnechuk's power base of Martinsville. While Martinsville was a fairly large city by Midwestern standards, it was hardly cosmopolitan. Steve's brash worldliness stood out.

Steve was actually from Bay Ridge, a quiet, residential neighborhood full of tree-lined streets in the south side of Brooklyn. It has more in common with the New Jersey suburbs than the mean streets people associate with Brooklyn, but that didn't matter to the guys in Springfield. In their minds, Steve was a New Yorker with all the rights and privileges that held. And he knew how to play it up. He'd go from spouting a ridiculous parody of Brooklynese ("dese," "dose," and "dem") to speaking in overly complicated English—sometimes in the same sentence—whenever he thought it would give him a psychological advantage.

He hadn't wanted to go back to Springfield. He considered it being sent to the minors—going to the boondocks to babysit a bunch of idiot yokels. But Mehelnechuk painted an entirely different picture of the Springfield assignment. Steve wouldn't be a babysitter, the boss assured him; he would be a general, heroically carrying the Sons of Satan banner into a war he was sure to win. Ivan also, subtly, indicated that once the city was secured, it would be his to plunder. Schultz readily accepted and, in a short time, he had achieved impressive results.

By the night on which he spoke with Lessard, Johansson and young Ned Aiken, Steve had turned the Death Dealers into the Sons "puppet" club and made them a force to be reckoned with in Springfield.

As they discussed the nuts and bolts of the phone-card scam, Connie's show was coming to a close. "Let's have a big hand for Lexus. Lexus, everyone," the DJ intoned as Connie crawled around the stage on all fours picking up the crumpled bills that had been thrown at her. There were a few minutes of awkward silence as the DJ waited until she was finished before starting his spiel to introduce the next dancer.

There was a smattering of applause. Most of it came from two guys who stumbled in halfway through Connie's act, when she was already nude. Jason Sugarman and Tyler Heath barely knew each other. They were junior employees at a local television station who had stumbled into Foxes toward the end of six-hour binge following a work function earlier that day.

Tyler, who was drunker, got right into it. Connie, or "Lexus" as he knew her, was exactly what he imagined "his type" to be and he fell for her act. Once he had gathered enough nerve, he abandoned Jason and took a seat up close to the stage. He lured Connie over to his area with five and ten dollar bills and very nearly touched her a few times. When she left the stage, he applauded loudly and even hooted a few times before returning to his seat beside Jason, whose anxiety was obvious.

The DJ threw on a song with heavy synthesized bass. As it got louder and louder, he growled into the microphone: "Gentlemen . . . please put your hands together for Destiny . . . Destiny joining us for her first time at Foxes, gentlemen, it's Desssssssssssssstiny."

Lessard nudged Ned, and said, "You may want to watch this." And pointed at the stage.

Destiny was none other than Ned's girlfriend Kelli. She was dressed in what appeared to be a hard plastic corset and matching miniskirt, and was prancing nervously around the stage. She studiously avoided eye contact with any of the men.

Ned was shocked to see her there, but did his best not to let the other bikers notice.

The crowd gave her the benefit of the doubt through the first song, but began to get restless during the second. Tyler voiced their disappointment with her unwillingness to take her clothes off. "Take it off, you fuckin' bitch!" he shouted. "I didn't come here to see your fuckin' face!"

Jason tried to get him to simmer down but that actually egged him on more. "Look you fuckin' skank, I paid my fuckin' money and I came here to see some skin, not some dancing," Tyler shouted as he imitated Kelli's tentative steps. "Do your fuckin' job!"

Kelli, who was extremely nervous to start with, lost it. She retreated to the back of the stage and started crying.

"Jesus fuckin' Christ," said Tyler with an exaggerated flourish of frustration. "Do I have to come up there and show you what you have to do? Do I?" With that, he put his right foot up on stage and prepared to climb on.

That was enough for Ned. He bolted for the stage. Lessard started to go after the kid, but Steve grabbed him.

Ned was no bigger than Tyler, but a lot stronger. He seized him by the shirt with his left hand and threw him back into his chair. He didn't say anything. Ned turned to look at Kelli, but she looked away. While he had his back turned, Tyler lunged at him, hitting him in the hip with his shoulders. Ned bounced off the stage as Tyler slipped and landed in a heap. Enraged, Tyler got back up and let out something of a roar as he lunged back at Ned. Instinctively, Ned grabbed a beer bottle by the neck and slammed it into the back of Tyler's head as hard as he could. Tyler went down hard and didn't get back up again.

Everyone was silent. The DJ cut the music. Kelli ran off the stage. Two dancers came out of the change room to see what was going on, then turned around and went back. The Chinese guys with the turned up collars ran out of the building and down the street. Grizzled old Hank remained seated at his place in back and pretended to have suddenly acquired an interest in Major League Baseball as it played on the bar monitor. Buddy looked at his feet and waited for it all to be over.

Jason was in shock. He couldn't talk, couldn't move. Ned sprang past him to see what condition Tyler was in. He'd landed face-first on the lip of the stage, chipping both of his front incisors, then had fallen on his right side on the tiled floor. A pool of thick, dark blood was slowly widening around the back of his head. Ned put his hand under Tyler's head to take a look at his face. He was surprised at how light it felt, how little resistance his neck gave to his lifting and turning of Tyler's head. The skin on Tyler's face was a pale color Ned had never seen before, almost blue. His eyes were rolled up into his head so that only the white showed. Ned instinctively knew that if Tyler wasn't already dead, he would be soon and that nothing could stop it from happening.

Without thinking, he turned at looked at Jason. When their eyes met, Jason snapped out of his trance.

"You killed him!" he shouted. "You fucking killed my friend! Call an ambulance! Somebody call the police!"

Annoyed, Steve excused himself from what remained of his meeting and walked over to the scene. Johansson followed him. Steve then put his arm around Jason, turned him away from Ned and Tyler, and said: "Don't worry, son, your friend is going to be fine; why don't you come with my associate here and we'll take care of your friend." Steve then turned to Johansson and said, "You make sure our friend here has everything he needs, I'll initiate CPR and call the police and ambulance."

Johansson put his arm around Jason and led him to a door behind the bar that had an "employees only" sign taped to it. Confused and frightened, Jason neither struggled nor agreed; he simply complied.

Once Jason was out of the room, Steve stepped over to where Ned was still holding Tyler. "It's a shame when these drunks fall over and hurt themselves—but accidents do happen," he announced, loud enough for everyone to hear. Buddy laughed nervously. "Alright, let's clean him up; until we're done here, everybody gets a free trip to the VIP room and two . . . no, three free drinks."

As the patrons and dancers filed out of the room, Lessard went to guard the bar's front door and Steve dialed his cell phone. Ned couldn't make out exactly what he was saying, but he could tell that he was ordering someone to come to the bar immediately. He understood from his tone that Steve was more exasperated than worried.

When Steve finally hung up and came over to Ned, he just glared at him.

"I'm sorry, man . . ." Ned began.

Steve wouldn't let him finish. "I'll say you're sorry," he scolded. "You are indeed a very, very sorry sight." He shook his head and rolled his eyes. "Not only do you kill a guy in my bar, making a huge fucking mess, but you did it in front of witnesses," he continued. "And do you know what the worst part of it is? You did it over a fucking woman. What an asshole. You should know by now no woman is ever worth putting yourself in danger for."

"I—I think he's still breathing; maybe we should call an ambulance."

Steve sucked air between his clenched teeth. "Uh—that's not going to happen," Steve shook his head. "He's dead, or just about—he's way too far gone. Even if by some medical miracle they kept his heart and lungs going, he'd be a fucking vegetable—and nobody should have to live like that."

"So what do we do?"

"Well," Steve paused. "I guess it's up to you to put him out of his misery."

"Kill him? I can't do that. I've never..."

"Sure you have—you've actually already killed this guy," Steve told him. "All you're doing now is making it easier for everyone, including him."

"How do I do it?"

"Do I have to do everything around here?" Steve asked, as though Ned were a petulant child who refused to clean his room. "I would suggest you do it quickly and quietly—look, he's not moving, never will again—just put a damp cloth over his mouth and nose to cut off his breathing."

Ned walked over to the bar and grabbed the bar rag. He went back to Tyler and held the white cloth—already stained red from the blood on Ned's hands—to the young man's nose and mouth.

Just as Ned began to apply pressure, he heard a loud bang. Startled, Ned dropped the rag and fell backwards into a table, knocking it, and three chairs, over.

Steve started laughing. The noise had come from some of his men—Dario Gagliano, Dave Peters, and "Little" John Rautins—coming into the bar to help. Gagliano had a habit of making big entrances, and he kicked the bar's outside door open. He figured that the situation inside the bar would be tense and thought it would be funny to scare the shit out of whoever was in there.

Lessard positioned himself by the door. Gagliano immediately recognized what was going on. Although many in the Death Dealers considered him a total asshole, he had a knack for acting without fear or remorse in tough situations. He was a bold and decisive man, and that's why Steve depended on him for jobs like this. "Looks like we had a little accident," he said, laughing at his own half-joke.

"Don't step in," Steve said. "He's got to take care of this himself."

Ned, surrounded by the other men, knew he had to go through with what he started. He picked up the bar rag and held it over Tyler's nose and mouth. He pressed silently for about two minutes. Tyler convulsed once.

"Dude," Peters said quietly, "I think he's done."

Everybody but Ned laughed.

"Okay, now for the hard part," Steve said, once they all quieted. He instructed Peters and Rautins to clean up the place. They both knew the drill and started unpacking the mops and sponges from a nearby closet, complaining all the while.

Ned sat in a chair. He just wanted to sit and collect his thoughts. Steve wouldn't allow it. "Get up, lover boy," he ordered. "You made this mess, you have to take care of it— pick him up and follow me." Without looking back, Steve went back to the employee washroom.

"Well, pick him up," said Gagliano impatiently. Ned put his arms under Tyler's neck and legs. "Not like that, faggot!" Gagliano shouted. "He's not your girlfriend—over your shoulder." Peters and Rautins laughed. Ned complied.

He followed Gagliano into the room Steve was in and paused. "Throw him in there, asshole," Gagliano growled, pointing at the bathtub. Steve sighed in an exaggerated display of exasperation. Ned had always wondered why Foxes had a bathtub in the employee washroom. He originally assumed it was for the dancers, but they had their own washroom attached to their change room. He placed Tyler down in the tub.

"Yeah, put him down gently," Gagliano scoffed. "You don't want to hurt him."

Regaining his composure, Ned looked at Gagliano. "Okay, what do we do next?"

"'We' don't do shit; other than watch you clean up the mess you made. Here." He handed Ned a knapsack. "The head and hands go in this. Tie up the rest and wrap it in this chicken wire—you'll find the wire cutters . . . uh . . . over here—then wrap it in a blanket and come get me."

He got up to leave, and turned his head. "Don't come out until you're done," he cautioned. "And clean yourself up for Christ's sake."

He tossed Ned a large black garbage bag, and then threw in a T-shirt, tan canvas pants, socks, shoes, and a faded blue sweatshirt. "Put all your clothes in the bag, and throw this stuff on when you're done," he said. "You can keep your underwear."

As Steve headed into the VIP room, he saw Kelli, who had put her street clothes back on, leaving the bar. He didn't try to stop her. He asked Peters how long it would take them to get the bar back in shape. They told him forty-five minutes. He grabbed a beer and went into the VIP room.

Back in the washroom, Ned asked Gagliano if he had ever done this sort of thing before. "Sure," he answered. "It's part of the job." Ned offered him five hundred dollars if he'd do it for him now. Gagliano laughed. "No fuckin' way—Steve said you had to do it, so do it." Though trying to sound amiable, his speech still came out threatening. "Besides, you should keep your money; there are a lot of people helping you out tonight—including me—and they are all going to expect something in return." He turned pensive. "Think about it, Peters and Little Johnny are in there cleaning up the blood and shit you spilled, and I'm in here teaching your stupid ass how to stay out of jail, ya stupid fuck." He laughed. "If you were a full member, no problem, we'd do it out of love; but you aren't and if you don't smarten up, you never will be—so get cutting."

Ned picked up the hacksaw, lined it up on Tyler's right wrist and started to cut. "You're probably gonna need a couple of blades to get through—gets tough when you hit the bone."

Gagliano stood back to let Ned get on with the job, then asked, "So what's the deal with you, anyway?"

"Whaddaya mean?"

"You know what I mean. I know you work for Steve and I hear you make good money," he paused, and then he lost interest before the kid could answer.

"Ah, don't worry about it," He waved off his question and went back to instructing Ned on the proper way to disassemble a corpse.

***

After closing, Johansson, Lessard, Gagliano, Peters, and Ned sat silently at the bar drinking beer. Nobody felt much like talking. Steve came out of the VIP room and approached them. "You know what you gotta do," he said. "So go do it; I'm headed home."

Peters stood up. "I feel like partying," he said. "Who's coming to my place?"

Everyone left with him, except Gagliano and Ned.

"Okay, lover boy, let's go," Gagliano said. "We got some work to do; I'll pull the car around and you bring out the package."

Ned winced and ran his fingers through his hair. But he knew he had to do what he had to do. He went back into the washroom and assessed the package—or packag*es* to be more precise. Tyler's head and hands were in a knapsack, his body was wrapped in chicken wire, and a blanket and Ned's own clothes were in a garbage bag. Ned correctly assumed that the head and hands were separated from the rest of the body because they were much easier to identify. Put together in a smaller package, they would be much easier to dispose of than an entire body. The body, without its head and hands, could be just about anyone.

He tried to pick up the body and couldn't. The chicken wire had not only made him much heavier, but had also stiffened him, making him a much more awkward package. Ned grabbed the knapsack and the garbage bag and headed outside.

Gagliano was waiting for him in the driver's seat of a black, six-year-old GMC Jimmy. Ned motioned for him to lower the passenger-side window. "It's too heavy," he said.

Gagliano couldn't hear him. He was listening to Black Sabbath's "Paranoid" at full volume.

Ned shouted again. "The body—it's too heavy!"

Gagliano put his index finger up, indicating that he wanted Ned to wait until the song was over. Once he was satisfied it was, he turned the radio down. "Alright," he said. "What is it?"

A chill went up Ned's spine. He was standing at the corner of Cannon and Wellington, one of the busiest intersections in the city during the day. Sure, the only people on the streets at this time of night were the homeless, and cars only went by every two minutes or so, but the cops could happen by at any second.

Gagliano snapped him out of it. "What . . . the . . . fuck . . . is the problem?" he shouted.

"The body is too heavy," Ned said. "I can't lift it by myself."

"Do you mind my saying that you are the biggest fucking pussy in the whole wide world?" Gagliano shouted. "It's not like he was Robert Earl Hughes!"

"Who?"

"Robert Earl Hughes." Gagliano was pissed. "Fattest man who ever lived—fourteen hundred pounds. Look at *The Guinness Book of World Records*, you idiot. He was buried in a piano case. Everybody knows that, you stupid asshole."

"Okay, fine, he's not Bob Hughes or whatever the fuck his name is," Ned replied. "But he is too heavy for me to move, and if you want to get him out of the bar, you are gonna help me."

Gagliano knew he had no choice. He sighed, turned the ignition off, and turned the hazard lights on. He started laughing. "You are a fuckin' mother fuckin' son of a cocksucking whore," he said while opening the tailgate. "Throw that shit in there and I will help you, you fucking little girl you."

Ned threw the bag into the back of the truck. He realized it was a human head and hands and, he also realized, he didn't give a damn anymore. "Just get your faggot ass in there, cocksucker." Gagliano patted him on the back and laughed.

Inside, Gagliano grabbed Tyler's feet and Ned grabbed his shoulders. Gagliano admitted that he was kind of heavy after all.

As they went out the door, Ned asked his partner if he was scared of being caught. "Not really," he answered while throwing the package into the back of the truck. "If the cops stop us, they have to ask if they can search and I can say no."

"Really?"

"Yup, unless they have probable cause," Gagliano said. "And unless you wrapped him all fucked up, with a foot or something sticking out, we have nothing to worry about." He sat on the back bumper and passed Ned a joint he'd just fired up. "Besides, most of the cops around here know better than to fuck with Steve."

Inside the car, Gagliano turned the radio back on. It was a commercial for discount furniture. "I know that fucker," he said. "Gay as a French trombone. All I have to do is not tell his wife about his little boyfriend and I get $250 a month; fucker even gave me a nice dining-room table for Christmas." He laughed. Ned joined in.

After about ten minutes in which they talked mostly about sports, Gagliano pulled up in a gravel parking lot near the lake. Ned remembered when he took Kelli to the very same spot to make out. He laughed when he remembered how freaked out she was by all the dead fish. "Uh, Dare, we can't get rid of him here; he'll just wash back up again tomorrow," he said.

"You know what I like about you? No matter how fuckin' stupid I think you are, you can always say something that will amaze me," he said. "The beach is on that side, the canal is on that side."

Above all, Springfield is a port town. While most of the population knows "the point" as a wooded area with a beach, they rarely think of the other side of the peninsula. But that's the important part. Facing Springfield Harbor, the west side of the peninsula—what locals call "the canal"—drops off sixty feet straight down to allow the mooring of giant Great Lakes freighters. But since the steel business has been slow in Springfield for the last decade or so, the west side is now generally occupied by a few rusting tugs and thirty thousand or so gulls.

Again, Gagliano grabbed Tyler's feet and Ned took the other end. The walk through the woods took maybe three minutes. Gagliano clearly knew the way. Ned was surprised by the view from the west side of the point. The factories, massive and reaching upward, had a strange beauty. He marveled at the huge, purple and blue flames the steel plants spat out. When they finally got to the water's edge, Gagliano told him to put him down.

They sat, one on each side of Tyler. Gagliano lit another joint and leaned back on Tyler's body, using his chicken-wire-wrapped thighs as a makeshift pillow. "This is where Steve's genius comes in," he said.

Ned asked him what he meant. "Remember when we were at war with the Chain Masters?" he said. "Well, Marcus O'Brien—the old boss, before Steve—had four of them put down. He told his men to get rid of them, so they put each one in a sleeping bag—you know, like for camping—weighted them down with bricks and threw them in the harbor."

"Yeah?"

"Well, a few weeks later they started floating to the surface—the fuckin' sleeping bags disintegrated in the filthy polluted water," he continued. "The bodies were black and bloated, but were all easily identifiable—six friends of ours are in jail, went to prison, and Marcus ran away to Thailand or some other fuckin' place."

He took a long drag on the joint and offered it to Ned. Ned was grateful and took the hit. "But Steve learned from that," Gagliano told him. "He wraps them in chicken wire—the fuckin' stuff not only weighs them down, but allows the catfish and suckers and other fuckin' bottom feeders to eat them piece by piece. A week later, there's nothin' but bones surrounded by rusty wire." He laughed. "They're like piranhas, those fuckers—got a taste for human flesh." He flicked the butt of his joint into the water as though he saw a particularly fearsome catfish just beneath the surface.

With that, he stood up and Ned understood he meant to throw Tyler into the water. When they had each grabbed an end, Ned asked: "On three?" Gagliano agreed.

Ned threw on three; Gagliano was a beat late. Tyler's body bounced off the concrete ledge but eventually disappeared under the black water with a cascade of bubbles. Gagliano wiped his hands together triumphantly and said, "That's that."

"What about the knapsack and the garbage bag?" Ned asked.

"Aw fuck," Gagliano replied. "I fuckin' forgot. Good thing you were here. C'mon, follow me."

They went back to the car, and Gagliano drove Ned home. "Don't forget your package," Gagliano said, holding up the knapsack.

"What the fuck? I thought you were going to take care of it."

"Uh uh, it's yours; I'll throw the garbage bag in a dumpster, but the knapsack is all yours," he laughed. "We'll take care of it tomorrow—right now, I'm going to sleep; see you in the morning."

Ned didn't have a lot of choice; he grabbed the knapsack and carried it into the house. It was close to four a.m., and he was dead tired. Kelli wasn't there, but that didn't really surprise him. Whenever they argued, she would stay over at her friend Mallory's.

He went downstairs and opened up the freezer. Kelli's uncle had given them his old freezer when he got a new one. But Ned wasn't really into buying great quantities of frozen meat, so it was usually empty or close to it. He opened the door and threw the knapsack in. He turned to go upstairs, but changed his mind and lay down on an old couch next to the freezer. It was too short for him—he was six-foot-one—and it had a broken spring. But it beat the floor, and he wasn't leaving the basement as long as the knapsack was still there.

As tired as he was, Ned just couldn't sleep. The cops had never come to his house before, but he couldn't stop thinking that he had been seen. Gagliano was so calm, so sure of himself that he seemed sure they'd never get caught. Maybe, Ned thought to himself, Gagliano was more sloppy and foolish than confident. Ned knew that he'd been to jail at least a couple of times before, so he couldn't be all that smart. And, if he was so confident he wasn't going to be caught, why did he make him take the knapsack?

All those thoughts and more kept tumbling around in Ned's head all night and well into the morning. Although he never really fell completely asleep, he was about halfway there most of the time. He rose twice to check on the knapsack. Although he was relieved to see it was there both times, he also wished it wasn't there, that it had all never happened. The third time he woke up, he didn't even get close to sleep again.

From about 9:10 until 10:15, he did nothing but stare at the freezer. The doorbell knocked him out of his trance. He raced to the basement's front window and looked outside. He could see Gagliano's car and boots.

Ned ran up the stairs and to the front door. He looked out the window to see if Gagliano was alone. He was. He saw Ned and waved goofily. Ned opened the door and Gagliano walked in. "Nice place here, a little feminine, but not too bad," he said. Ned ignored him. Gagliano waited. "So, no coffee? No eggs? Not even a hello?" he complained. Then he sat on Ned's couch and looked him up and down. "You look like a huge pile of shit—rough night?"

"Rough night? You try . . ." Ned realized what he was saying was ridiculous. He could tell from Gagliano's face, demeanor, and conversation that sleeping next to a severed head and hands was not a huge deal for him—or anything new. Ned forced out a laugh. "I didn't get a ton of sleep; fuckin' couch down the basement."

"She sent you down the basement?"

Ned wondered how to answer that. A number of bikers had shown disgust at how pussy-whipped they thought he was. He knew Gagliano had done some research on him and didn't want to reinforce any negative opinions.

"No, I just wanted to make sure the package was safe."

"Don't be such a fuckin' dork all the time; it wasn't going to walk away by itself ."

"I know, I know, but it makes me nervous—can we get moving?"

"Yeah, sure, but Vladimir doesn't leave for work until twelve-thirty, so we should probably get a bite to eat first—bring your new friend along."

"No fuckin' way!" Ned protested. "What if we get caught? What if it starts to smell?"

"We won't get caught; didn't you wrap it in plastic? I know you did. I saw you do it." Gagliano shrugged in exasperation. "Where is it now?"

"In the freezer . . . downstairs."

"In a fuckin' freezer all night and you think it'll smell—like what, hamburger? You are such a fuckin' chickenshit. Grab the bag, grow a pair, get in the car, and take me to Smitty's; I'm starving."

Ned laughed, hit his friend on the arm, and headed downstairs. Gagliano shouted after him: "And bring money, lots of money—you've got some people to pay."

When he returned, Gagliano laughed at him. "So you keep your cash in the bedroom? Bad idea, first place I'd look."

They drove about five minutes to a family-style restaurant. Gagliano knew the waitress. She was a heavyset woman in her middle forties, although she looked somewhat older. She was ordinary in just about every way, although an ace of spades tattoo on her left wrist betrayed some wayward history.

"What's good today, baby?" Gagliano asked. "Besides you?"

"How about the usual?" she said. "And what will your friend have?"

"Nothing, just coffee," Ned muttered.

"Bullshit!" Gagliano shouted, disturbing a nearby table of elderly ladies. "Get him two eggs over easy, bacon, home fries, white toast, coffee, and orange juice—I have to order for him, sweet pea; I'm still teaching him to be a man."

The waitress looked at Ned. He returned her gaze sheepishly and said, "Yeah, yeah, that's fine, but could you make it grapefruit juice instead?"

After the waitress left, Gagliano started scolding Ned much the way Steve had. "You act like this has all been thrust upon you when you actually did it all yourself and we are just helping you out," he said. "We know what we're doing. You have to trust us; it's your only safe way out of a situation you created—so suck it up, grow some fuckin' nuts, and do what the fuck I say."

"You're right; I know you're right," Ned said. "I just wish it never happened."

"Wish in one hand and shit in the other—see which fills up first."

"Yeah, you're right."

"Damn right I am."

"So what happens next, I mean ..." he cut himself off when the waitress returned with their drinks.

"Thanks darling," Gagliano said, unconcerned by what else she may have heard. "Well, we take your package over to Vladimir's and he gets rid of it; then you show your gratitude to some of the people who helped you out last night."

"And that's it?"

"That's it."

Gagliano then shot Ned a look that made him feel even worse. "What's the deal on you?" he asked.

"What do you mean?"

"You show up, you're a big earner like the next day," he said. "No offense or nothing—but the rest of us had to come up through the pipe."

"The pipe?"

"Yeah, the fuckin' pipe," Gagliano was clearly getting angry. "I started hanging out with these guys when I was thirteen; I wasn't even in high school and I got a guy to weld an extra couple of forks onto my bike to make it into a chopper."

He paused. "Yeah, I wanted to be a biker even back then— hell, younger'n that, maybe even—nine, ten." He was really getting into it now. "I wore a fake leather vest and used to give myself tattoos with a ballpoint pen."

"Yeah, so?"

"So, I worked my way up, first as a lookout, then a messenger boy, then a delivery boy—just like everyone else," he said. "And here you are, just showed up one day and you're dealing big right out of the box."

"Hey, I had to earn it."

"Like fuck you did," he said. "The rest of us really had to earn it, doing all kinds of hard work for the members—beating up witnesses, setting fires, robbing warehouses—you ever do any of that shit?"

"No."

"Didn't think so—but we all did; they treated us like slaves, kicking our asses for years until we earned their respect and got to do some pushing around of our own," he said. "And your waltzing in the way you did hasn't exactly made you that popular with the boys."

"What do you mean?"

"Well, I ain't gonna name any names, but some people have raised some suspicions about you," he said.

"Suspicions? Like what?"

"One guy thought you might be a cop, but that's ridiculous—you're too young and I've seen you smoke weed, and cops can't do that, even undercover."

"Of course I'm not a . . ."

"Yeah, but that doesn't mean you're not an informant," Gagliano pressed on. "Y'know, maybe you got in a little trouble at school and you thought you could deliver them Steve or one of us to save your ass . . ."

Ned felt like punching him, after all he'd been through, but he knew it was the worst thing he could do at the moment. Instead, he let him trail off, letting the obvious question hang in the air like a cloud.

"Do you believe that?" he finally offered.

"Not after last night," Gagliano laughed.

There was little Ned could do but grin goofily.

"But I am telling you here and now that there are people in our little group who don't like you, don't trust you, and are keeping their eyes on you," Gagliano said. "One of them especially does not like you."

"Who?"

"That will make itself clear in time," he said. "Now eat your fuckin' eggs before I do."

When they finished their meal, the waitress placed the bill in front of Ned. "Lesson number . . . actually, I've lost count of how many lessons I've taught you today—anyway, this lesson is that I never pay for fuck all," Gagliano grinned.

"That's true," added the waitress. "He never pays."

"Leave her a big fuckin' tip."

Back in the car, Ned noticed they were driving back to

the city's north end, where the steel factories are. The houses here were mostly small and falling apart, and the air was thick with soot from the giant blast furnaces. "Yeah, Vladimir will totally fuckin' take care of you, but there are some ground rules," Gagliano said. "First is never disagree with him, and never, ever make fun of him, his house, or anything at all associated with ... actually, y'know what would work best? Why don't you just keep your mouth shut; maybe say 'thank you' or something."

"Sounds like a bit of a psycho."

"You are paying the man to dispose of a severed head and hands for you—don't expect Mary fuckin' Poppins."

They stopped in front of a dirty white bungalow with a collapsing roof. Gagliano slammed his flat hand against the ancient wooden screen door. "Vladimir? You in?"

"Yeah, yeah," a voice rumbled from inside.

The bikers entered. The place smelled of sweat, urine, and food gone bad. Vladimir was sitting on the couch with a video-game controller in his lap. He was wearing faded purple sweatpants, work socks, and no shirt. A huge, but not quite obese man, Vladimir's body was covered in thick gray hair, which stopped where his collar would be. His head was shaved, revealing a fading black tattoo of a two-headed eagle. Although Vladimir was flabby and clearly out of shape, Ned could tell he was immensely strong. Vladimir's one eye stared intently at the TV screen, while the other appeared to be fixated on a spot near the base of a lamp on the opposite side of the room. He nodded at Gagliano, but did not acknowledge Ned.

"You better get ready for work; you have to be there in twenty minutes," Gagliano said.

"Two seconds to throw on a fuckin' T-shirt, two more for a hat," Ivan growled, not moving his attention from the video game.

After a long pause, in which the only sounds came from the video game, Gagliano said: "We got a job for ya."

"I know, I know, your boss . . . ah, fuck, you got me killed! Son of a bitch!" Vladimir glared at Ned. "Gimme the package."

"Here ya go," Ned said politely and handed him the knapsack, which was still a little cold from its time in the freezer.

"What did you say?" Vladimir stood up and rushed towards Ned. He was hovering over him, no more than six inches from his face. "What did you say to me?" he shouted.

Before Ned could speak, Vladimir smiled. "I'm just fuckin' with ya . . . Steve said you were a total geek. I just wanted to have a little fun with ya."

Gagliano laughed before the other two did. Vladimir picked up the bag. He didn't open it, just held it up at about head level, as though he was weighing it. "Eleven hundred," he said.

Gagliano laughed. "Vladimir, my friend, you are magic," he said, patting the big man on his naked shoulder. "Pay the man, lover boy."

Ned peeled off $1,100 from the wad of cash he had with him. Vladimir took it and said: "Okay, you guys get out of here now—you'll never see this again . . . wait, you want the bag back?"

***

Once he got home, Ned realized he wasn't good for much. Kelli hadn't come back, and there were no messages on the phone. He sat on the couch and turned on the TV. He lit up a joint. Ned flicked through all the channels and decided there was nothing on. He left the news on, but was scared he'd hear about a head and hands being found, so he changed the channel.

He switched over to a game show, but found it too annoying, too intrusive for him to sleep through. Finally, he settled on a nature program—something about lions and hyenas fighting it out for supremacy on the Serengeti, while the zebras and wildebeest take it on the chin, as usual. He stubbed out what was left of the joint. After about five minutes, he nodded gently off to sleep.

He slept for five hours—weed always made him sleepy—finally waking when the phone rang. He struggled to get it.

"Get down to the Strip by seven." It was a voice he recognized, but couldn't quite identify. "And bring money, lots of money."

Cash was never a big problem for Ned. He'd been selling drugs for years now and had developed a nice little network. He always had at least $20,000 in the house at any given time. But he knew when one of these guys said "a lot" of money, he didn't have to bring more than $10,000.

* * *

When he got to the Strip, Ned was greeted in the parking lot by Lessard and Johansson. "Boss wants to see you," Johansson said. "Wants to see you now."

Ned wasn't great at judging people's motives, but he could tell Johansson and Lessard were deadly serious. He nodded, took the knapsack with the money in it, and followed them. He was so caught up with what was going on, he forgot to lock his car.

When they got to the purple, windowless metal front door, Ned noticed Dave Peters and "Little" John Rautins standing on each side of it. Both men were in full Death Dealers regalia and had their arms crossed in front of them. Neither acknowledged Ned, but both nodded at Johansson when he approached. Just at the edge of his peripheral vision, Ned could see Buddy standing on a corner a block away, playing with his hands and pretending not to watch what was going on.

Although the Strip was ostensibly open at 7:30 on a Sunday night, the door was locked. Rautins banged on it—three hits, then a pause, then two more. The door opened. The DJ, who had been setting up, slunk away as soon as he saw who was coming through. Ned was surrounded by a phalanx of silent and angry-looking bikers. Only Peters—who had a reputation as a ruthless psycho and had a look in his eyes to match—wasn't significantly larger than him.

Wordlessly, they paraded him into Steve's office. Steve was behind his desk, sitting next to a large, Hispanic-looking man in an expensive suit and lots of gold jewelry. The chair in front of the desk was open. Ned sat in it.

Steve didn't acknowledge his presence at first, instead shuffling papers and shaking his head. Finally, without looking up, he sighed and said: "You know, you really, really, really fucked up last night."

Lessard laughed. Just about then, Gagliano entered the room and apologized for being late. Steve rolled his eyes and turned his attention back to Ned. "You put us all in danger; you freaked out and you showed weakness," he said, still shaking his head and still not looking at Ned. "And you did it for a woman." He paused. "Well," he finally looked him in the eye. "What have you got to say for yourself?"

Ned ran his hands through his hair nervously and exhaled loudly. "Nothing."

"Good, that's what I hoped you would say," Steve said. "Because there is no excuse for what you did—what you displayed last night was weakness, and by trying to defend it, you would be piling weakness upon weakness . . . but today, right now, you showed me strength, real strength."

Ned was silent.

"The fact is . . . what is done is done," Steve continued. "One more useless fuck—taking up space, breathing my oxygen, probably not recycling . . ." Lessard laughed again and Steve grinned an acknowledgement of his henchman's appreciation. ". . . is no longer with us; that's not a problem." Steve paused. He came around and sat on the edge of the desk, just a few inches away from Ned's face. "What bothers me is why," he said, and paused. "You know why they won't let fags into combat?"

It wasn't a rhetorical question; he expected an answer. "No, I don't know."

"Because the generals are afraid that fags will form close personal attachments to their squadmates and that their subsequent emotions would prevent them from doing their duty," he said. "What you did last night was the act of a fag—you freaked out and acted out because of your close, personal attachment to that woman, didn't you?"

"I guess so."

"There's nothing to guess, you did or you didn't—choose."

"Okay, I did."

"Did you make a prudent, well-thought-out decision when you hit that worthless fuck in the head with a beer bottle?"

"No."

"And why did you put such an imprudent, poorly-thought-out plan into action?"

"Because he was abusing Kelli?"

"Because he was abusing Kelli," Steve mocked him in an annoying falsetto. "And that made you feel how?"

"I don't follow you."

"Your problem is that you let your little faggot emotions get in the way of your better judgment," Steve said. "You saw her up there on stage and that lowly bastard telling her what to do and you snapped."

"My friend, she's chosen one path and it's about time you chose another," Steve said. "There's lots and lots and lots and lots of pussy out there. I can get you anything you want from pretty well anyone you want; you do not need to link your future to hers."

"You're right."

"Say it again."

"You're right."

"Perhaps you'd like to elaborate."

Ned caught on. "It was wrong of me to act stupid when confronted with that situation," he said. "Kelli is a stripper, she took on a career choice that has certain drawbacks, and I have to live with that and move on with my own career."

"Exactly what I was thinking," Steve said. The assembled bikers laughed.

"Now we come to the small matter of how you are going to make up for your indiscretions of last night." He said something in what Ned took to be Spanish to the man beside him, who nodded but did not otherwise change the expression on his face.

"The first matter on the agenda is the custodial work done by young Mr. Peters and young Mr. Rautins," he said. "How long did you two work?"

"Two hours, at least," piped up Peters.

"Really? I spent two fuckin' hours in the fuckin' VIP room with those fuckin' losers and fuckin' skanks?" Steve feigned shock. "Two hours? That would be $500 to each."

"Fine," Ned peeled ten hundreds off his wad of cash and distributed them to Peters and Rautins.

"Alright then, now comes the matter of Mr. Lessard and Mr. Johansson," Steve said. "They provided essential security—$700 each."

Ned did as he was told.

"And, of course, we cannot forget our good friend, Mr. Williams," Steve motioned to the man sitting next to him, who made no indication there was anyone in the room other than himself and Steve. "For various services rendered, $1,500." Mr. Williams made no noise or gesture other than stick the index finger of his right hand up. Steve corrected himself. "My apologies, I meant $2,000."

"What did he do?" Ned protested.

"Profoundly important things you are not yet privileged to know about."

For the first time, Mr. Williams acknowledged Ned. He swiveled in his chair and faced him. Ned couldn't see through the lenses on Mr. Williams' sunglasses, but the older man appeared to be staring him down. Ned had no choice, he passed the man two thousand in cash. Mr. Williams then shook Steve's hand and left without a word.

"Be grateful," Steve admonished Ned.

"I guess that just leaves you and Dario . . ."

Gagliano stood up and addressed Steve. "I think it would be more appropriate for Ned to settle up with me at a later date."

"Wise," said Steve. Then he stood up and sat on his desk, facing Ned. He leaned in so that their faces were just a few inches apart. "As far as I'm concerned, you're just gonna have to do me a couple of little favors . . ."

"Like what?"

"I need to hear you say it's over between you and her," Steve growled.

"It is."

"Then you won't mind if I send a couple of guys to your house to remove all her stuff."

"Uh … no, of course not … where ya gonna put it?"

"Anywhere you want, just not your house—you okay with her parents? No, wait, Mallory's her best friend, right? How about her place?"

It occurred to Ned that giving Kelli's stuff to Mallory (who worked for Steve) would keep her uncomfortably close, but he didn't mention it. Instead, he said: "Yeah, yeah, sure."

"If I ever see you with her again, you may just never see her again."

"*Her?*"

"Yeah," Steve said adamantly. "She's the problem, not you … unless you really are, because if you are, tell me now."

"I'm not."

"Who is?"

"She is."

"Y'know, I spent some time in Texas, and the bikers down there have a saying that sums up this situation pretty well. They say, 'Jesus hates a pussy,'" Steve said. "To make sure you remember your promise, you're going to get a tattoo that says 'J H A P'—Mack will hook you up."

Ned agreed.

"Right, now we can proceed."

Steve stood up, and went back behind his desk. He took something out of the top drawer that Ned didn't see, and held it behind his back. Steve grinned broadly, stood up, and walked slowly behind Ned. "You really, really fucked up last night … you know that?"

"Yes, yes, I do."

"No, no, no, no, you don't understand … you really, really,

really, fucked up," Steve said, running his left hand through Ned's hair. Ned could hear Gagliano laugh.

"Look, Steve, I killed a man last night. I realize I fucked up."

Steve laughed. "Oh, killing a man—at least that man—is not a big deal," he said, patting Ned's chest with his left hand. "He was an asshole; maybe he didn't deserve to die at that moment, but it was going to happen sooner or later . . . trust me."

Gagliano laughed first; the others joined in soon thereafter.

"No, no, no, no, the problem was not that a man died; the problem was that things were going along according to plan and your lack of backbone fucked it all up." By this time Steve had his head on Ned's shoulder and his big left arm around his neck.

They all stopped laughing.

"But you are never ever going to do that again—never ever going to fuck up my plans ever again are you?" Before Ned could answer, Steve loosened his grip on his neck, patted Ned on the chest and stood back up. "You won't be able to—because of this." He whipped out what he had hidden behind his back. Ned jumped. Everyone else in the room laughed uproariously.

It was the top rocker for his Death Dealer's patch. Ned was shocked. "What . . . what does this mean?"

"It means I want you to be a Death Dealer—full member," Steve said, and shook Ned's hand. "You showed me a lot of things last night—you can use force when necessary, you kept your mouth shut, you did what you had to do . . . and you didn't piss your pants a minute ago." Again the other bikers laughed. Steve smiled to them and got back behind his desk. "Look, you have always been a good earner and a sharp kid. I wanted you to be a Death Dealer right from the start, but there was always one problem." He looked Ned directly in the eyes. "With her gone, you're now free to be the man you can be . . . and don't worry about women. I can get you all you want."

"So am I really a Death Dealer?"

"Yep. After—what's it been?—a year or so of prospective membership, you made it," Steve slapped him on the back. "With one little condition—and I don't have to tell you what that is again, do I?"

"Well, that's . . . that's great," Ned said. He was genuinely happy. "But I was told that there had to be a vote for a prospect to get a full patch."

"You are confusing the Death Dealers with the Sons of Satan, my friend," Steve looked angry again. "I'm a Son of Satan. I went through all that bullshit; but I am president of the Death Dealers—we play by my rules." He stood up again, as he delivered his homily. "If I say you are a member, then you are a member." Then he smiled and looked at all the other men in the room. "Okay, fine, we'll have it his way," he said. "Gentlemen, I put it to a vote—do you accept Lover Boy Aiken as the newest member of the Death Dealers?" Steve interrupted himself. "Wait, I don't like the handle 'Lover Boy'; he should put all that shit behind him," he mused, grinning. "Gentlemen, do you accept Ned 'Crash' Aiken as a Death Dealers member?"

Gagliano shook a can of beer and opened it in Ned's face, covering him in a shower of foam. There was a huge roar as the other men joined in. Johansson, who was already profoundly drunk, picked Ned up, put him on his massive shoulders and spun him around a few times, before tottering and almost falling down. After regaining his balance, he placed Ned as gently as he could on Steve's pool table.

"Tonight, gentlemen," Steve announced. "We party."

***

At about the same time Ned showed up at Foxes, Vladimir went to his locker at the blast furnace and grabbed the knapsack. It raised no eyebrows when Vladimir took the bag into the steel factory. Not only was he a very large man who consumed enormous amounts of food and often brought big bags full of bread and sausages into work, but Vladimir was also well known as someone who was not to be messed with. Such was his reputation that he could bring a herd of school children into the factory, and nobody would have the courage to say anything about it.

When his dinner break rolled around, Vladimir went back to his locker. He waited a good ten minutes until the other guys retrieved their lunches before he went into the room. He grabbed two bags—the knapsack Ned had given him and a plastic shopping bag he had stuffed full of kielbasa and crusty bread. He wolfed down the meal and carried the knapsack to his work station. He noticed that Gordon, the guy who worked next to him, saw him. Vladimir stared him down.

Once he was sure the shift had gotten back up to speed again, Vladimir heaved the knapsack into the furnace full of molten metal. Tyler Heath's head, hands, and every part of the mostly nylon knapsack other than the metal pulltabs on its zippers disintegrated in midair just before they would have hit the molten metal.

Vladimir looked over at Gordon and saw fear in his eyes. Vladimir grinned and knew it was all over and done with. He'd made $1,100 for just five seconds' work.

CHAPTER 2

You could say that Ned Aiken's road to Steve Schultz and the Death Dealers began with his twelfth grade English teacher, Mr. Lambert.

"I'm not supposed to say this—no teacher is—but I really, honestly don't think you will ever amount to anything," Ned's English teacher shouted at him in the hall. "I really don't think you ever will."

Ned thought Mr. Lambert had had it in for him since Ned had corrected him on some detail in geography class in ninth grade and all the kids laughed at him. Three years later, Lambert was getting his long-simmering licks in. He had been trying his hardest to impart to the class what his teacher's guide told him was the enduring influence of T.S. Eliot's "The Wasteland," when Ned and his crew erupted into gales of laughter. Lambert knew Ned was the ringleader, so he pulled him out of class for a discussion.

"Seriously, I don't think you ever, ever will amount to anything unless you straighten up and fly right," Lambert spouted as he turned bright red.

Ned looked at Lambert long and hard. He was short— maybe five-foot-six—and bald, with a shoulder-length fringe of hair surrounding his big, freckly scalp. He wore thick, dark blue worsted slacks—which had that day's brown paper lunch bag in the back pocket every afternoon—and a checkered, western-style shirt he thought made him look cool.

Lambert lived two blocks away from Ned, so Ned knew that he'd been through two failed marriages and was living with a borderline obese woman whose children wouldn't speak to him. He drove a seventeen-year-old Subaru that sounded like it was farting every time he pressed the gas, and he had a hobby of flying radio-controlled airplanes.

Ned normally zoned out when the teachers criticized or scolded him. But this time, he hung on Lambert's every word. And as he listened, Ned realized that Lambert's advice—at its very best—would land Ned exactly where Lambert himself was; if he worked hard, applied himself—straightened up and flew right—he could be just like Lambert.

The realization made him laugh out loud, and Lambert exploded with anger. "I'm gonna expel you!" he shouted.

Ned just stared at him with a smirk. "You can't do that," he said. "I *know* you can't do that."

Lambert stammered. "Yeah, yeah, yeah, yeah, tough guy, I can't expel you, but I can fail you," he taunted and grinned broadly.

It wasn't much of a threat: Ned was already failing every course except Phys Ed and Calculus. He thought hard on what he should do next. Punching Lambert would have gotten him expelled for sure—exactly what Lambert wanted. So Ned did what he thought would bother the teacher most. He walked away, more determined than ever to use everything in his power to not end up like Mr. Lambert.

***

Ned gravitated to the unofficial smoking area just outside the school fence. He was surprised to see none of his friends there yet, so he just sat there, thinking.

Eventually, two of his best friends, Gareth and Cameron, came out laughing. "Mr. Aiken ... you're never the first one out here," said Cameron. "What's up?"

"Kicked out of Lambert's ... again."

"Yeah, he's such a dick," Gareth said.

"This time's permanent."

"What'd you do?"

"Same ol', same ol'."

"Yup," Cameron and Gareth both nodded.

"So ... got any weed?" Cameron asked.

"Nope, just hash," Ned told him.

"Fuck! You know I can't smoke hash," Cameron said. "Makes me cough like I'm hocking up a lung."

"Too bad, it's all I got."

"Can't you go talk to André?"

"Quiet," Gareth interrupted. "The cops." He was actually referring to a group of "good" girls, ones they could not trust not to tell on them if they knew what was going on.

"Ladies," Gareth said as they approached. "Can I interest you in a few moments of indescribable pleasure?"

"Gareth, you are so gross," Lily Hogenboom sneered at him.

"Aw, don't be that way," Gareth continued. "I'll go easy on you. You'll hardly feel a thing."

Lily started laughing, even though she didn't want to. The group of girls with Lily included Kelli Johnson. Ned had harbored a crush on Kelli for years. Even when he had steady girlfriends throughout high school, it was obvious from how he looked at her, how he got quiet whenever she was around, and how often her name came up when he was drunk or stoned, that he was really interested in Kelli.

But there were complications. Although Ned was generally seen as a relatively popular guy around school, he was also considered something of a loser when it came to academics and a future after high school. Kelli, on the other hand, was the daughter of Augie Johnson, a math teacher at their school, and she was one of the school's hardest-working and most gifted students. She was a regular winner of academic awards and was likely to be the graduating class's valedictorian. She was everyone's most-likely-to-succeed girl and not exactly in the same social circles as Ned.

And, the opinion that Ned was at least a part-time provider of weed and hash had filtered throughout the school. Kelli and many of her friends generally considered contact with him to be tantamount to aiding and abetting a felon.

As Gareth and Cameron continued their clumsy but amusing flirtation with the girls, Ned joined the conversation. But, as usual when Kelli was around, he found himself unable to be very assertive. Clumsily, Ned made a stab at asking her out.

"I don't think my boyfriend would like that very much," she told him politely.

"You don't have a boyfriend, Kelli," said Lily, grinning broadly.

Kelli's eyes widened. "Yes I do!"

"No you don't; you haven't even been on a date in months," Lily continued, giggling a little.

"Shut UP!" Kelli's face was turning red.

Ned was too dumbfounded to react, but Cameron assessed the situation pretty succinctly. "Weak," he said, then took his friend back to where they were sitting in the smoking area.

Getting shot down always hurts, but Ned was in a bad way after his run-in with Lambert, and Kelli—the girl everyone knew he'd always wanted—turned him down in front of his best friends. Cameron and Gareth, in an attempt to make their friend feel better, started talking about whatever came to mind—from Cameron's dog's fight with a raccoon to Mr. Ditmar's need for a new toupee.

It didn't help Ned's mood any. After a few minutes of sulking, he left for the one place he knew would make him feel better.

***

André's townhouse was a cool place. Ned liked how simple and straight-to-the-point it was. In the living room, there was nothing but a huge flat-screen TV, a video-game console and a long, low, white leather couch. Nothing on the walls, nothing in the way, just pure simplicity. And André was always happy to see him. They'd hang out, spark up a couple of joints or have a couple of beers and talk.

André was twelve years older than Ned. They met when André was dating Brianna, Ned's youngest aunt. Brianna had just divorced her insurance agent husband and was going through what Ned's mom called her "wild phase." And André was a very big part of that. Born and raised in the mountains of northern Maine, André had long, wild hair, tons of tattoos, and he rode an insanely loud Harley-Davidson. He never told anyone what he actually did for a living.

Ned was fifteen at the time, in tenth grade, and he thought André was the epitome of cool. He followed him around and aped his mannerisms. But when André took him aside at a party, Ned was cautious, even afraid, at first. André took him into an empty bedroom, but Ned calmed down when his new friend showed him a huge spliff which he called the "universal joint." They sat and smoked and talked and—like many people who smoke up together—found out they had a lot in common.

The bond lasted long after that first joint. Whenever the family got together, André and Ned would often greet each other, find a place far away from the rest of the crowd and spend their time talking and laughing, usually oblivious to what was going on around them.

A little more than a year after they started dating, Brianna caught André in her bed with another woman. When she told him she never wanted to see him again, he just shrugged and left.

But André and Ned stayed in touch. André lived about four blocks away from Ned's school, and Ned would frequently drop by to talk or smoke. As Ned brought more and more friends over, André realized he could make a few bucks by selling them weed or hash instead of supplying it for free. So he told Ned that his friends weren't welcome at his house anymore, but that he could front him some hash and weed to sell to them. At first, Ned didn't like it—he felt like he'd been cut off—but he eventually came around when he realized he could make a few bucks off his friends at school and still smoke for free at André's.

On this particular afternoon, Ned felt he could use a pick-me-up at André's. He was stinging from the brush-off he'd gotten from Kelli, and, to his surprise, the confrontation with Lambert was still bothering him. André could tell something was up.

After they started smoking, André stared hard at Ned, making him feel uncomfortable.

"What?" Ned asked.

"What 'what?'"

"What do you want?"

"One thing," André asked. "To know what's up with you."

Ned sighed loudly. "It's that fuckin' English teacher," he said. "He's gonna fail me, even though I'm doing okay in his class."

"What? You're good in English?"

"Okay, I suck. I could be good at it, but I find that all the other stuff—skipping class, getting in late, talking with my friends, y'know, all the stuff that pisses teachers off—is making it tough."

"So why do you do that stuff?"

Ned didn't hesitate. "The teacher, he's a total asshole; it's always gotta be his way—like we all owe him something and we have to please him—the work seems totally secondary, not just to us, but mostly to him."

Now it was André's turn to sigh. But unlike Ned's sigh of frustration, André's was that of world-weary boredom. "Y'know what?" he said. "That's the way it will always be."

"What do you mean?"

"Every teacher, every boss you will ever have will be like that."

"What?"

"You're a naturally smart kid, but you aren't prepared to play the game."

"What?"

"The game, man," André shouted. "You don't know about the game?"

"What game?"

"Yeah, I hate to be the one to tell you this, but it doesn't matter how good you are at English," André said. "It matters how well you behave."

"Behave?"

"Yeah, you gotta act the way they want you to for them to accept you," André told him. "You gotta walk their walk, talk their talk if you want a job from them; and even if you get that job, they will make your life miserable, no matter how much you try to please them."

"I don't believe that."

"Okay, who's the biggest fuckin' suck-up in your class?"

"Danny Forte."

"Does your teacher treat him with respect? Does he seem happy?"

"No, but he's got a lot of reasons to be unhappy, and a lot of reasons to be treated without respect."

"But does he get good marks?"

"Yeah, why?"

"Okay, I'm not getting through to you; let's go to the garage."

Without questioning, Ned followed André to his garage and then into his truck.

Ned really, really, really liked André's truck. Like most things André owned, the truck was bright white. And inside, it had an outstanding stereo and the softest leather seats that Ned had ever felt. He would have loved the truck even if it didn't have the dirt bikes, jet-skis, or snowmobiles that were usually in the back.

André pressed the button that moved his seat all the way back and put his feet up on the steering wheel and encouraged Ned to do the same. He put the key in the ignition and turned on the stereo. Led Zeppelin's "Misty Mountain Hop" filled the cabin, and Ned (who had never heard the song from such a high-quality stereo before) marveled at its depth, texture, and complexity.

As the song ended, André turned the volume down a little and asked Ned: "So, what do you want to be when you grow up?"

Ned giggled.

André pressed on. "No, really."

"I guess I could be a pretty good accountant," he said. "Good steady job, decent money."

André moved his seat back into driving position, opened the garage door and the big GMC crept onto the road. André didn't tell Ned where they were going and Ned didn't ask. They turned left.

André turned the stereo off. "So you are telling me that what you'd like to do is to graduate from high school—which is actually not looking all that likely—then follow that Herculean effort with four more years of absolute misery at some college you have to pay for, just to count some other motherfucker's money?"

"What?"

"Yeah, you know all that shit you hate about your English teacher's class?" he said. "You just told me that's how you want to spend every waking second of the rest of your natural life."

"No, no, it's not like that."

"Sure it is," André said, grinning. "You can be as good as you want at English, but what matters is how well you please the boss—'ya-suh, no-suh, whatever-you-say-suh.'"

Ned just sighed.

André continued. "What did you want to be when you were seven years old?"

Ned didn't hesitate. "An astronaut," he said.

"You wanted to travel thousands, even millions of miles into the unknown to discover new worlds ... and now you want to count other people's money," André said. "Do everything they say, then get a tiny, tiny bit of it for yourself." Ned could hear him sneering. "Like a fuckin' rat, begging at the table for scraps."

Ned didn't know what to say.

André told him to pull down his sun visor. On it, there was a video monitor playing hardcore porn. André pressed a few buttons. Suddenly, AC/DC's Brian Johnson was screeching "You Shook Me" so loud it shook Ned's innards. As he was enjoying the show, he was pleasantly surprised when André turned on the massager in his seat.

"You can be an accountant, or a teacher if you go to college," said André. "And live 'the good life'—or you could consider an alternate route."

Ned waited for him to continue, but he didn't. Instead, they drove into the parking lot of a brown low-rise commercial building with a few, dark-tinted windows. It had no name, but had a sign indicating which business was in which unit. Ned noticed that many of the businesses were just numbers or nonsensical acronyms and the few that had real names sounded either Chinese or Arabic. André hit the button for No. 14, or GTMA Financial LLC. "Seymour!" he shouted into the intercom. "Let me in!"

Ned heard a buzz as the aluminum door unlocked. André bounded up the stairs and opened a windowless door with the letters GTMA stuck on it.

"Seymour! How's it goin', buddy," André said as he slumped into a chair facing a desk with a small man behind it and put his feet up on the desk. "I want you to meet my good friend Ned."

The small man stood up.

Ned was surprised at how soft and timid Seymour's handshake was, and how he looked him in the eye for only the briefest of glances. "How you doin', Seymour?"

"Oh, my name's not Seymour; it's Eugene," the small man grinned. "He just calls me that." He gestured at André.

"André slapped Ned on the back. "Seymour here is my accountant," he told him. "Mine, as in I own the motherfucker." Eugene grinned timidly. Then he softened and looked at Ned in a way that Ned realized he should understand, but didn't. Then André said: "I call him Seymour because he sees more than he puts into the books."

"Yeah, yeah," Seymour started laughing nervously.

"You'd better," André warned him sternly. Seymour stopped laughing and looked at André silently.

"It's a pretty good gig you got here, eh?"

"Oh yeah, I do okay."

"What, you work about eight hours a day?"

"More like ten, since the divorce—it's been rough."

"Right, she got half of everything . . . even the dog, right?"

"No, she got all of him."

"Child support bad?"

"We never had kids."

"Yeah," André paused. "I thought you would take her name off the business."

"Costs too much."

"Yeah, but doesn't it remind you?"

Seymour knew he was being abused for André's pleasure, but there was nothing he could do about it. André was by far his most lucrative client and a large, unpredictable man who had some pretty seedy business interests. "It didn't really," Seymour replied. "But it may start to now."

André laughed. "Sorry, dude; you still got that minivan?"

"No, head gasket blew about three weeks ago; it'd cost more to fix it than the damn thing was worth."

"Sorry to hear that, man, but it was pretty old . . . so how you getting to work these days?"

"I ride my bike."

"Not the same one you had in high school?"

Ned was surprised to hear that the two went to high school together. André was no fashion model, but Seymour looked about ten years older.

"No, no, that was stolen years ago; I got this one at the police auction."

"Ain't that just like Springfield PD? Trafficking in stolen goods."

"Yeah, yeah," Seymour laughed nervously again.

"What you gonna do when winter comes?"

"I'll cross that bridge when I get to it."

"Just gotta keep on peddlin'."

"Yeah."

"Well, we just popped in to say 'hello'; we gotta go."

"Well, it was nice meeting you Ned and always a great pleasure to see you, Mr. Lachapelle."

"Yeah, yeah, don't you work too hard there, Seymour."

As they walked out to André's truck, Ned said: "Very subtle."

"You like that?" André grinned back. "You still wanna be an accountant?"

"They aren't all like that."

"Basically they are," André disagreed. "Some make more money than others, but it's more or less the same fuckin' thing—working your ass off for some richer motherfucker."

"It can be a decent way to live."

"Yeah, if you don't want a life or dignity or a chance to make it big or any of that other unnecessary stuff."

Ned exploded into something of a tantrum. "What the fuck do you expect me to do?" he shouted. "Be an astronaut? The only decent marks I have are in math and the fuckin' business college is the only one who'll fuckin' take me!"

André laughed. "Who says you have to go to college? I didn't."

"That's different …"

"Why? Because I'm a drug dealer? A criminal? I'd like to remind you, Sonny Jim, you're one too."

"Yeah, but . . . I couldn't do what you do."

"Maybe you could or maybe you couldn't, but that's not what I'm talking about."

"What are you talking about?"

"You could come work for me," André grinned. "Make more money in the first month than Seymour or your English teacher do in a year."

"I dunno, man, I don't think I could do it," Ned stammered. "There's some bad dudes out there and there's the cops and . . ."

"You think I'm asking you to stand on a street corner with a bag of weed and yell 'Drugs for sale! Drugs for sale!'" André scoffed. "Is that how you think it works?"

"I . . . I . . . I don't know how it works."

"It's actually real easy." I have a delivery boy—nobody ever suspects him because he has such a sweet face and he's underage anyway, so no big deal—who takes the product to bars."

"Yeah."

"The bartender or some other employee or associate then distributes the product in the bar," he continued. "Only to people he knows."

"So how do you get paid?"

"That's where you come in."

"What do you mean?"

"I need someone to go to all the bars and collect the cash."

"That's it?"

"That's it—and you get five percent. I'd figure it out to be about eight hundred dollars a week."

"I had no idea you made so much money."

"Don't kid yourself, I have lots of expenses."

"All I have to do is go to bars, grab bags of money, and bring them back to you."

"Yeah, and once you get the hang of it, you can get your

own customers—and I'll only take ten percent of that, plus my expenses, of course."

"What's the catch?"

"There isn't one. But there are rules," André stopped the truck by the side of the road and put on the hazard lights. "You treat all my customers with respect, and you give me every penny I deserve."

"Of course I would."

André continued as though he hadn't heard him. "That means if the package is supposed to be $10,000, I get $9,500, no matter what."

"Makes sense."

"If the package is light, that's got nothing to do with me; if I am expecting $9,500 and you get less than that, it's your responsibility to make it $9,500," André continued. "No excuses, no credit, no 'I'll pay ya later'—you give me my money, all of my money, on the date due."

"What if they don't want to pay?"

"Well, that's why the job pays so well—those fuckers never want to pay—your job is to convince them to pay."

"How do I do that?"

"The easiest way for you," André said as he started driving again, "would be to remind them who they are actually paying. Believe it or not, I have a little bit of respect in this town."

"So when do I start?"

"How about next week?" André answered. "I'll take you on a little tour, introduce you around."

"Then I can start?"

"Then you can start," André grinned. "You can use your bike or the bus at first and, if you do well enough, I'll see what I can do about getting you a set of wheels."

"That would be awesome."

"Alright, big fella, don't mess yourself," André laughed. "Anyway, school's out, where do you want me to drop you off?"

Ned really wanted to go home, but he knew his mom would freak if she saw him come out of André's truck. "Here's good. I was going to go to Cameron's anyway," Ned said. "Which reminds me . . . could you spare a little cake of hash?"

André laughed and stopped the truck. "I'll tell you what, I'll do better than that," he said. "Why don't you take this package—but don't open it up until you get into your buddy's house."

"Sure."

"No, really, is that clear?"

"Absolutely."

"Good, then get the hell out."

Ned laughed and took the package. It was a sealed manila envelope with no markings. As Ned felt it, he was relieved that it was spongy and not lumpy. "Great," he thought. "Weed, not hash."

As soon as Ned shut the door, André sped off. Ned, happy, began to walk home when a patrol car pulled up to the curb, then stopped. Two cops emerged from the car and approached him.

One of the cops was a fat bastard who needed a shave. The other wasn't much older than Ned himself.

"Did you just exit that vehicle, sir?" the fat one asked.

"What vehicle?"

"Oh, okay, smart guy," the fat one continued. "Do you mind if we take a look at that envelope you have in your hand?"

"Yes, yes I do," Ned stammered.

"Thank you, sir," the younger one said as he pried the envelope from Ned's hand. "Most people we stop are not quite as helpful as you."

"Asshole," Ned mumbled under his breath. The fat cop backhanded him across the jaw. Ned tried his best to pretend it didn't happen, but he could taste blood in his mouth and instinctively checked his teeth with his tongue to see if any were loose.

The young cop turned the envelope over in his hands, as if trying to find clues from the outside.

"Just open the damn thing," the fat cop scolded.

Ned sank.

A puzzled look crossed the cop's face. He pulled out a fist-ful of shredded paper.

Ned couldn't help but smirk.

"Oh, yeah? Oh yeah, tough guy, you think you're something?" the fat one shouted just before he gave Ned a whack in the ribs with his baton. "Not so fuckin' smart now, are you punk?"

Ned collapsed and curled up with the pain. The cops laughed; the little one gave him a small, impotent kick. Ned tried to laugh at him, but it hurt too much.

***

The last time Steve Schultz was this excited, it was Christmas morning and he was five years old. He was bursting with the exact same kind of anticipation because he knew he was going to get his patch that night. It wasn't just a matter of pride. Once he was a full-patch member of the Sons of Satan, he would be allowed much more autonomy in business, and he would no longer have to be at the beck and call of the guys who had rank on him.

The one notable exception was Ivan Mehelnechuk. Steve didn't like the short and ugly little tyrant at all. Ever since Steve showed up, Mehelnechuk started pushing him around. He'd call him up, any time of the night or day and make him do something. From getting him a pizza to roughing up a debtor, there was no job too mundane for Steve to do. And he never paid him anything, never even said thanks.

But it was time for the annual meeting of the Sons of Satan and it was the Martinsville chapter's turn to play host, so Steve knew he would have to keep playing ball for now. Steve had been a prospect for the club since last year's meeting. Not that many prospects get promoted to full member after just one year, but Steve was confident he would be.

In that year, he had brought the club a lot of revenue. His two escort agencies—Heaven's Angels Executive Escorts and AAAAA Budget Escorts—yielded a lot of untraceable cash and supplied dancers for local strip clubs. And he had done what many bikers had tried and failed at for years; he infiltrated Martinsville's gay village, supplying cocaine, meth, ecstasy, and steroids to a small network of four competing bars.

But that didn't seem to matter much to Mehelnechuk. The night before Shultz knew he was to get his patch, he got a text message from the boss, instructing him to help some fat middle-aged guy from out of town who was celebrating something and throwing some big bills around at the Wild Flower dance bar.

Steve had helped in more substantial ways in the short-lived and one-sided war between the Sons of Satan and the Lawbreakers in Martinsville. He had supplied his associates with C4 plastic explosives which he'd bought from a second cousin in the army. He had also helped dispose of the corpse of a Lawbreakers-associated drug dealer who'd been killed by a Sons of Satan-associated drug dealer after a beer-fueled softball game.

Steve knew the Sons of Satan were in desperate need of men like him. There had been many arrests lately. By the time the annual meeting came around, four of the most senior

Martinsville Sons of Satan—including long-time national president James "Jimbo" Masterton—were in jail awaiting trial. With Masterton behind bars, the club needed a president. Two of the primary candidates came from Martinsville.

Marvin "Big Mamma" Bouchard and Ivan "the Flea" Mehelnechuk could not have been more different from one another. Bouchard was tall, strong, handsome, and charismatic. He was French-Canadian—from Maisonneuve-Hochelaga, the roughest neighborhood in Montreal—but spoke English with only a trace of an accent because he had been in the U.S. for almost thirty years. He had a reputation for getting things done his way, and that way almost always involved violence. He'd been arrested forty-three times in the last ten years, but through fancy lawyering and other circumstances, he had spent less than nine months in total behind bars.

Mehelnechuk, on the other hand, had only been in jail to visit his friends. He was small—no more than five-foot-five—and funny looking. He had been no pretty picture to start with, but when he was thirty, about the time he became a member of the Sons of Satan, he was shot in the face.

It was a freak accident. Mehelnechuk was instructing a pair of young associates on how to intimidate a witness. After he was done his demonstration, one of his pupils threw a handgun to the other. Excited, the kid accidentally squeezed the trigger. The bullet flew out of the barrel and hit Mehelnechuk in the top left canine tooth. The tooth shattered, but it stayed intact long enough to deflect the lead. It shot backwards, tearing the flesh of his face in such a way that it split it five inches back. Mehelnechuk's cheek was slashed open from his mouth to his ear.

From that point forward, the right side of his face showed his real emotions while his left side displayed an insane grin—not unlike the Joker from *Batman*—no matter what the situation.

A few months earlier, nobody would have given Mehelnechuk a snowball's chance to be president. Not only did Bouchard look more like the man in charge, he was well liked and widely respected. Mehelnechuk had many members' respect, but it was a grudging respect, and few would call him a friend.

Things changed pretty quickly in his favor. Bouchard was arrested again, just two months before the meeting. A pair of Martinsville's finest were tailing him when he forgot to signal a lane change. A quick flash of lights, a brief conversation, and a couple of frisks later, Bouchard and his lieutenant Mickey "Wino" Godel were behind bars for possession of unregistered handguns.

Though they were bailed out quickly, Bouchard came home to find a pair of men in cheap suits sitting on his porch. They were from immigration. Bouchard had lived in the United States since he was nine, but he'd never bothered to file for citizenship. Because he had never attended college, gotten a job, filed a tax return, or crossed the border, he had fallen through the cracks—until now, as the annual meeting drew near.

With Bouchard fallen on hard times, his old buddy Mehelnechuk came to the rescue. Not only was he the one that came up with the bail money—he also let it be known that he would find a way to get Bouchard a Green Card. Bouchard, grateful, had no objection to Mehelnechuk's plan to host the annual meeting.

It was an elaborate affair. Mehelnechuk was originally from Springfield and still owned a bar there, even though it was a Lawbreakers' town and the Sons of Satan didn't hold much sway there. Well, he didn't actually own the bar—it was registered under the names of two old friends with legit businesses—but everyone in town whose job it was to enforce or break laws knew it was his.

Johnny Reb's was a Confederate-themed bar in a northern town. On weekends, it drew huge crowds. Many came to dance to the live country or rock acts—usually cover bands. Mehelnechuk had a fondness for the music of his youth—but far more came to blow off steam or get shitfaced. And a few came to make deals in Mehelnechuk's back-room office. He didn't have a huge amount of business in Springfield—the Lawbreakers saw to that—but it was worthwhile. Besides, he came home pretty well every weekend to escort his elderly mother to the Eastern Orthodox church where they attended mass in Ukrainian.

When he let it be known that this year's annual meeting would be held at Johnny Reb's, many members were surprised that Mehelnechuk would risk having it in what most considered to be enemy territory. But, as the idea circulated, more and more members realized what a powerful statement it was. There were maybe two dozen Lawbreakers in Springfield. At the annual meeting, Mehelnechuk could muster several hundred Sons of Satan and associates. He could have more firepower on the door than the Springfield Lawbreakers could put together in the whole town.

And it was a hell of a party. Bikers and their associates were greeted at the door by bikini-clad hostesses—most of them hired from Steve Schultz's dancer and escort agencies—who offered them drinks and hors d'oeuvres. Buddy Boy and the BJs—a country-punk outfit who flirted with national fame until Buddy Boy's alcohol and cocaine problems derailed them—played all their well-known songs and a few old covers Mehelnechuk had specified.

The bikers, the drug dealers, the enforcers, their wives, girlfriends, and other hangers-on were having a great time when

Mehelnechuk made his entrance. Two burly, leather-clad bikers flung open the front doors. Buddy Boy and the BJs fell silent, as they had been instructed earlier. Immediately, the stage lights lit up the door and Richard Strauss's "Also Sprach Zarathustra" boomed through the speakers.

In strode Mehelnechuk—all five-foot-five of him. Despite his odd appearance and his scarred face, he had something of a regal bearing that night. He wore a floor-length wolf- fur coat, a white silk shirt unbuttoned enough to show his many gold chains, soft leather pants, and ostrich-skin cowboy boots. It wasn't subtle, but it was a profound show of wealth and success to a very impressionable crowd.

As he entered, an assistant took his coat and the music stopped. He announced: "I trust everyone is having a good time." The crowd roared its approval. "Well then, let's make this a party." He clapped his hands twice, and all of the hostesses removed their bikini tops and let them drop to the floor. The crowd went wild and Buddy Boy and the BJs cranked up a powerful version of ZZ Top's "Sharp-Dressed Man."

One of the first to greet Mehelnechuk once he was seated was Bouchard. He whispered something into the host's ear, then shook his hand and left with a smile on his face. One by one, the other players in the Sons of Satan—some from as far away as California and even England—approached Mehelnechuk to wish him well.

About an hour later, a couple of prospects were sent to tell all of the collected Sons of Satan members that it was time to vote. One by one, they filed into the back office to write a name down on a piece of paper and stuff it in a box.

About fifteen minutes after the last one was finished, a prospect was sent to tell Buddy Boy to cut the music. Paul Potter, a 420-pound monster with a beard down to his belly button and a tattoo of a rattlesnake on his shaven head, strode to center stage. Potter was a much-respected member of the Sons of Satan. He was a good earner and a feared enforcer who would have been a viable candidate for president himself if only he hadn't been a similarly powerful member of the Lawbreakers only a year earlier.

Potter cleared his throat at the microphone and simply said, "It's Ivan." As if on cue, Buddy Boy and the BJs thundered into their rendition of "Street Fightin' Man."

Mehelnechuk did little but grin. Bouchard, sitting next to him, clapped loudly and cheered. He shook Mehelnechuk's hand, and the smaller man whispered something in his ear. Bouchard nodded and beamed.

Steve Schultz approached Mehelnechuk. The new national president laughed. "Don't look so sad, Hollywood," he said. "There's lots of room for a guy like you."

CHAPTER 3

Ned was sweating as he drove over the sun-bleached asphalt on his way to work. André had delivered on his promise to get him some wheels, but the car Ned was driving offered precious little more than basic transport. Made from a mix of parts cannibalized from a derelict Dodge Omni and a mechanically identical Plymouth Horizon, André had dubbed it a "Hor-ni," bought it from a mechanic friend for four hundred dollars, and given it to Ned.

It was a horrible little car: one headlight shone up at an angle of forty-five degrees; the skinny, bald tires made driving in rain, snow, or even moderate winds a death-defying adventure; the speedometer didn't work, but since the car began to shudder violently at forty-eight miles per hour, speeding wasn't really an issue. André explained that, if he drove a more expensive-looking vehicle, his mother would realize he had quit school. In fact, Ned's mom had long ago come to that conclusion, but in the interest of avoiding a conflict, played along.

Today, Ned was driving to Torchy's, a hillbilly bar located in an ageing strip mall in suburban Springfield. It was across the bay, but since Ned didn't trust the Horni to cross the high and windswept Bay Bridge, he had to go around, adding an extra forty minutes to his trip.

Torchy's was part of his route. Ned had accepted André's job, and was collecting cash for him from bar managers and bartenders around the city. But it wasn't working out as well as he'd hoped.

To a man, the dealers absolutely hated to pay. They'd whine and make excuses or argue. They'd short him or not be around when they said they would be. There was not a single week in which he received as much money as he was promised and he would occasionally have to dip into his own pocket to get the package up to the level André expected. Instead of eight hundred dollars a week, he was averaging around three hundred and fifty.

And he absolutely hated going to Torchy's. Not only was it far away, but the only day the manager would meet him was on Tuesdays. None of the other guys were available Tuesdays, so it meant he had to blow a whole day on just one call. Worse than the distance was the manager. Pat Wells was a total dick. A big, ugly guy who smelled bad, Wells was the worst of the bad lot Ned had to deal with. He argued about every nickel and dime and always, always, always shorted his package. Experience had led Ned to count the money in the envelope before leaving the bar, which always prompted loud complaints from Wells about what an asshole Ned was for not trusting him.

Today's trip was tolerable, though, because Ned had brought a friend along. Leo Babineau had been a pal of Ned's since fourth grade. He quit school about the same time Ned did, but didn't have any plans beyond getting stoned and playing video games.

Leo was totally out of weed, was bored with his games and was being harassed by his mom and stepdad to get a job, so he was delighted to hear Ned wanted him to tag along. It was something to do, a great relief from the nagging, and a great opportunity to score some free weed.

As they pulled into Torchy's parking lot, Ned said: "Be prepared, this guy is a total asshole."

"Can't be worse than Conrad," Leo said, referring to his stepfather. "Won't bother me, I'm just here to watch—but I got your back, buddy."

As soon as they opened the door, Wells snorted: "Aw shit, look who it is." He was alone in the empty bar except for his equally robust pal Pete Mulligan. They looked very much the same—big men with even bigger bellies. Both had mustaches, buzz cuts, thick necks, and powerful tattooed arms. Mulligan laughed.

"Hey, Pat," said Ned with a forced jocularity. "You know what I'm here for."

"No, what?"

"André's money," Ned said, hoping that the mention of who was actually getting paid would help make Wells comply.

"André's money? I don't know any André. You know any Andrés, Pete?"

Mulligan shook his head.

"C'mon, Pat, why do you have to put me through this song and dance every week?" Ned whined. "You get your product on time, don't ya?"

"Listen to this little fuck coming into my place and telling me what I can and can not do," Wells was yelling so loud and so fast that gobbets of saliva orbited his head. "That's not a very wise move on your part, you little shit."

"No it ain't," piped in Mulligan.

"All I know is that André expects his cash."

"All you know? You don't know shit."

They stood there, all four of them, staring at each other. Ned was at a loss. There was no logic to what Wells was saying, nothing Ned could work on. It was pure macho bullshit. Worse than that—it was psychopathic. The man wanted product and didn't see any reason why he had to pay for it. That made negotiations difficult.

Wells broke the silence. "Listen, you little bag of shit, I'll tell you what I'll do," he said while piling up a stack of bills which, to Ned's eye, appeared short of what he owed. "I'll stand beside you over there, and if you can grab the money before I do, it's yours."

Mulligan laughed stupidly.

"What are you talking about? The money is André's."

"André ain't here—but you and I are."

"This is bullshit."

"Do you want your money or not?"

"I want André's money."

"Then come and get it, you little shit."

Out of options, Ned lunged at the stack. As he leapt, Wells thrust both fists into his ribs. Ned toppled over a barstool and fell to the ground. Wells then ran over and kicked him in the gut. Then he grabbed the collar of Ned's shirt and his belt, dragged him over to the door, and threw him into the parking lot.

He came back and stood in Leo's face. "What do you have to say, faggot?" Leo said nothing, just ran out the door. Wells and Mulligan laughed.

Once outside, Leo helped his friend to the Hor-ni's passenger seat and got into the driver's seat. He asked Ned for the keys.

"You gonna be okay?" Leo asked his friend as he started the car. "Do you need to go to a hospital or something?"

"No, no, no, I'll be okay," he said.

They both laughed. Ned instructed Leo to drive him to André's. Leo, still pining for a little free weed, grinned.

André sighed after they told him the story. "I know I told you not to come to me with this type of problem, but I'm actually glad you did," he said. "If this sort of thing gets out, nobody will ever feel like they have to pay you and that would reflect very badly on me."

He lit a joint and Leo sighed contentedly. "I just can't allow this to happen," he continued. "And, luckily, I have a solution."

He led them down into the basement, passing Leo the joint. André instructed the boys to move the couch about a foot back. Then he lifted up the rug. Underneath it was a trapdoor that opened to reveal a small, deep storage space. In it, Ned could see some little glass vials with maroon rubber tops and red buckets full of yellow and white tablets. Ned hadn't passed either chemistry or biology, but he knew what they were when he saw the prefix "testo-" on some of the vials.

"Now, the liquid works faster, but I don't want you two idiots playing around with needles." André said as he groped around the storage space for two white plastic bottles. He counted sixty pills into each and handed them to the boys.

"Okay, Dr. Dré says to take one of these beauties every morning with breakfast—and you will start eating breakfast or they won't work as well; I suggest eggs, they're full of protein and collagen," André instructed them. "And y'know Kennedy's Gym downtown?"

They both nodded.

"You both have lifetime unlimited memberships," André said. "Just show up and tell the manager—make sure it's Dave you talk to—that André says you have the run of the place."

Although neither boy had ever been committed to anything before (unless you count Leo's pot smoking), they enjoyed their weightlifting. They spent about two hours a day at the gym working upper bodies and lower bodies on alternate days. And they saw almost immediate results. Within six weeks, they were already bigger, hairier, and more aggressive. They even saw their tastes in music and movies change.

Ned had returned to work the day after his meeting with André. There were a couple of changes, though.

He no longer went on trips without Leo. It cost him a little—he generally paid Leo in weed and handed him a twenty every once in a while—but it helped ensure that debtors paid in full and on time. The same people who had scoffed at the skinny lad with the shitty car were now ready to work with the two suddenly bold and well-muscled young men who made it clear they meant business.

And he cut Torchy's out of his rotation. It cost him a lot—in fact, almost two-thirds of his own net from collections. Torchy's was still receiving deliveries from André's other guys but not paying for them.

Ned made up for that deficit and more by finding customers of his own. Leo had a wide circle of weed-hungry pals. It wasn't really worthwhile for Ned to visit them all, getting ten bucks here and twenty there, so he set up an André-style distribution center at an independent record store where one of them worked. That, in turn, led to another distribution center at a mens' residence at the Springfield campus of the state university. André got his ten percent plus costs, and also supplied them with steroids to supply their weightlifting buddies at the gym under the usual terms.

* * *

Ned was on his way to the gym when he received a call from André. He told Ned to grab Leo and come over to his house. As he was just about to pull into the gym's parking lot, he saw

Leo and called him over. "Hop in," he said. "Big meeting up at André's." Leo jumped into the passenger seat and held his door closed for the whole trip.

André met them out front and told them to get in the pickup. "And park that piece of shit around the corner," he said. "Don't want my neighbors to think I hang around with riff-raff."

They didn't talk much as they got on the Interstate in André's pickup, instead preferring to listen to music. When they did talk, it was mostly about how much weight they were lifting or sharing anecdotes about the stupid or crazy stoners and dealers they had to deal with.

They were twelve miles from the Canadian border when Ned told André he didn't have a passport. André said he wouldn't need one where they were going. Then he drove down an offramp that indicated it led to the road to Millersville and Ondasheeken.

"Where we going?" Ned asked.

"Ondasheeken," André answered.

"What's there?"

"I'm taking you there to meet the FBI."

"FBI?"

"Yeah—Fuckin' Big Indian."

Other than what he saw in a few hokey cowboy movies and a hazy memory of something he heard in history class about maize and longhouses, Ned didn't know much about Native Americans. So, when they drove onto the Indian reservation, he intently studied everything. Ondasheeken looked like all the other little towns he had seen in the county. There were the usual clapboard houses and trailers made into permanent residences. There were clotheslines, above-ground gas tanks, muscle cars, and big angry dogs tied to stakes. But the kids playing by the side of the road were often bronze colored, and many of them had very long, always black hair. The businesses had long, Japanese-y names with lots of consonants. And every sign had an eagle or a turtle or some other dumb animal on it.

André turned onto a dirt road with a few mailboxes on it. He reached one shaped like a largemouth bass with the name "Wilson" on it and turned.

As they approached a fairly large low-slung ranch style, Ned could see that there was a small group of men out front. Most had long black hair (some in ponytails) and all wore some combination of jeans, wifebeaters, and/or plaid shirts. Their skin tones ranged from copper to milky. They were clearly having a good time smoking and drinking. There was a fire with meat cooking over it. And every single one of them (including a boy who appeared to be about ten) was carrying a gun.

One of them—a big guy, maybe six-foot-four, and all muscle—saw André's pickup and let out a piercing shriek. When he was done, he grinned broadly.

André lowered his window, and grabbed the man's left hand in a grip that looked like they were arm wrestling. The big man walked alongside the truck as André slowly guided it into what he determined was an appropriate parking spot on the grass.

"How you doin', man?" the big guy said, obviously happy to see André.

"I am screwed, blued, and tattooed, chief," André answered.

"I told you not to call me that," the big guy answered. "That word means something to these guys." He motioned at the men behind him, many of whom also seemed very happy to see André.

"Fine, fine, fine," said André. Then he paused. "Chief."

The big guy laughed. The rest of his crew gathered around.

Ned found them menacing despite their smiles, but André clearly had their respect.

"Yes, yes, yes, gentlemen, Santa Claus has arrived," André said as he came out of his pickup. He dug out and threw clear plastic bags full of weed to the big guy. Then he threw one full of white pills. And then two full of small translucent shards, which Ned (correctly) assumed were methamphetamine.

The big guy looked into the cab of the pickup—where Ned and Leo were still buckled into their seats—and said, "Boo!" He laughed when they both flinched. He turned to André and asked, "Who's the ballast?"

"Oh, these are friends of mine; good friends of mine in great need," he said. "They need some . . . uh . . . cantaloupes."

The big guy smiled broadly. "That's good," he said. "I just got a load of fresh 'cantaloupes.' Come inside."

André followed the big guy inside, and Ned and Leo came after. Ned overheard him ask André why he never wore his colors anymore but couldn't make out André's response.

Inside, the house looked very much like any of their own, but with more animal body parts used as decoration. There was a tiny old lady on the couch who stared off into space and tore cardboard into increasingly smaller pieces. An ancient and obviously arthritic dog of undetectable lineage cuddled up against her.

The big guy, whose name was Willie Wilson, sat with his three guests at a Formica and stainless steel dining room table. A heavy-set young woman—possibly stoned—walked out of one of the bedrooms to see what was going on.

Willie shouted to her. "Debbie, get these guys something to drink—and get Mom outta here." She walked over to the fridge and bent down to see what was inside. Ned instinctively looked to check out her ass, but instead found himself focusing on the tattoo on the small of her back. It said "Roberto" in Gothic letters.

She straightened up, turned, and threw Ned and Leo each a Budweiser. She handed a Miller to André. He kissed her on the cheek.

"That'll be enough of that," Willie chuckled. "I don't want her getting the jungle fever."

"Keep yer feathers on, Pocahontas," André shot back.

"You are so lucky you have drugs," Willie said. His jocularity hadn't waned a bit. He seemed to enjoy being insulted by André. "What can I do for you, my French fried friend?"

"It's not me, I'm fine, I'm totally self-sufficient, all I need is cash—oh, and you, Debs," André said as he turned to acknowledge the stout girl who was now fighting the old dog for room on the couch. "It's the boys. I don't know what to do with them."

It was at that point that Ned realized he hadn't spoken since he had arrived at Wilson's compound. He didn't want to appear afraid, so he spoke without really thinking. "We just came along for the ride."

After a beat, both of the older men laughed. Willie smacked André on the back. "They're not with me," André deadpanned as he shot a disappointed look at Ned.

Willie stiffened up. "Look guys, I know why you're here," he said. "I can take care of you."

The problem was that they didn't know why they were there. Willie then asked André: "What are you looking for?"

"Something small and clean," he replied.

There was a knock on the door. Willie snickered at the sight of Ned and Leo stiffening, then yelled, "Come in!"

It was one of the guys from outside. He was tall and thin with black hair down to his waist. He was carrying a rifle with a scope. "Fuckin' Winston just called," the young man told Willie. "He wants to know if you can get him something this weekend."

André laughed. "Not Winston from Canada?"

"Yeah," Willie said. "And that makes him a priority customer."

"What? That fat Jamaican asshole? I've known you longer and bought you more product—and he gets priority?"

"Yup, he gets priority because he lives on the other side of *your* border," Willie said. "See, on this side of *your* border, guns are easy to get—and on *his* side, they are much, much harder to get."

"And since the reserve is on both sides of *our* border— which you don't recognize ..."

"Well, let's put it this way," Willie said. "What would you give me for a ten-year-old Makarov that may or may not have been used in an incident in West Palm Beach?"

"I'd kick your ass for such an insult."

"Really? Because that fat Jamaican fuck in Toronto will give me eight hundred bucks."

"And the cops don't get on you?"

"Not really," Willie said, smiling. "The cops on this side are happy to see the guns go and the Canadian cops know they won't be staying in their neighborhood; they're going to Montreal or Toronto or Vancouver. They're all like 'fuck it, let those guys deal with 'em.'"

"Well, never let it be said that I stood in the way of free enterprise," André said. "And say 'hi' to Winston."

Willie snickered and shook his head. Then he told the kid with the rifle, "Look, call Winston back and tell him I'll be free in an hour ... and tell him Dré says 'hi.'"

As the younger man left, Willie turned back to André, and said, "Okay, you have my undivided attention."

"Good," André said. "They will need good products, something that will work when asked to do so and not fail," he said. "And, since they live on the sugar-coated side of the border, they will have to be clean."

That meant that the guns André was hoping to buy for the boys could not have been linked with any crime in the U.S. That cut the choices down considerably and jacked up the price accordingly.

Willie didn't take time to think. "I have two you'll like," he told André. "They fit your description—and they are nice products."

"Yeah?"

"Yeah, one of them is el Glocko and the other has been provided by my good friends—Mr. Smith and Mr. Wesson," he said. "You will like them—really, really like them."

"Careful what you say," André shot a look at Ned and Leo, then sighed. "And you're sure they're clean?"

"Would I lie to you?"

"Aggressively and repeatedly . . ." André paused. ". . . but never about product. You honest injun."

"Jesus, Dré, knock off all that Indian stuff," Willie sighed.

"Okay, okay, okay, can we get back to business?" André asked. "Are you absolutely sure we can talk here?"

"We are in the middle of a fuckin' Indian reservation!" Willie said. "It would be an act of war to bug my house." He walked over to the door, opened it, and shouted: "My name is Willie Wilson and I sell drugs!" It was immediately followed by hoots of approval and a few shots in the air by the young men outside. He grinned and returned to the table. "I got a Glock 17 and a very nice Smith & Wesson SW1911; I like the Smith. The Glock looks a bit coppish to me," he said. "They are both slightly used, but in pristine condition."

"Sounds awesome, can we see 'em?" André asked.

Willie mumbled something in a language none of the guests understood. Debbie groaned a mild protest, but got up from the couch, walked into a bedroom, and brought back a hockey bag with a Boston Bruins logo on it. She put it on the floor between Willie and André. Ned and Leo got up from their chairs.

Willie unzipped the bag. In among some pants, sweaters, and T-shirts, there were two cardboard boxes. Willie picked up one, and André picked up the other. From a lining of foam pellets, they both pulled out black automatic-style handguns. Ned couldn't see much difference between them, but he could tell that Willie and André could.

"I see what you mean; this is a nice piece of iron," André said. "Don't get me wrong, the Glock is a quality product, but the Smithie has a much nicer design." He handed the gun to Ned, who almost dropped it because he didn't realize how heavy it would be.

Ned stood up and posed with the gun. He was careful not to point it at anyone. As he held it, he began to understand why some guys really, really liked guns. He looked at Leo and said, "Dibs."

Leo protested with a half-whined, half-shouted stream of invective.

Willie silenced him. "You gotta pay for quality like that," he said as he handed the Glock to Leo. "It's a prettier gun, it don't work any better, don't kill no quicker, it's just prettier; and—as people who look like Dré learn to understand—you gotta pay for pretty."

André chuckled. "That's true, that's true. If I didn't have lots of cash, I'd never get laid," he said. "So how much of the pretty stuff are we actually talking about?"

"Well, the Glock retails for five-something, so that's a bill," Willie told him. "And the Smithie retails for seven-fifty or eight, so I'll do fourteen for it—but only 'cause I like you."

"Twenty-four hundred for two lousy used and abused popguns? I have half a mind to take my business elsewhere," André exaggerated taking offense. "Will, Willie, William, can we come to some kind of civilized deal?"

Willie pointed to Ned and Leo, who were posing with their guns in the living room. Debbie had wisely vacated the house. "You gonna say no to them?"

André shrugged. "But Willie, I'm your drug dealer—to you people, that's like family."

"Twenty-*five* hundred," Willie said, then chuckled. "Dré, Dré, Dré, what am I gonna do with you? Okay, okay, it's a rare win for the French—for you, two bills and I am literally cutting my own throat on this one."

"Yeah, I'm sure. Probably cost you about twenty-five dollars for the pair," André said. "But you got 'em and I want 'em—so what will it be, cash or product?"

"Product," he said. "School's starting up again, that's the hot season for weed."

"Hey, assholes," André shouted. Ned and Leo put their guns down and fell silent. "This is coming out of your allowance."

He was serious. André would connect the boys with Willie, negotiate the deal, and front them the money, but they would pay him back. In full. With interest.

"Okay, put those tools away and get to work," André ordered. "Get the stuff out of the truck and bring it in here." He threw the keys to Ned.

André had a false floor put into the bed of his pickup. It was shallow enough to make it hard to detect, but generally held enough to make a single trip worth the gas money. Ned opened it and the herd of young armed men who were surrounding the truck marveled. It was the most drugs any of them had ever seen. A few of them offered to help Ned and Leo carry it into the house, but the boys politely refused.

When they got inside, they saw André counting a large amount of cash. When he was done, he shook Willie's hand. As he headed out, the guys outside crowded around him. "Hey Santy Claus," the most stoned-looking one said. "What did ya bring us?"

"Be a good boy, and you'll find out," André said, to a smattering of laughter. He and the boys got back in the truck and headed for home.

About fifteen minutes into the trip back, André smacked himself in the forehead. "Jesus, Leo, you don't even work for me, do you?"

"Nope," he said. "I work for *him*." He pointed at Ned.

André laughed. "He doesn't have enough to pay for your piece and his own," he said. "From now on, you work for me."

"Awesome."

"What can you do besides smoke up and look stupid?"

"Pretty good at video games."

"Okay, okay, can you carry a small package to a hotel bar once a week," André asked.

"How small?"

"Oh, shut the fuck up, the bag is smaller than a sandwich—can you fuckin' do that?"

Leo got serious very quickly. "Of course, sure."

"Okay then, I want you to take a small bag to a friend of mine at a hotel bar once a week," André said. "You can't get caught, you can't fuck up, and you can't steal from me."

"Understood."

"I'll pay you one hundred dollars a week," he said. "But to make up for the gun, it'll be seventy a week for the first year."

Leo didn't bother to do the math. He agreed.

"Can he still work for me?" Ned asked.

"Not a problem," André grinned.

CHAPTER 4

Daniel "Bamm Bamm" Johansson was falling asleep in Ivan Mehelnechuk's hot tub. Who could blame him? He'd been drinking scotch-and-waters like they were Kool-Aid for four hours. As he grew less and less conscious, his grip on the glass holding the expensive Glamorgan scotch and water grew less and less firm. As he finally gave in to sleep, the heavy glass dropped to the deck and smashed into millions of tiny shards.

This presented a couple of problems. Mehelnechuk didn't like to waste anything. And while the glass was still in the air, he saw it falling and instinctively calculated the value of what was about to be wasted. The glass: $41.99. Two ounces of Glamorgan: approximately $19.

Crash!

The second problem was that there were now millions of shards of broken glass on the deck. Johansson dogmatically knew he had to clean it up. He also knew he was far too drunk to do a decent job.

The third, and most important, problem was that Johansson had fallen asleep while Mehelnechuk was talking to him.

Their relationship had begun about four years earlier. Mehelnechuk arrived at the only strip joint in Stormy Bay. He made an impressive entrance. Even though he was small and not very muscular, he commanded respect as soon as he walked in the room. While a big part of that could be attributed to his full Sons of Satan gear—the gang was widely known and feared—his bizarre facial scar and his obviously malicious demeanor completed the package.

He sat alone at a table near the stage, but cast only a cursory glance at the girls. He ordered a club soda from the waitress without looking at her or even allowing her to speak. Then he called her back and told her to get everyone in the bar whatever they wanted . . . on him.

It took Johansson—a foot taller and full of muscles—about a half hour to work up the nerve to approach him. He sat at a table next to Mehelnechuk's, close enough so that they could talk. "Buy you a drink?" he asked.

Mehelnechuk chuckled. "I seem to have one already," he paused and when Johansson could offer no retort, continued. "You important around here?"

"You might say so."

"Is it safe to talk here?"

"Three years in business, no arrests."

"Yeah, I know," Mehelnechuk acknowledged. "You had a little bit of trouble when you ran with the South Main boys, though, didn't you?"

Johansson was too stunned to react. After a moment, he looked down and mumbled, "Yeah."

"Well, I'm happy to hear things are going better now," Mehelnechuk said, grinning. "Let me buy you a drink; then we can talk business—you have a place?"

"Yeah," Johansson said and went over to have a short conversation with the bartender. After a few nods, Johansson smiled and called Mehelnechuk over. Mehelnechuk pretended he didn't see him. Johansson then walked over to the biker chieftain and invited him into a private room behind the bar.

It was a fairly lush office by Stormy Bay standards. Johansson sat in a leather swivel chair behind a big wooden desk. He was surprised to see that Mehelnechuk didn't sit in the chair opposite him, but rather on the couch a few feet away. Johansson awkwardly rolled his chair over so that he could face him.

"So, what goes on around here?" Mehelnechuk asked.

The waitress knocked before entering. Before she could speak, Johansson asked for a bottle of Jack Daniel's, then motioned towards Mehelnechuk who indicated he didn't want a drink.

After she left, Johansson stretched to show his massive, tattooed biceps and replied, "I'm pretty much it around here—weed, meth, coke, H, ladies, you name it."

His guest chuckled. "From what I hear, you sell a little hash when you can get your hands on it and farm out a couple of local sluts part-time," Mehelnechuk said. "The rest is fencing, muscle for hire, and the occasional B and E."

Johansson realized later that he probably should have laughed or said something clever, but at the time he tensed up and said nothing.

"But that's why I'm here," Mehelnechuk continued. "I can get you all of those things and more."

"Yeah?"

"You can distribute 'em in the area for me—make some real money."

"What's the catch?"

"No catch. In fact, the opposite of a catch—an opportunity."

Johansson looked puzzled.

"If you do a good job, bring in some cash, stay quiet, I may have some work for you with me in Martinsville and on the road—you interested?"

"Who wouldn't want to work for the Sons of Satan?" Johansson said. "It's like going up to the big leagues."

Mehelnechuk was true to his word. Starting the following weekend, a Martinsville College sophomore took a train to Springfield and showed up at Johansson's apartment. She didn't look like anyone who'd ever knocked on his door before. A little blonde with a high ponytail that never seemed to stop moving, she looked more like a cheerleader than a drug mule. She had a backpack full of weed and a manila envelope containing some small plastic bags full of cocaine. Johansson invited her in, but was disappointed when she made it clear she had no interest in him.

Her name was Ellie, and she came back again two weeks later with another backpack full of drugs. Before she would give it to him, she wanted Mehelnechuk's money. "You owe the boss $6,550," she said. "You want drugs, you better have the fuckin' money." She was tiny and he hated being pushed around (especially by a woman), but Johansson knew better than to cross Mehelnechuk. And he actually did have the money. He managed to sell every leaf of weed and every granule of coke—except that which he had taken for personal use. In fact, he had more money than he had ever seen in his life. So he counted out the $6,550 and handed it to the girl. Then she emptied the backpack.

It went on like that for a few months, and Johansson later recalled that he had never been happier. Not only did he have more money (and drugs) than he had ever dreamed about, he had the respect of his community. He was the *man* in Stormy Bay. He bought himself a jacked-up Jeep—one so high, he had to help most passengers get in—and a Harley.

He'd never had an interest in motorcycles beyond riding his cousin's dirt bike when he was young, but after Mehelnechuk's visit, he felt it appropriate to buy one. Mehelnechuk had never given him any kind of patch or anything, so Johansson went ahead and made his own.

He knew a guy, Randy something, who was an artist. Years ago, Randy had airbrushed a mural on the side of his stepdad's van. Johansson hadn't seen him in years, but knew he could track him down at the flea market where he sold romance novels along with his original artworks. Not only was Randy willing to make a patch for Johansson's jacket, he was delighted.

About two weeks later, Johansson was adding a running board to his Jeep when he was approached by two men in Sons of Satan jackets. The first asked him: "You Johansson?"

"Yup."

"Boss wants you in Martinsville."

"That's great, but I got a lot of work to do here."

"That's why we're here."

"What?"

"We're gonna run this town while you're gone."

"What?"

"Jesus, man, you're going to Martinsville to see the boss, until you get back, we run this town; it's not rocket science."

Johansson knew better than to argue. He finished his job and exchanged pleasantries with his visitors. He was instructed to show them who his contacts in town were and to pack his bags. They also handed him five hundred dollars "for his trouble."

As Johansson put his jacket on, one of the Sons of Satan asked: "What's that?"

"What's what?"

"That, on the back of your jacket—the Mad Vikings."

"It's not the Mad Vikings, it's the Mad Viking—that's who I am, the Mad Viking."

"So . . . your patch is all about yourself?"

"Yeah."

"So your club is the Mad Vikings and . . . you are the only member?" They both broke into gales of laughter.

Johansson seethed, but said nothing.

* * *

Since he didn't have a job, Ned couldn't qualify for a loan. So when he replaced the Hor-ni, he had to pay cash. But business had been so good that he could buy a pretty decent ride anyway. When he saw the bright yellow, four-year-old Chevy SSR pickup on a lot, he was shocked by how little they wanted for it. It was a V8, a pickup *and* a convertible. He bought it without negotiating.

The following day, he and Leo went out collecting. Leo quietly wondered why, but didn't say anything. After all, it was Tuesday, and they never went collecting on Tuesday.

Thirty minutes into the trip, Leo realized where they were going. "You sure?" he asked Ned.

"Oh yeah," he replied. "Should be fun."

Leo laughed.

They pulled up to Torchy's at about three, exactly when Pat and Pete would be setting up the bar.

Ned kicked in the door. "Hey Pat!" he shouted.

Pat, who was wiping down the bar, dropped his rag and started laughing. He walked right up to Ned and said: "Hey Pete, lookit what the cat threw up."

Ned bashed him in the face with his gun, breaking his nose.

As Pat was rolling around on the floor in pain, Leo ran up to Mulligan and twisted his arm around his back so violently it fractured in two places. He marched him over to Ned. Ned looked at the scared man and said: "He's yours, Leo, do what you want."

Pat had made it up to his hands and knees when he started vomiting violently. Ned laughed, then kicked him in the face.

When Pat stopped moaning, Ned said: "Hey, Pat, I think you owe me a few bucks—not André, but me."

"What?"

"Yep, I been calculating every cent you owe," Ned told him calmly. "You actually owe me a little more than $17,000—before interest—and . . ."

He was going to continue, but Leo interrupted. Ned hadn't noticed, but Leo had been beating Pete violently with his fists and his gun since they had parted. Consequently, Pete's face was purple, swollen, and bleeding. Leo, child-like, was trying to get Ned's attention.

"Lookit, lookit, lookit, Ned!" he shouted, as he plunged the barrel of his pistol into Pete's mouth, breaking one of his front incisors. "It's just like that show!" Then he turned to Pete and mock-angrily scolded him: "Tell me where the drugs are, Ramirez, or you'll be snorting in hell!"

"Okay, okay, that's great, Leo," Ned told him. "But I'm doing business here." Leo left dejectedly, dragging a now unconscious Pete behind him.

"So, Pat, you wanna talk business?"

"I don't have no $17,000."

"$17,162 and change."

Pat started weeping.

"Aw, come on, don't cry, big fella," Ned mocked him. "You owe me a lot—I mean a lot—of money, so what are you gonna do about it?"

"I don't know."

Ned hit him in the knuckles with his gun. Pat screamed. "I think you better figure something out," Ned said. "Right now."

Pat moaned and whined.

"Now!"

"Okay, okay, okay, okay, I can give you the ten thousand now," he managed. "Then a hundred a week after that."

Ned grinned. "A hundred a week?" He asked. "That's less than minimum wage. Gimme three hundred a week on top of what you'll be buying—and if you want drugs, remember, they come from me; you go to the cops, you're dead; you go to another dealer, you're dead; you give up selling altogether and you're dead. You got it?"

"Okay, okay, okay," Pat said. "It's a deal ... so will you call me an ambulance?"

Ned laughed. "Fuck that," he said. "We had a deal before and you fucked me over repeatedly ... you reap what you sow, Pat." Then he kicked him in the face. "Now, where's my ten thousand?"

Pat sputtered and said something nonsensical. Ned shook him. "It's in, it's in, the bar fridge," he finally admitted, pointing to the correct door.

Ned dropped Pat and went to the fridge. It was full of beer bottles. He threw them to the ground, smashing most of them. Nothing.

Then he looked in the ice tray. There was a manila envelope inside. He opened it; it was full of cash.

Satisfied, Ned looked up at Leo, who was still beating an unconscious Pete. "Yo, Leo, we really gotta get outta here," he said.

Leo looked at him like he was asking him to leave an amusement park. After a few seconds, Ned nodded toward the door and Leo complied. He didn't stop laughing until they were past the Bay Bridge.

***

Johansson didn't know what to expect as he followed the bikers' directions to the office. When he finally arrived at 317 Barridge Street, he was surprised that the only Harley he could see was the one he had ridden in on.

What he did find was a medium-size rectangular building packed among the factories and auto wreckers that dominated the area. The building was painted black and red (the Sons of Satan colors) and had a sign above the door that read: "SOSMC Martinsville."

Johansson could not recall ever seeing a building that large entirely without windows. He did notice that there were video cameras on each corner and a number of satellite dishes and other antennas on the roof.

As he passed by the stumpy concrete barriers that surrounded the building, he approached a thick, red metal door. He heard it buzz open before he rang the bell. He was surprised at how heavy the door was.

Inside, he saw what looked like the reception area of an office designed by teenage boys. The old furniture was in rough shape, there were posters of nude women on every bit of wall not covered in graffiti, and the detritus of a party—beer cans, cigaret butts, pizza boxes, and snack food wrappers—littered the floor.

Two men greeted Johansson. They looked pretty much like how he pictured bikers—long hair, beards, and leather jackets—but they were both very young (perhaps in their early twenties) and very slim. The bigger of the pair told him it was an extremely bad idea to keep the boss waiting, and he took Johansson through another metal door that buzzed when it opened. It led to a meeting hall with a full bar.

He was led through another door and up a staircase. At the start of the corridor, he saw a door with a sign that read, "Keep Out." The biker who came up with him knocked on the door.

"Send him in," said a voice from inside.

The biker opened the door and Johansson walked in. He was surprised at what he saw. Mehelnechuk was sitting behind an expensive wooden desk in a tidy, professional-looking office. It was the only place he had seen inside the building where the walls were not covered in pornography or graffiti. Instead there was just one framed photograph of a group of men in leather jackets holding up the Sons of Satan logo. Mehelnechuk and Marvin Bouchard (whom Johansson recognized from a couple of stories he'd seen on TV) were in the center.

"Thanks for coming," Mehelnechuk said without raising from his seat or offering his hand. "Can I get you something?"

"No thanks, I'm fine."

"Good. How are things in Stormy Bay?"

"Awesome, I'm selling everything you can supply . . ."

"Except for personal use, of course."

Johansson chuckled. "Yeah."

"Just weed, though, no coke or meth, right?"

Johansson recalled that Mehelnechuk took a dim view of coke and meth. Of course, he dealt both, but he would not allow his men to use either. He said he had seen them fuck up too many people. The penalty for coke or meth use on Mehelnechuk's watch was severe and, Johansson had heard, potentially fatal. So he lied: "No way, profit margin's too rich." Then he continued. "The bar is packed pretty well every night, I've got some big plans for . . ."

Mehelnechuk interrupted again. "That's chump change; if you want real money, you'll make it here in a bigger city."

"What do I have to do?"

"I'll let you know."

"Uh . . . okay."

"Don't worry so much," Mehelnechuk smiled for the first time in Johansson's presence. "You're going to Springfield to join a club called the Death Dealers—it's all set up—but you have to come back to Martinsville whenever I need you."

"Here." Mehelnechuk handed Johansson a leather brief-case, its elegant design ill-suited to the scruffy young man who received it. There was an awkward silence that only broke when a frustrated Mehelnechuk ordered Johansson to open it.

Inside, he found a sawed-off handgun, a cellphone, and five thousand in cash. He grinned.

"Use the money to get yourself a place to stay and some decent clothes—the guys out front can help you with that," Mehelnechuk said. "Keep the other two things with you at all times—and keep the phone charged up. Don't worry about the bill; I have a connection in the business."

"What will I be doing?"

"Making money."

Months later, in Mehelnechuk's hot tub, Johansson real-ized that he was making a lot of money. Although he was mak-ing it by performing for his master, he was okay with that. He'd have liked to be his own boss again some day, but for the time being, he was content to follow orders and rake in the bucks.

* * *

Jamie Roblin knew on an intellectual level he had to eat, but he just didn't feel like it. He paced around his apartment, just as he had a million times before, trying to think of something he could eat that would have a tiny bit of appeal for him. He'd been pacing for about two-and-a-half hours when he finally decided upon a box of Froot Loops and a two-quart bottle of orange soda.

He was just digging into his meal when he heard a knock at the door. It was the secret, coded knock he instructed all of his business associates to use, but it still made him nervous. He grabbed a handgun and approached the door slowly. He heard the knock again. He looked through the peephole and grinned.

It was none other than Marvin "Big Mamma" Bouchard. The big man himself had come to pay Jamie a visit. He'd been dealing with the Sons of Satan for a couple of years now, but had never met any of the important ones. And everyone who was anyone knew who Bouchard was. He was in the paper and on TV all the time. For a small-time meth cook like Jamie, a visit from Bouchard was something of an honor. It must, he thought, be something big. So he put away his gun and opened the door.

"Mr. Bouchard . . . uh . . . nice of you to come."

Bouchard smiled warmly, shook Jamie's hand, and walked in with three other big bikers. "Sit down, sit down, Jamie," he said. "Relax."

Jamie did as he was told. Two of the big bikers sat beside him on the couch. It was a small couch and they were big guys, so it was a tight fit.

"You do a pretty good business with us, don't you Jamie?"

"Oh, yeah . . ."

"I mean, we pay you lots of money for lots of drugs and it works out pretty good, doesn't it?"

"Yep."

So why do you sell to the fucking Lawbreakers?"

"Oh, that . . . them . . . I always sold to them, I have been selling to them for years . . . I sold to them long before you guys . . . they're small-time, not like you guys . . . it was the deal . . ."

Bouchard grinned and shrugged. "Well, my friend, it's not the deal anymore."

Jamie panicked. He tried to stand up, but the bikers held him down. Each grabbed one wrist and held his hands on the coffee table. The other biker, who had been behind the couch, emerged with a large claw hammer in his hands.

Jamie screamed.

"Stick something in his mouth, Lou," said Bouchard. The biker with the hammer wadded up one of Jamie's T-shirts from the floor and shoved it in his mouth. He knew better than to spit it out. "Jamie, Jamie, Jamie, the reason you have that filthy old T-shirt in your mouth is because you have a nasty habit of interrupting, and I have something important to tell you." He sat down. "I'm telling you because you are a popular, likeable guy," he said. "You know everyone. You can get my message out to everybody in the business."

Jamie nodded.

Bouchard smiled. "Here it is—if anyone deals with us, they cannot deal with the Lawbreakers," he paused to make sure Jamie understood. "And if you don't deal with us, you will die." Then he chuckled. "Pretty simple, eh?" he said. "You got it, eh? You'll tell everyone, eh?"

Jamie nodded and smiled the best he could with the T-shirt in his mouth.

"Good, that'll save us so much unpleasantness," Bouchard said. "Go ahead, Lou."

Lou took a swing at Jamie's left pinkie, shattering it. He swung again, missing his fingers and hitting the table. Jamie was screaming through the T-shirt. Lou swung again, hitting Jamie's left thumb, but it was just a glancing blow.

Bouchard sighed. "I'll be waiting in the car; come down when you're done."

***

According to her parents' strict standards, Kelli had been acting irresponsibly lately. They attributed her unprecedented lack of discipline to the fact that it was her senior year and that some of her friends were encouraging her to cut loose a little.

But they were having none of it. Augie Johnson had seen a documentary on a TV newsmagazine about "tough love"—a concept in which parents use strict, zero-tolerance punishments to put their kids back on the right track. It hadn't been getting the results he wanted, but he knew that if he stuck with it, it would.

Kelli wondered why her parents had totally turned on her just because she missed one school assignment and a couple of curfews. Augie had explained "tough love" to her, but it sounded more like tough luck. All she got out of her parents these days were orders, criticism, and recrimination. Home was like a boot camp. She found herself staying away from it more and more often.

She was reluctant to leave Lily's, but knew she'd be in big trouble if she stayed any longer. Her parents had confiscated her bike because they had seen her riding it without a helmet, so she had to walk home. About halfway there, it started to rain—just enough to be annoying. When she finally made it to the front door, she found it locked. She rang and rang the doorbell, but there was no response. She could see the light on in her parents' bedroom, so she knew they were home. She phoned them—no answer. She started pounding on the door and yelling.

Augie's plan was to make her freak out for about fifteen minutes, then let her in and give her a good talking to. He decided to intensify the experience a little by having his friend

Harvey Giamatti—a drama teacher at another high school who sported a long beard and wild hair—hide in the hedges and approach her.

Harvey emerged just as it was dawning on Kelli that she was in all likelihood, going to have to find someplace to sleep that night. Doing his best imitation of a deranged homeless man, Harvey stepped very close to Kelli and said: "I don't think they're home, lady." He was about to follow up by asking her for some spare change, when she let out a horrified scream and ran. She ran down the block without any particular destination. About two hundred yards from her house, she saw a familiar face.

It was Ned, getting into his car after stopping at the corner store to buy some snacks. Kelli rushed up to him, screaming: "I'm locked out of my house and there's a crazy man after me!"

"Hop in."

After she calmed down a little, Kelli sighed. "I can't believe I'm asking you this," she said. "But can I stay at your place tonight?"

Ned, trying to act nonchalant, said, "No problem."

"Really? Your mom won't mind?"

"Mom? I have my own place."

"Ooooh . . . maybe this isn't such a good idea."

Ned laughed. "Look, I have an extra room, there's no bed in it, but I have a sleeping bag and lots of pillows—there's no lock, but you can prop up a chair or something."

"That's okay, you won't try any funny stuff—I have a black belt in karate."

Ned looked at her and started laughing. A moment later, she joined him. "You—a black belt in karate?" he chuckled. "A black belt in ballet, maybe . . ."

She playfully punched him in the right bicep and said: "You just watch yourself, Mister. We ballerinas can get pretty nasty."

CHAPTER 5

Ned's hand was actually shaking as he slid the key into the lock. He knew André often slept late, was somewhat paranoid, a heavy sleeper who went to bed every night with a handgun. Although the likelihood of getting shot wasn't great, Ned didn't like the idea of waking up his boss.

But he had to. That's why he had a key to his house. André's habit of sleeping in had made Ned and other employees late for deliveries before. To prevent this from happening again, André gave Ned a key. He gave it to Ned, he said, because he was the only one he didn't expect would rob him blind while his back was turned.

So when Jackson—one of the underage delivery boys—couldn't get André to answer, he called Ned. Jackson told him that he had to hit the downtown bars before they opened. Ned knew that the key to Jackson's continued success was stealth—he ran under the cops' radar—so he quickly agreed to come and open the door and wake André up.

Getting in was easy; waking André up and staying unharmed was another. As a heavy drug user, he tended to go into very deep sleeps at any time of the night or day and could often be angry, paranoid, and even violent when he was awakened. And, as a successful drug dealer, he tended to be heavily armed and desperate to protect his stashes of both product and cash.

When he got there, Jackson was sitting on the front step playing with a Nintendo DS. He complained about both André's sleeping and how long it took Ned to get there. But Ned didn't pay him any attention. Jackson was just a little punk kid, maybe even a fag. And he was much farther down the org chart, so Ned didn't have to listen to him and they both knew it. Ned made fun of Jackson's emo haircut—a long sweep of poorly-dyed black hair that covered his right eye, curving to a point near his jawline—and his "girl's pants." Then he pretended he had forgotten the key. When Jackson started freaking out and began throwing a tantrum, he quickly found it and slowly, methodically, unlocked the door. He pushed it in hard so it would bang against the wall. Then he stomped in the hall as hard as he could, shouting "Dré! Dré! It's us—Ned and Jackson!"

There was no answer and the pair looked at each other. "No, no, no, I'm not going up," protested Jackson. "I heard Dré once accidentally shot a guy right through his eyeball."

"Okay, okay, ya little puss, I'll do it."

As Ned approached the closed bedroom door, he could see light coming out from underneath. Clearly, Dré had fallen asleep with the lights on again. And as he inched even closer, Ned could hear what he identified as classical music coming softly from inside the room.

"Dré! Dré! It's Ned! I'm coming in!" He knocked loudly on the door.

Fed up with his own cowardice, Ned barged into André's bedroom, prepared for the worst.

What he saw knocked him to the floor.

André was still in bed, but the once pristine white sheets were drenched in thick, already browning blood. The back of his head was mostly obliterated. What remained was a mass

of matted hair, sticky blood, and what Ned correctly took to be brain tissue.

Stunned, Ned stepped backwards until his back hit a wall, and he sank until he was sitting. He brought his hands up to his face, then dropped them to the ground. He looked at André again and threw up.

The violence of his retching drew him out of his stupor. He stood up and ran down the stairs. He grabbed Jackson, who was in a chair, by the shoulders and stood him up. "We gotta get outta here, right now," he told him. "Dré's been shot."

"Then call a fuckin' ambulance."

"It's too late for that."

After Jackson figured out what that meant, he looked at Ned—wild-eyed, sweating, covered in vomit—and ran.

Ned went after him, locked the door as nonchalantly as possible and hopped into the SSR. He started it normally and drove away observing all speed limits and road signs. He wondered if the police could identify people from the DNA in their puke.

* * *

Vince Tate, the editor in chief of the *Springfield Silhouette*, couldn't believe what he was hearing. John Delvecchio, his veteran crime reporter, wanted to be reassigned.

The two men had never gotten along. Tate was just thirty-eight and still full of ambition when he came to Springfield. As a deputy editor at the *Martinsville Daily News*, he had brought sweeping changes into the paper that had garnered it acclaim in the industry and praise from readers and advertisers. His reward was the editor-in-chief job at the *Silhouette*. The challenge, as he saw it, was to drag the rapidly declining paper into the twenty-first century—kicking and screaming, if necessary.

Delvecchio quickly became one of his primary obstacles. The thin, nervous crime reporter had never been promoted despite having spent more than thirty years in the position. They had never even bothered to create a senior reporter position for him. So, by the time Tate took over, reporters' meetings at the *Silhouette* would always feature about a dozen ambitious twenty-somethings and one cynical bald man approaching sixty.

Although they were all officially equals, Delvecchio was paid a lot more than the other reporters. The union saw to that. And it was the *Silhouette's* strong union that kept him employed.

A few weeks after he started at the *Silhouette*, Tate wanted to get rid of Delvecchio. It wasn't his writing, which seemed acceptable, but his attitude. More than anyone else in what seemed to Tate to be a building full of unimaginative, change-resistant drones, Delvecchio fought Tate's initiatives. If there was a new technology, Delvecchio refused to learn it. If there was a new protocol, Delvecchio refused to follow it. He continued doing things the way he had for the past sixteen or so years, making life hell for the copy editors and page designers who had to work with him. He openly criticized Tate's ideas and changes, often calling him a "politically correct fascist." He frequently told co-workers that "once management woke up and fired Tate, everything would go back to normal."

As annoying as it all was, Delvecchio's little protests were too petty for Tate to build an insubordination case against him. In fact, Delvecchio had been there so long and had built up so much union protection, Tate couldn't even take him off the crime beat. So when Delvecchio volunteered, Tate had to hide his delight. He knew that Delvecchio's second wife had just left him, but avoided the subject. "Why the sudden change of heart, John?"

Delvecchio fixed Tate with a strange look. "No reason," he said. "Just looking for a change."

"That's cool, John," Tate said. "But where would I put you; where would you want to go?"

Delvecchio didn't hesitate for a second. "I understand the religion spot is still open."

Tate didn't know the *Silhouette* even had a religion reporter. In fact, it didn't. About ten years before Tate was hired, Hugh McAllister, the *Silhouette*'s religion reporter, retired. He'd never been replaced, so the job was technically open.

Tate thought about it. It seemed like a good deal. Not only did it allow him to sideline Delvecchio, but the whole thing made it look like Tate had done him a favor. He had no idea what had scared Delvecchio off the crime beat, but he didn't want to look a gift horse in the mouth, either.

* * *

Johansson was in the hour of perfect anger, between drunk and hung over, when the phone rang. He was furious, but cautious. "Yeah," he said.

"Boss wants you at the Springfield airport for six a.m.," a voice he didn't recognize said. "Be at the gate for Pearson Air, looking for the flight to New Hamburg—bring a bag of clothes and picture ID."

"This mandatory?"

"Everything the boss says is mandatory—you need the instructions again?"

"Let me get a pen."

Johansson was some pissed off. Not only wouldn't he get any sleep that night, but he would have to pack his shit in record time.

And when he thought about it, he was not impressed by the destination. New Hamburg was about six hundred miles away from Springfield and no bigger or more important than Stormy Bay.

* * *

Ned was sitting on the steps of a stranger's house when his cell phone rang. He answered without looking at the caller ID. "Yeah?" he said.

"You work for me now."

"What?"

"You heard me."

"What the fuck? Do you really think that . . ."

"Meet me at the food court in Westend Mall."

"Fuck you!"

"I really think that's the wrong attitude to take."

Ned was silent.

"Okay, meet me at the food court at Westend Mall—you'll know who I am."

Ned said nothing.

"It really is in your best interest."

Ned still didn't speak.

"I'll be here for a half hour. After that, things kinda have to change, and neither of us wants that to happen."

"I'll be there."

* * *

When he arrived at the airport, Johansson was delighted to see Mehelnechuk. The boss was sitting there, waiting for the flight to board and reading a book called *The Art of War*.

"You're reading?" he asked, chuckling.

"Yeah," Mehelnechuk replied without looking up. "You should try it some time." He went back to reading.

"What is it?"

Mehelnechuk sighed and put down his book with an exaggerated motion. "It'd take a long time to explain it to you ... hmmm ... let's call it a how-to guide," he said. "It's something I read every once in a while, something that calms me down, makes me happy."

Johansson was dumbfounded. The very idea of a biker reading books—hard books!—was very foreign to him. A big part of why he'd chosen the life he had was a hatred of things like books. He had a strong desire to make fun of Mehelnechuk, but his instinct for self-preservation quelled it. Instead, he grunted.

Mehelnechuk sighed again and told Johansson that Martin would take care of him and went back to reading.

Martin was a small and eager fellow Johansson hadn't noticed until Mehelnechuk pointed him out. He had a clipboard in his hands and glasses he kept pushing up his nose. "Mr. ... Mr. ... Mr. Johansson," he stuttered. "You're, you're, you're in the wrong, wrong place."

"What?"

"Mr. ... uh, uh, uh ... Mehelnechuk, he, he, he, always travels business class and ... uh, uh, uh ... your tick ... tick ... ticket is in ... uh ... economy."

"So we're not sitting together?"

"No, no, no, that never happens," Martin said, not looking up from his clipboard. "Mr. Meh ... Meh ... Meh ..."

"Mehelnechuk!"

"Yes, yes, Mr. Mehelnechuk always travels alone. In fact, he often books the seat beside his so he can read on the plane." Martin paused. "He finds it very relaxing."

Johansson privately seethed. He had been six-foot-five for many years; he knew what an economy seat would do to his legs.

***

Against his will, Ned showed up at the Westend food court. It was Springfield's oldest and smallest shopping mall, and there was rarely anybody there on weekdays aside from the elderly who walked zombie-like around the mall whenever it wasn't full of teenagers.

It didn't take long for him to spot his contact. Steve Schultz was a big guy with long hair and a leather jacket. He was sitting, talking, and laughing with three other men who were wearing similar clothes. There was another man with them. He was somewhat older—bald with glasses—and he was wearing khakis and a pressed blue shirt. They were the only ones in the food court except for an older lady who kept muttering to herself.

"Ned!" Steve called out, grinning broadly. He stood up and motioned for Ned to come to the table.

Ned was confused. He considered running out of the mall, but realized it wouldn't do him any good. Instead, he walked over to the table wordlessly trying not to betray any fear on his face.

"Well, sit down, big fella," Steve said. "We don't bite."

Ned hoped they couldn't see him shaking. Steve introduced Little John, Pete, Dario and the older guy, Bradley, giving no more information than first names. They all greeted Ned like he was a friend.

"Terrible tragedy," Steve said.

"André?"

"Yeah, awful what happened to him."

"You didn't do it?"

"Me? Why would I do something like that to my top earner?"

"Your ..."

"Yeah, you didn't know your boss worked for me?"

"Uh ..."

"Where do you think he got his product from? The tooth fairy?"

The bikers laughed. Bradley looked nervous.

"I never asked him about it," Ned said. "I figured his business is his business and the less I knew the better."

"See?" Steve said to Pete, Little John and Dario. "This is why I love this kid—you don't have to teach him the basics."

The bikers laughed. Ned grinned.

"Look, I brought you here to make you an offer."

"Okay."

"In light of André's disappearance, it has become necessary for me to find someone to fill his role," Steve said. "And I think you're the perfect candidate." Then he turned to the older guy, and asked: "What do you think, Bradley?"

"I can offer no opinion on your business dealings at this time," he answered. "I am not even aware of what you do for a living."

Steve laughed, and faced Ned. "Basically, you'll take over for André," he said. "You'll do everything for me that he did, and you'll get what he got."

"Really?"

"Yeah, Little John will take you back to the house—once it's all cleaned up—to show you how to take over."

"André's house?"

"André's house, he says!" Steve laughed. "Get a load of this kid; that's not André's house, it's my house . . . and my pickup truck, my motorcycles, my TV, my everything."

"What?"

"André worked for me, so I took care of him," Steve said. "And I'll take care of you. You already have keys to the house, the rest of the stuff is there—I'll get Bradley to take care of insurance, utility bills, and stuff like that."

"You mean, I'm going to live in André's house?"

"There he goes again," Steve laughed. "You can call it your house if you want, but it's my house."

"And the truck?"

"Yes, the truck," Steve said. "One other thing—you know the Harley André used to ride?"

"Yeah."

"You're going to ride it now; not all the time, just some-times, when it's appropriate . . . it's kind of a thing we have."

"Sure, I'll have to learn how first."

"Make sure you do. And we have a jacket for you; you don't have to wear it all the time, just when we need you to."

The length of the subsequent pause and the look on Steve's face indicated to Ned that he'd better do what he said.

"So, I think this was a successful little meeting," Steve said. "Don't you, Bradley?"

"I really can't comment on that," he said.

Steve chuckled. "Fair enough. Little John, you ready to take him over there?"

"What about the bod . . ." Ned stopped mid-word when he saw Steve's reaction. "I mean, what about André?"

"André has disappeared; I have no idea where he has gone," Steve said. "I have some friends over at the house cleaning up and collecting his personal effects for safe-keeping—he can get them back when and if he returns." He paused. "You'll make sure of that, won't you, Bradley?"

"I will arrange for Mr. Lachapelle's personal belongings to be stored securely," he said. "When he returns to either Mr. Schultz or myself, they will be returned to him. Any cash or negotiables will be held and any interest accrued on them will be awarded to Mr. Lachapelle at that time ... minus a small handling fee, of course."

* * *

When Johansson arrived from the luggage checkout at the New Hamburg airport, Mehelnechuk was already surrounded by a group of local Sons of Satan. Out of respect for the national president, the local bikers had arranged to bring him a Harley to ride into the clubhouse. Johansson rode in the pickup truck that had brought it.

After a few pleasantries at the clubhouse, Mehelnechuk had a closed-door meeting with the local club's president and two confidantes. Johansson waited at the clubhouse bar and tossed back a couple of beers with some local prospects. One of them asked him why he and Mehelnechuk were in town.

Johansson told him that he wasn't exactly clear why they were there.

The New Hamburg prospect was surprised and told him that their small chapter was having a war with a local independent gang—the Devil's Own—and they had called Mehelnechuk to put a stop to it. So they were surprised he didn't show up with a little more muscle and firepower.

Johansson was taken aback. He knew that his size and aggressiveness were what Mehelnechuk wanted him for, but he wasn't sure exactly what that meant. Was he expected to fight an entire gang?

He was pondering that question when Mehelnechuk emerged from his meeting. "We've got a few hours before we have to go," he told Johansson. "So you can amuse yourself with these guys—but don't be drunk; I'm gonna need you tonight. Can you be back here by nine?"

"Sure," he said. "What's going down tonight?"

"A party."

* * *

Little John drove Ned back to the house. It looked pretty much exactly as he remembered it, although a few things were missing. He toured around, eventually stopping at the master bedroom. There was more missing from it than any other room.

"Looks like you're gonna need a mattress," said Little John.

"Yeah."

"Makes you wonder; what kind of guy . . . when he skips town . . . takes his mattress with him."

Ned looked at Little John's face to see if he was joking. He saw no sign of it.

"Some people are strange," Little John finally said. "Anyway, there's a 1-800 place that'll deliver today—you need cash?"

"No, no, I'm fine," he said. "I think we've got some work to do."

* * *

Vince Tate had to hire a new crime reporter right away. *Silhouette* readers liked their crime stories and he didn't want them on his case.

He called in Frankie Kerr, his managing editor. "I saw John come out of your office looking more relieved than I've seen him in years," he said. "Did you promote him to super reporter or something?"

Tate chuckled. "No, no, no, he kinda demoted himself," he said. "He volunteered to give up the crime beat."

"Really? I wonder who got to him."

"What do you mean?"

"John loved the crime beat, thought it made him something of a celebrity," Frankie told him. "And in my experience, crime reporters cling to their beats like barnacles, unless there's pressure from outside."

"You think John's being threatened?"

"Wouldn't surprise me—he's not the most likeable guy out there, nor is he the most imposing."

"Nah, you're just being dramatic. I read John's stuff; it's basically pumped-up police reports with some bystander reaction. I don't think he's in any danger."

"So, who's taking over?"

"I was thinking about Lara Quinn."

"Miss Thing? You realize she's about fifteen years old?"

"Look, she's aggressive. She's the type."

"Yes, and she's also really, really pretty."

"That has nothing to do with it."

"No, no, I'm not accusing you of anything . . . but she is plenty good looking. Don't you think that's inappropriate for the crime beat. Don't you think she'll kind of stand out amongst Springfield's undesirables?"

"Whaddaya mean?"

"She looks like she just fell off a fuckin' wedding cake; you don't think she might be a bit obvious in . . . oh, let's say a strip joint or a leather bar?"

"Like John didn't? He looks like a frickin' zombie."

"Nobody notices a zombie; everyone will notice Lara."

"Yes, yes, yes, I know what you're talking about . . . but I really think her looks will be more disarming than they are a problem."

Frankie gave Tate his most concerned look. "Yeah," he said, "I guess you're right."

But he didn't believe it.

***

It didn't take long for Ned to get comfortable in what he had known as André's house. He sat in the big leather couch in front of the big TV and flicked through the channels. Bored, he decided to call Leo.

"How's it goin'?"

"Where you been, man?"

"I got a new place."

"Wait, you got a new place? But I live with you, man; I'm in our place."

"That's not our place anymore; why don't you get over here?"

"Where's here?"

Ned sighed. "André's."

"What?"

"I'm the new André."

"Really, what's André think about that?"

"Look, you asshole, I got the house, the truck, the Harley, the TV . . . everything."

"You got the drugs?"

"Oh, I have the drugs, my friend."

"Party on, Wayne."

"Party on, Garth."

* * *

Johansson was at least relatively sober when he set off to meet with Mehelnechuk that evening. Since he'd been in a plane, he hadn't been able to bring any weapons with him, so he'd borrowed a .22 and a hunting knife from his new friends in New Hamburg. He was confused when the bikers at the clubhouse told him that Mehelnechuk had already left.

And Johansson was more than a little surprised when the guys he was riding with stopped their car in front of a bar. He was sure he was headed to a clubhouse. "What? Are we stopping for a drink?"

"Kind of, this is where the meeting is."

"Here? At this place?" Johansson asked of nobody in particular. "Won't people get hurt?"

The prospect who was driving the truck looked at him quizzically. "Not unless somebody does something stupid."

Johansson grunted and went into the bar. He was surprised by what he saw. There was Mehelnechuk at the head of a long table with a bunch of Devil's Own. They were laughing and having a good time.

Johansson approached him. "Everything okay, boss?"

Mehelnechuk looked at him like he was an idiot. "Hey, Bamm Bamm, tonight's all about having a good time," he said. "Why don't you go up to the bar and tell them I just bought you whatever the hell you want?"

"Really?"

"Really," he said. Then he brought the big man close and told him: "But don't get drunk . . . and keep your eye on that big motherfucker by the door." He motioned toward a 350-pound man with a tattoo on his face.

"Got it." Johansson noticed that his boss was drinking club soda.

* * *

When Leo arrived, he looked like a kid in a candy shop. Ned couldn't help but be proud. When he opened the door, Leo ran in, almost screaming. Ned managed to calm him down enough to get him to sit in the couch. Throwing a little hardcore porn on the big TV helped.

"So this is all yours?"

"Yeah, I guess."

"And I can stay here?"

"Sometimes, I guess; but this is my house, man. I'm not living in the fuckin' apartment with you any more—it's all yours."

Leo laughed. "Fuckin'-A! I can't believe this, you fuckin' live here . . . wait, is all this stuff yours?"

Ned couldn't help wonder why Leo hadn't asked about André. "Yeah . . . I guess so."

"Well, let's make the most of it, my friend. Call Kelli. Let's have a paaaaaaar-tay!"

"Yeah, yeah, yeah . . . y'know what, we could have a party," Leo was like a kid on Christmas morning. "We got the space, we got the drugs . . . we got the drugs, don't we?"

Ned nodded.

"Then we got the party; you call Kelli, I'll call Patsy, and we'll have a good ol' time."

* * *

Johansson was confused. He simply didn't understand what had happened in New Hamburg and he wanted to ask the boss what was going on.

"There was a war going on in New Hamburg, right?"

"Sort of, it was kind of what we call a 'cold war,' nobody was actually shooting, but the two sides were considered enemies."

"So you showed up and started buying people drinks and supplying hookers . . ."

"Well, what would you have done?"

Johansson was formulating an answer when there was a knock on the door.

Two bikers escorted Bouchard into the room. Mehelnechuk stood up and greeted his old friend with a hug. He dismissed Johansson with a wave.

"So, how was your trip to New Buttfuck?" asked Bouchard.

"They are on board," said Mehelnechuk. "As are Harriston, Mount Wayne, and Goresport."

"And not a single casualty."

"That's how I do business, my friend; better to buy your rival a beer than kick his head in."

"I wish sometimes I was like you, but I find the best way to beat our enemies is to get rid of the troublemakers."

"You exterminate, I enthrall—it ends up the same."

"I only know one way to do business."

"And that's why you have the job you have. So tell me, what's going on in Springfield?"

"Well, we had some great success. Because Roberts has a good friend in the Marines, we have managed to gain some eleven pounds of C4 plastic explosives and two LAW rocket launchers."

"I'm sorry, what? Rocket launchers? What exactly are you trying to accomplish?"

"For us to succeed, the Lawbreakers must be gotten rid of."

"Or brought to our side."

"Sometimes that's not possible."

"I understand that, that's why our partnership works so well."

"And I personally know of at least two Lawbreakers from Springfield who will never be brought to our side; you remember Gabe? Fat blond guy?"

"Yeah, yeah, I used to ride with him back when I was with the Horny Devils."

"You won't ride with him anymore."

"Should I ask why not?"

"Apparently when he turned the key in, his car—the whole thing went up in flames."

"Sad, very sad," said Mehelnechuk. "Keep up the good work, my old friend."

As they were talking, Tim Collier, president of the Springfield Lawbreakers, was putting his kids to bed. He kissed Troy, five, and Tricia, three, good night and headed to his big armchair where he planned to watch *SportsCenter*. He hadn't quite gotten to the chair when he heard his doorbell ring. He looked out the narrow window beside the door to see who it was. It was a little guy with glasses, long hair, a pizza box and a baseball cap from a regional pizza chain. Collier hadn't ordered a pizza, but he had often gotten mail and deliveries for the Guptas at 24 Chateauguay Circle because he lived at 24 Chateauguay Court, about a hundred yards away.

He swung the door open and started to tell the guy he had the wrong address, when the pizza man dropped the empty pizza box, revealing a sawed-off shotgun. Earl "Geronimo"

Hayes pumped two shells directly into Collier's chest. The big man staggered and fell backwards. Satisfied, Hayes threw the shotgun and the pizza hat into the house and ran.

The following day, the regional media was ablaze with stories about Collier's death and how it linked to the other Lawbreakers' murders and disappearances. Jake Levine, a former biker cop turned author, came from Martinsville and was interviewed on both Springfield TV stations. On each he told the same story: Springfield was under the grip of an all-out biker war being directed through the Death Dealers by the man they called the Sons of Satan's national president—Marvin "Big Mamma" Bouchard.

***

Two days after Collier's death, some of the furor created by it had died down. Lara was starting her first solo day as the *Silhouette*'s crime reporter when she received a phone call from a blocked number. "*Springfield Silhouette*; Lara Quinn speaking," she answered.

"This the crime reporter?"

"Yes."

"Well, I want to report a crime."

"Oh … okay … don't you think you should call the police?"

"That would not be in my best interest."

"I see," she said, but really didn't understand why he had chosen to talk to her instead of the police. "So what would you like to report?"

"Well, I can't say exactly, but I can tell you that if you look in the back seat of Frank Vanden Boom's car, you'll get your story."

"Who?"

"You sure you're the crime reporter?"

"Yeah, but I'm new. Can you spell the name?"

The caller did.

"And, can I get an address?"

"No, I'm not gonna do your job for you," he said, and hung up.

***

Ned knew Kelli would be excited about the new place. They'd been dating with increasing regularity since she spent the night over at the apartment before Leo moved in. They were surprised at how much they had in common and really enjoyed each other's company. The fact that her parents really hated him impressed her even more.

Patsy, Leo's girlfriend, arrived before Kelli did. Patsy made Ned more than a little nervous. André had introduced them a few months earlier, and Leo immediately fell for her. She was about fifteen years older than he was gaunt with a leathery, withered face, and had worked as a dancer at a bar André frequented. She made no secret of the fact that she had occasionally worked as an escort—something that instilled great pride in Leo. "It's like being with a porn star, man," he said enthusiastically. "She can do things you wouldn't even imagine."

As soon as she walked through the door, Leo was all over her. Ned wasn't crazy about watching them kiss, but when he called her "lover," it made his skin crawl. He excused himself to get some beers.

Patsy excused herself to the washroom, and Leo went in with her. Ned could hear them laughing and snorting in there. When they came out, they were sniffling and giggling.

"You shouldn't be doing that," Ned said. "Remember what André said about coke."

"Yeah, so what does André say about it now? André is gone, my friend."

Patsy giggled.

"Yeah, I guess you're right . . . I guess I'm the new André."

"So, boss, what about the coke?"

Ned couldn't say no to his old friend he'd been through so much with recently. "Sure, okay, but keep it under control. Don't let anyone else know about it, and pay for it yourself."

"Yes!"

Patsy giggled again.

When Kelli arrived, she asked why they were meeting at André's house. She wasn't crazy about André; he was lascivious and vulgar.

"It's not André's house anymore; it's mine," Ned told her.

"No way! That's awesome!" she shouted and kissed him.

"Hey, yo, you two, get a room," said Leo, laughing. "What do we have planned tonight?"

"Well, I have some DVDs in my backpack, we could make dinner, and watch a movie," offered Kelli.

"What kind of movie?" asked Patsy.

"A couple of romantic comedies," Kelli enthused. "I have that new one with Kate Hudson in it."

"Pass," Patsy said, and Leo echoed her thoughts with an imitation of a game show buzzer.

"I think we should have a night on the town, and let you two love birds enjoy your new house," Leo said, getting his coat.

After they left, Kelli and Ned enjoyed a quiet evening. The following morning, when he asked her to move in with him, she enthusiastically agreed.

***

When Lara mentioned Frank Vanden Boom to her police contact, she was quickly connected to Mike Clegg, Springfield's ranking biker cop. Clegg told her to tell him everything she knew. After about twenty minutes of negotiation, she got him to agree to let her come along on the call in exchange for her information.

In his car, Clegg explained who Vanden Boom was. "Y'know the Lawbreakers? The biker gang?"

"Of course," she said, offended by the idea that she—a crime reporter—hadn't heard of him.

"Well then, you know about Collier and the other murders?"

"Yeah . . ."

"Well, Vanden Boom is . . . I mean was . . . the ranking member of the Lawbreakers in Springfield," he said. "I don't think he had any kind of title or anything, but he was the only one left who had the nuts to take over; the rest of them are idiots or pussies."

"Why are you using the past tense?"

"He's dead."

"How do you know?"

"Well, the Sons of Satan pay their members and associates for murders of their enemies," he said. "But the only way they can get credit for a murder they claim to have committed is through media coverage."

"So that's why I got the call, instead of you."

"Yup, that thing you were supposed to find in Vanden Boom's backseat is probably Vanden Boom—the murderer called you because he was tired of waiting for someone to stumble upon the body."

Clegg went over to the *Silhouette*'s office and picked Lara up. They drove to Vanden Boom's address. Clegg parked in front of Vanden Boom's house and went around back to the garage. There was a black Lincoln inside. Lara looked in the back window. There was something large covered with a blanket. She nodded to Clegg. She tried the back door; it was unlocked. As it swung open, a sawed-off shotgun fell onto her feet. The smell of rotting flesh was strong enough to push her back a few feet. "Whoa!" was all she could say.

Clegg laughed. "Delvecchio puked when he saw his first body . . . and his second and third; I think he fainted on the fourth," he said. "See that shotgun—that's a Sons of Satan touch—they always leave the weapon at the scene."

"Why?"

"None of the weapons are ever registered to them, and there's very little chance of getting fingerprints off them, so they're not very meaningful as evidence," he told her. "But if they got caught with a weapon—especially one that could be linked to a hit—after a crime, they'd go down for good guaranteed."

CHAPTER 6

Ned's cell phone was ringing. Kelli was getting ready to go to her parent's house and Ned was in the shower, so she picked it up.

After she said hello, a voice on the other side asked: "Who the fuck are you?"

Taken aback, she stammered: "I'm Kelli . . . Ned's girl-friend."

"Put him on."

She went into the washroom and handed Ned the phone. She went back into the bedroom, but she could still hear him apologizing for letting her answer the phone and promising never to let it happen again.

After he was finished berating Ned, Steve told him he had a job to do. After Ned took over André's position, he learned about a few complications. André wasn't just a drug dealer. He was a biker. In fact, he was what's called a prospect for Steve's gang, the Death Dealers. A prospect, Ned found out, is some-one who works with or for the gang, but is not yet a full mem-ber. André had been a full member of another motorcycle gang, the Chain Masters, but was bumped down to prospect status when they were taken over by the Death Dealers.

That didn't just mean Ned got a leather jacket with a patch on the back. He also had to learn to ride the Harley.

Little John told him that the motorcycles were more than just a symbol; they also made the Death Dealers a legitimate common-interest club and much harder to prosecute under organized-crime legislation.

It also allowed him access to the Death Dealers clubhouse, except during some meetings. And when they were on, he and the other prospects were expected to stand guard outside the building no matter what the weather.

Officially, Death Dealers prospects are required to do anything a full member asks them—no matter how stupid, dangerous or, paltry—but they usually took it easy on Ned. A few of them had him go to the store for them late at night and other little jobs like that, but nothing major.

But they leaned heavily on Leo. They used him as muscle, they used him as an errand boy, and they used him for entertainment. The irony was that he didn't know he was doing the work for nothing. Unlike a prospect like Ned, the Death Dealers had already labeled Leo as a "hangaround"—what the cops, lawyers, and media call an "associate." He was considered someone useful to the gang who technically could become a prospect. But in reality, he had little if any chance of ever becoming a member.

That didn't dampen Leo's enthusiasm. He carried out every task the members asked of him, often for little pay and sometimes for none. He specialized in using his strength or gun to intimidate debtors and witnesses.

So when Steve gave Ned a job that required muscle, he suggested he take Leo along. The premise was simple. There was a witness that needed intimidating. And to make it easier, it was a woman in her early thirties who lived alone with her great-grandmother in a big house in what was beginning to become something of an iffy neighborhood.

Ned didn't have a choice. He picked up Leo and drove to the address. Leo had tried to dress like what he thought a "normal guy" looked like, but Ned found his attempt comical, so he decided that he'd take over the initial part of the operation. They walked up to the house. Leo hid on the veranda while Ned knocked on the door. A young woman who matched the picture he'd been given answered. Without an explanation, Ned shoved the door open and barged inside. Leo followed.

Ned held the startled woman up against the wall by putting his meaty forearm against her neck. Leo, wild-eyed and ridiculously dressed, sized her up. "Guess what?" he said. The victim didn't answer. He continued: "No ... guess."

She stammered.

"No, no, no, you can do better than that."

She began sobbing uncontrollably.

"Don't take it like that—it's nothing personal; all we have to agree on is that you won't testify."

She closed her eyes.

"No, we need a deal here," Leo continued. "I need to know that you will not testify."

She nodded.

"I mean it," he said. "Because if you testify, things could get very, very bad ... not just for you, but for your whole family ... you know what I mean?"

She nodded again.

"Okay, glad we could reach an agreement."

Ned lowered his arm. Free, the woman ran into another room.

"Let's go," Ned told Leo.

"Not yet," his friend said, just before throwing a lamp at a mirror that was hanging on the wall.

"We gotta get out of here," Ned said seriously.

"Almost, almost ..." Leo said as he started looking through the room. After a brief search, he found a little stereo, grabbed it, and ran out the front door. Ned ran after him. He noticed Leo was laughing. "That was pretty fuckin' easy," he said.

* * *

Lara was shocked at how many people were at Siobhan O'Farrell's wedding. Tate had sent her there because Siobhan was the only daughter of Gerard "Big Gerry" O'Farrell, last remaining star from Springfield's branch of the Irish mafia.

She was marrying Jacob Weitzmann, a prosperous local real estate investor. He had—as far as Clegg, Tate, and her other contacts knew (Delvecchio refused to help her)—no organized-crime connections other than his illustrious father-in-law-to-be.

As Lara stood in line outside the gates of Leonardo's Banquet Center, she gave the rest of the crowd a once-over. It was an older group than you'd expect for a twenty-four-year-old marrying a twenty-six-year-old, but there are always lots of relatives at weddings. It was all dark suits and evening gowns, a lot of gold and plenty of fur, despite the eighty-degree heat.

The exceptions to the dress code were a bunch of young men wearing T-shirts, jeans, and leather jackets. She could tell that some of them were Death Dealers from their patches, but most had no patches at all. A few of them had a patch from another gang. It was Black-somethings, but she couldn't read the second word because the old gothic typeface made it illegible to her.

When she got to the front of the line, a well-muscled guy in a tuxedo asked her for her invitation.

"I don't have one ..."

He interrupted. "You alone?"

"Yes."

"You got a boyfriend in there?"

Her first instinct was to say yes to justify her presence, but his body language told her to say no. She did.

"Go right ahead, miss, and have a great time."

Once inside, she approached a big-haired group of women about her age. She correctly guessed they were Siobhan's friends. She stood near them, pretending not to listen to what they were saying. It was mostly about gifts.

Eventually, one of them broke off from the crowd, so Lara said "hi." The young woman smiled and introduced herself as Maria Mascarello. She asked where Lara was from, because she didn't seem like she was from Springfield. Lara told her, truthfully, that she was from the West Coast.

As they began to get along, Maria gave Lara a tour of the facility and pointed out some of the young and single men. None of them were bikers. Lara pointed out one biker she thought was pretty good looking, and Maria made a face. "You like that sort of thing?" she said. "Not for me, thanks."

Then Lara asked her about a group of casually dressed people just outside the fence.

"Them? Ugh, those are what my dad calls 'the bloodsuckers'; you know, like reporters, the media," she said. "Every time anyone who is anyone tries to do anything anymore, they show up and try to ruin it. Fuckin' paparazzi."

"Is Siobhan famous?"

"Not yet, but she has an awesome demo tape—it'll blow you away," said Maria. "It's her dad who's famous. He's a big-time businessman."

"Oh, what business is he in?"

"I dunno. Business."

Just then, Lara saw the only person she recognized at the party. It was Marvin "Big Mamma" Bouchard, holding court in full Sons of Satan colors. He was surrounded by four or five other men, mostly in their forties and fifties. They were wearing expensive suits.

Lara took a deep breath and walked up to him. She could smell his leather jacket. "Hello, Mr. Bouchard."

Bouchard smiled and returned the greeting. The other men left without a word.

"What can I do for you, turtle dove?" he asked as they sat at a table. A waiter brought two glasses of champagne without being asked.

"My name is Lara Quinn . . ."

"You look like you are a friend of the groom's, but your name sounds like you are a friend of the bride's."

"Actually, I'm neither . . . I'm a reporter from the *Silhouette* . . ."

"A reporter? Really?" he was grinning very widely, almost laughing. "And they let you in?"

"Yes."

"And you just walked up to me and started talking?"

"Yes."

"This is indeed a strange, strange world," he chuckled. "Okay, Scoop, what do you want to know? Consider me your source on the inside."

Lara stammered.

"Okay, you can tell your paper that the notorious Marvin Bouchard is happy to attend the wedding of these two fine young people," he said. "And wishes them the utmost in health, happiness, and prosperity."

While they were talking, another man approached. He was short and stocky and walked with a slight limp. Although he was wearing an impeccably tailored Armani suit, he ruined the effect by matching it with a black shirt with no collar and about a half-dozen gold chains. His face was marred with a strange scar on his left cheek that looked like his mouth extended back and upwards. Lara tried not to stare.

He sat down beside Bouchard, facing Lara. He was not smiling. Though his eyes never left Lara, he asked Bouchard: "Who's your little friend, Marv?"

"This is Lara Quinn . . ."

"I know who she is."

". . . and may I present . . ."

"You won't present anything," Mehelnechuk interrupted. "I don't think it's a very wise idea for you to be speaking with such a pretty young girl when your wife is here. Come with me, Marv."

They both stood up. Bouchard excused himself.

Seconds after the two men left, two others—much younger and much bigger—stood on each side of Lara. "Miss, we're gonna have to ask you to leave," one of them said. "And it would be better for everyone if you didn't make a scene."

Lara got up and left. She thought about talking to the other reporters, but decided against it.

* * *

Ned walked into Steve's office at the Strip. "You get the job done?" he asked.

"Yeah, it was easy," Ned replied. "No problem really; didn't even need Leo—in fact, I wish I hadn't brought him."

"Why?"

"Well . . . can we talk in front of him?" he said, motioning at Bradley Myers, who was sitting on a nearby couch.

"We can only talk in front of him," Steve chuckled. "See, Bradley here is my lawyer, and if the cops or some other smart-ass tapes me or bugs me or even overhears me, it's inadmissible in court because of attorney-client privilege—I can say I killed Jimmy Hoffa and they couldn't do shit."

Ned laughed. "Okay . . . well, he stole something on the way out . . ."

"Aw, c'mon, you can't begrudge him a little extra; he doesn't make much and he does everything you say. 'Course I don't condone stealing, but that's his problem."

"Yeah, yeah, yeah. So why did we have to do that job anyway?"

"Well, a couple of our guys fucked her, and now she's pressing charges."

"Pressing charges? Do you mean they raped her?"

"That's what she says, but my boys say it was all consensual, so I have to believe them," Steve said. "Besides, that's up to the courts to decide."

"And if she doesn't testify . . ."

"Our two friends don't go to jail."

Ned rubbed his face in frustration, then sighed.

CHAPTER 7

Mehelnechuk had been grooming Sean Feeney for a while. He liked the kid. He wasn't very big, but he had presence. In fact, he reminded him a little of himself.

Feeney attracted the attention of the Sons of Satan when he was selling drugs for the Screaming Eagles, a New Devon-based gang controlled by the Martinsville Sons of Satan. They'd seen him sell drugs, seen him intimidate witnesses, and even seen him set fire to a Lawbreakers bar. But what really impressed Mehelnechuk was the fact that Feeney had gone to prison, done hard time, for something that wasn't his fault. He very easily could have gotten off if he talked, but he decided to take one for the team. Mehelnechuk was aware that not too many twenty-three-year-olds with two young children at home would have done that. Mehelnechuk wanted to reward him.

That desire dovetailed perfectly with another one of Mehelnechuk's plans. The Lawbreakers were no longer invincible in his hometown, and he wanted to take advantage of it. So he decided to start a new gang in Hagerstown, on the other side of Springfield—deeper into Lawbreakers' territory.

Feeney, he decided, would be the one to lead it. He was a tough kid, dedicated to the cause and a proven earner.

Mehelnechuk wanted to organize the effort himself, but he was too busy with other pressing expansion operations, so he recruited his old and trusted friend, Ray "Toots" Vandersloot. Toots did the organizational work, then collected some nonessential members and prospects from the many regional gangs that the Sons of Satan controlled, and assigned them to Feeney.

* * *

Ned noticed that Kelli had been acting differently lately. She'd cut off all contact with her parents and saw few of her old friends once she moved in with Ned. Since her parents refused to pay for college, she was growing increasingly bored and restless on the many nights Ned was out selling, collecting, negotiating, and performing other duties for the Death Dealers. He had what amounted to a full-time job with night-shift hours and she was afraid she was turning into a housewife.

So she made new friends. Steve had come to tolerate her presence and had started bringing Connie along, so the pair could talk while he and Ned did business. Kelli was surprised at how much she liked Connie, who was very articulate and even a bit erudite, despite her profession.

Eventually, Connie started inviting Kelli along on her girls' nights out, which usually consisted of a nice meal, a lot of talking, and then getting smashed, followed by a lot of laughing. Kelli had come to appreciate the company of many of Connie's other friends. She became close to one in particular, June O'Malley (who went by the stage name Pepper).

On one drunken night out, June introduced Kelli to the joys of cocaine. Kelli was reluctant at first, but when she saw that June wasn't crazy or suicidal or any of the other things they tell you drugs make you, she thought she'd give it a try— just this once. Besides, Connie said, it helped you lose weight.

* * *

Vandersloot's meeting with Feeney went exceedingly well. Not only did Feeney want the job, he couldn't hide his boyish enthusiasm. He even asked if he could name the gang. They became the Satan's Favorites after his own initials. Feeney also told Vandersloot to make sure he thanked Mehelnechuk for the opportunity and to tell him he wouldn't let him down.

Vandersloot, a veteran of too many wars and operations to get very excited about this kind of operation, assured him he would do well. Then he introduced him to some of his new gang. Feeney had never met any of them before, but they seemed like a big, tough lot, so he was impressed.

The plan was for Feeney to drive into Hagerstown. He would get his hair cut and wear a suit to rent a clubhouse. Then the rest of the gang would ride in on Harleys in full colors.

But there were problems from the start. Instead of an obscure and easily defended industrial or commercial space, Feeney rented a luxurious three-bedroom apartment in Hagerstown's fashionable Ironworks district. While the Satan's Favorites wanted to be noticed, their target market was hardly well represented by the young couples, families, and seniors they rode up and down with in the elevator.

And the Satan's Favorites found very little success on the ground. The Lawbreakers had been firmly entrenched in Hagerstown for more than a decade, and between them and their associated brokers, they had the drug and vice markets pretty well cornered.

That would have been a tough situation for even the best bikers to crack, but Feeney didn't have the best bikers. The men he got were expendable from other clubs because they weren't much good at anything. Their clumsy attempts at making contacts with those likely to buy product from them were met with laughter or scorn.

And Feeney himself wasn't much help. He spent a lot of time in Hagerstown's small but thriving gay village because, he said, it was an affluent, drug-using crowd, which the Lawbreakers avoided out of prejudice. If he could establish a beachhead in the gay community, he maintained, he could get cash and connections to make inroads into the rest of the town.

But his actual motives were quite different. A brief fling with a transvestite in prison had proven to him that he liked sex with men even more than sex with women. And while he was doing his best Mehelnechuk imitation in Hagerstown's gay village by buying drinks and showing off his wealth to make lots of friends, he really hadn't sold any drugs.

* * *

Lara was a little bit miffed when Clegg asked her to wait outside the police station for him. She thought it was rude of him not to invite her in. She was even less impressed when five minutes had passed their appointed time and he still hadn't shown up. Then she heard a car horn.

It came from a Suburban, painted in police colors. When she stood up, she could see Clegg was inside. "C'mon, kid," he shouted. "I don't have all day."

She climbed into the Suburban and was surprised at how cluttered the front seat was. Besides Clegg himself—a former college football player who had gotten no smaller over the years—the seat held his utility belt, two computers, and two shotguns.

As soon as she was in, he sped off. "Sorry we had to do it this way," he said, "but this is the only time I had. Besides you'll learn more this way." When he saw from her face that she needed an explanation, he continued. "Union rules state that every staff sergeant has to go out into the field and supervise his or her officers at least once a month."

She seemed satisfied, so he continued. "Okay, this is downtown, where most of the drug sales happen," he said. "You see any?"

"No."

"You won't. This isn't like TV, where there's a dealer on the corner—I'm sure some places are like that, but not Springfield," he said. "The drug sales happen inside—in bars, in nightclubs, in discos . . ."

"Who's behind it, the mafia?"

"To some extent, but less and less every year," he said. "That was the way it worked in the old days, but the mafia has fallen apart these days, most people think it's the arrests and the FBI, but it's not."

"No?"

"No, you met Siobhan, didn't you?"

"Not really."

"Well, you know who she is, right?"

"Yeah."

"Well, her dad is in the mob, her grandfather was in the mob, and three of her five uncles were, but she ain't and neither are her two brothers, and only one fucked-up waste case of the sixteen or so cousins that I know of."

"Why not?"

"Organized crime is a dirty, dangerous business. These kids, they don't want that kind of life. They're happy to take Daddy's dirty money and use it to start legitimate businesses. The only ones who stay in are the idiots and the psychos, and they're pretty easy to catch."

"So who is running all this? The Jamaicans? The Asians? The Hispanics? The Russians?"

Clegg chuckled. "You sound like you're from outta town."

"I am. I'm from ..."

"Los Gatos, California, I know," he said. "Anyway, as far as the Blacks are concerned, there's just too few of them—there are a few black kids and just as many Whites who call themselves Bloods and Crips, but they generally just steal chains and iPods from one another, nothing major. Sometimes they'll deal, but nothing better than street level."

"It's basically the same story with all the others—the few of them that are here will mostly fight among themselves and won't talk to us," he said. "Sometimes the Southeast Asians can get pretty fuckin' violent—sick fucks, some of them—but they keep it all in-house."

"So who is it?"

"Well, think about why you thought of all of those groups; what do they all have in common?"

"They're tight-knit ethnic groups who are generally poor and feel locked out of mainstream society."

"And in a cold, ugly, beat-up industrial town where the favorite sport is getting wasted, who does that describe?"

"Everybody?"

He laughed. "You've got a point, but the correct answer is white trash," he said. "They're poor, they're angry, they feel left out ..."

"So they band together and start committing crimes to get ahead ..."

"Yeah, I guess you could say it's a cycle."

"In their own strange way, they're trying to make life better for their children."

"I wouldn't go that far," Clegg sneered. "These guys get a

girl pregnant and leave ASAP; I've never seen one who was good to his kids."

"I guess there's no shortage of potential recruits."

He laughed. "What else are they gonna do?"

"They become bikers, why?"

"Mostly because it's the established way white trash bond in these parts—lots of people here who aren't involved with crime at all think the Sons of Satan are heroes, you know, rebel outlaws—and the bikes give them some legitimacy as an organization."

As he toured her around the downtown and industrial areas the bikers and their associates frequented—pointing out bars and other hotspots—he explained how the gangs worked, how the war against the Lawbreakers was proceeding, and how he saw the gangs' org charts shaping up. He put Bouchard at the top of the Sons' organization.

Eventually, she asked him. "Do you know a small, funny-looking man with a scar like this?" She traced a line up her left cheek.

"Sure, li'l Ivan, he's from here. I used to give him a boot to the ass every once in a while."

"Li'l Ivan?"

"Ivan Mehelnechuk used to ride with some stupid-ass gangs around here until I—that is, we—cleaned 'em all up," he said. "He was sharp, but nobody paid him much mind. I hear he's in the Sons over at Martinsville now, maybe a full patch, even."

"What if I told you he was giving Bouchard orders at Siobhan's wedding?"

"I'd say you were nuts."

"I'm saying it."

"I still say you're nuts, but it's worth looking into."

CHAPTER 8

Ned was pissed off and a little bit drunk when he came home from his meeting at the Strip. Steve wanted him to talk with these two El Salvadorean guys he'd heard were trying to make a name for themselves as independent dealers. Unlike many other big-time bikers, Steve made a habit of working with illegal immigrants: they worked hard, he said; they had their own built-in and otherwise impenetrable markets; and they adhered to a very strict code of silence. But Ned didn't like these two little pricks and their affected machismo. At the meeting, he got what he wanted out of them—they would sell drugs to the growing number of Central Americans coming to the area in search of work—but it had taken forever and Ned felt like he had just sat through a bad, low-budget gangster movie.

After they left, he stayed at the Strip for a while and had a few beers, just to cool down. He idly watched the dancers. A few people he knew came to talk with him, but he wasn't really into conversation. He just sat and drank.

When he'd had enough, he hopped in the SSR and drove home. He wasn't surprised to see Leo and Patsy there, along with June, Kelli, and her new friend Mallory. Mallory, a stripper, was young and beautiful. She had long dark hair and green eyes; she didn't look like Connie at all, but her natural, unaffected beauty attracted almost as many fans.

She had just turned eighteen when Steve discovered her working at a fast-food drive-thru window. She was too young to work at the Strip without her parents' permission because it served alcohol. A false signature and a fictitious address and phone number on a couple of never-checked government forms gave her a license to strip.

Mallory's good looks and matching ego rubbed many of the other dancers the wrong way at first. While many of them had abusive—or at least controlling—boyfriends, Mallory was blissfully unattached. She drove a Cadillac, had a lovely, two-bedroom, rented condo in downtown's most fashionable neighborhood, and dressed in styles that had not hit Springfield before she brought them. The other dancers were jealous and they let her know it by ignoring her.

Pretty well every biker and other man associated with the Strip had made at least some sort of pass at her. And her lack of interest led most of them to believe she was a lesbian. They teased her, but she wasn't intimidated.

Patsy eventually attached herself to the young girl and the two of them often went out drinking. When Patsy learned, to her surprise, that Mallory was doing coke, the pair became fast friends. Before long, Mallory started tagging along with Patsy and Leo to Ned's house.

Mallory and Kelli hit it off immediately. They had common interests, similar personalities, and both of them were profoundly lonely for someone else like themselves. Within a week of meeting, the two of them would often have nights out or hang at Ned's house, usually by themselves, but sometimes with June, Patsy, and Leo.

When Ned came home after dealing with the El Salvadoreans, he knew Mallory was there because the house was pumping techno music into the street at a tremendous volume. The front door was not just unlocked, it was ajar. In the living room, Kelli, Mallory, and June were dancing, while Patsy made out with Leo on the couch.

Ned stormed in, shut off the stereo, and started yelling at Kelli for leaving the front door open. Mallory rolled her eyes and asked Kelli if she wanted to go to a bar with her. Ned looked at her sternly. Kelli smiled and told him they were celebrating and that she really wanted to go.

Leo broke the tension by saying: "Let 'em go, boss; we have business to conduct, don't we?"

"No, no, we don't Leo . . . just get out of here."

"So how'd your meeting . . ."

"Just get out, all of you."

Ned went to bed.

***

Johansson was pretty pleased with himself. Not only had the boss's meeting in Newchester gone very well—a local outfit called the Death Vipers had agreed to crush the Sons of Satan's local rivals in exchange for probationary status as Sons of Satan, Newchester—but he had let Johannson sit up front with him on the flight home if he promised to stay quiet.

What Johansson didn't realize was that Mehelnechuk only wanted him up there so he could complain about how the airline had canceled the direct flight to Springfield and put them on one that first flew to Martinsville and then connected to Springfield. The practice of flying into Springfield had never made sense to Johansson, who thought his boss would want to get to the Martinsville clubhouse as quickly as possible. He had always thought they flew into Springfield then drove to Martinsville because it was cheaper, but he was beginning to think there were other reasons.

On the drive from Martinsville airport, Johansson asked why Mehelnechuk always wanted to fly into Springfield. "Good business decision," he said. "I know all the airport security there and they're cool—and I get to see my parents sometimes."

"Oh, and why are we doing all this traveling? To move product?"

"Yeah," he said, and paused for a very long time. "You know what my dream is?"

"No."

"I want to see nothing but Sons of Satan patches from coast to coast—and in other countries, too," he said intensely. "I don't want to see Lawbreakers, or Death Vipers, or Devil Dogs, or anyone else." He continued. "I want this to be our country again; I want to see the Italians, and Mexicans, and Blacks, and every-fuckin'-body else working for us or buying our product. I don't just want to make money; I want to fix a lot of things that are wrong with this world."

Johansson took a moment, then said, "Yeah, me too."

Mehelnechuk chuckled and went back to his book.

***

Feeney hated to wait, but he knew he had to. He knew the Satan's Favorites were dying in Hagerstown and he had to do something quick before Mehelnechuk pulled the plug on the plan. He was waiting for the man who he thought would be the Satan's Favorites' savior. Kevin Burman wasn't much to look at, but he was valuable property. As one of the few meth cooks the Sons of Satan had who wasn't either crazy or dead, Kevin was a commodity to be protected. Feeney knew that and, before he could borrow him from the Martinsville Sons of Satan, he had to pay off a number of people, and make assurances to many others.

He needed Burman. Satan's Favorites hadn't sold a single ounce of drugs in Hagerstown and Feeney was desperate to put something positive in the ledger to keep his little gang alive. Convinced that Hagerstown was too hick to appreciate the drug deals the Favorites were offering, he decided to switch to meth—the white trash drug. Burman could cook pounds of meth, quickly and safely, from ingredients found at drug and hardware stores. Unlike many meth cooks, he'd never had an explosion, and he'd never gone completely mental. He was eccentric, sure, but that went with the territory.

So Feeney waited in a cheap-ass, nondescript car that looked like a rental. And when Burman—skinny, shaved head, covered in tattoos—finally came down, Feeney greeted him as though he was early. He even opened the passenger door for him and threw his stuff in the trunk.

Feeney drove at exactly the speed limit. He wanted to go faster, because Burman was driving him nuts talking about how great the Florida State football team was. Feeney didn't care much about football, and knew even less about Florida. But this was not the time to get stopped for speeding, so he simply smiled, nodded, and grunted agreement with all of Burman's emphatically stated opinions.

Feeney had planned to transfer Burman to another car at a fast-food restaurant halfway between Springfield and Hagerstown, in case he was followed into town. He pulled into a spot between two minivans and, just as he opened the door, he felt the cold ring of a gun barrel against the back of his neck.

"Freeze before I blow your head away, motherfucker!"

He knew it was cops. If it was a hit, he wouldn't have heard a thing. But cops—who aren't supposed to actually kill you—like to be loud about their threats. Feeney slumped forward and put his face in his hands. Burman tried to run but got a big cop's forearm in his face and went down like a sack of potatoes.

In the back of the police car, Feeney thought about his options. He'd been in jail before, for a felony, so no matter what happened, he was going to prison. But Burman—despite being a meth cook, small-time thief, and genuine lowlife—had never been arrested before. Sending him to prison would be a huge blow to the Sons of Satan—and to Feeney's own reputation. Feeney knew what he had to do. He had to take the fall.

The cops found twelve unregistered weapons, hundreds of rounds of ammunition, and eight Satan's Favorites jackets. Feeney admitted to it all, plea bargained, and got six months. Burman walked.

***

Ned's knuckles hurt. He'd had to discipline a recalcitrant bar owner and his punch caught teeth instead of jaw. Besides the normal bruises a bad punch can cause, he was also dealing with multiple lacerations. He debated going to the hospital, but thought it'd be better to go home to see Kelli, have a nice chicken dinner delivered, and a couple of bottles of wine.

But when he got home, he found a note. It read:

> *Mal got a diamond necklace from some old guy, so we're cele-brating. It's a big girls' night out at June's. Come if you want, but it's gonna be all girls 'cept you!*

Ned crumpled up the note and threw it in the recycling. Then he stepped out of the house and into the SSR. He drove downtown and went to a bar he'd never been to before. He just wanted something that was not on his route. He didn't want to run into Kelli and Mallory, and he definitely didn't want to see any of his contacts, or dealers, or collectors, or anyone involved with the Springfield drug trade.

Instead, he drank. He drank and drank. He ordered a plate of clams and pasta, but he didn't eat it. Four hours after he'd gotten there, Ned settled up his bill and laughed at nothing in particular. He walked out the front door towards the parking lot where he'd left the SSR, but realized he was too drunk to drive.

He was mulling over his options as he walked home when he heard the low rumble of a customized V8. He looked behind him. It was a bright silver pickup with exterior pipes coming at him at an outrageous speed. He started running as best he could. As soon as the pickup passed him, the driver slammed on the brakes. The truck skidded ninety degrees to a stop that blocked Ned's escape route. Three men jumped out of the pickup's bed and grabbed him.

He tried desperately to defend himself, aiming his blows at knees, eyes, and balls, but was too drunk to be effective against even one of his assailants. They pinned him to the bottom of the bed as the truck sped away. Nobody said anything until they got to the beach. Before the truck came to a stop, Ned was thrown into the sand. It was dark and he couldn't see his assailants at all, but he could tell they were big and smelled of beer and leather.

"You're Aiken, Aiken the dealer," one of them said. After a few seconds, Ned realized it was a question, but he still didn't offer an answer. He got a kick in the ribs.

"You gotta remember something," said another voice. "This here is a Lawbreakers town."

Ned tried to give them the finger, but wasn't sure if he managed it.

He took about a half dozen more kicks before he heard anything else. "Tell your boss this is a Lawbreakers town," someone said. "Unless you want to die, you're gonna stop selling in our town."

That last thing Ned heard before he blacked out was laughter.

* * *

The bikers from the Black Knights had never seen anything back in New Aberdeen like the spread Mehelnechuk had put together at Johnny Reb's. Not only was there a free bar, a huge buffet, and a live band, but there must have been three dozen strippers. Stan Bly, president of the Black Knights, had told his men that the Sons of Satan were the "Big Time," and now they all believed it.

Mehelnechuk was shaking hands and making small talk when Johansson rushed into the bar. Obviously drunk, Johansson walked up to Bly, mumbled something about money he owed him from back in Stormy Bay and punched him in the face. Bly flew back about ten feet. Mehelnechuk rushed to the scene and grabbed Johansson. The big man was about to shake him off until he realized who it was. His eyes met Mehelnechuk's and he fled.

Mehelnechuk spent the rest of the night trying to repair the Sons of Satan's relationship with Bly and the Black Knights. After a while and a lot of drinks, it was cool; they all started drinking and having a good time again. It all stopped at two-thirty in the morning when one of the Black Knights found Bly's cold body outside Johnny Reb's front door.

Just as all the Black Knights were coming towards Mehelnechuk look- ing for answers, one of his prospects yelled at him. Mehelnechuk couldn't make out what he said, but screamed "not now!" at him. But the prospect was ada- mant. "Ivan, Ivan!" he shouted. "Marvin's just been arrested for murder."

CHAPTER 9

A couple of days after she'd left, Kelli came home. She looked awful—her hair was a mess, her makeup smeared, and her face puffy. She was wearing some of Mallory's clothes and had that snickery look and stumbling gait of someone who wasn't quite high, but wasn't quite sober either. Even though she had a key, she rang the doorbell.

"Where've you been?" shouted Ned as he opened the door. He was still in a great deal of pain from the beating he'd gotten from the Lawbreakers. And he was pissed they'd stolen his gun—the one André had bought him—and almost seven thousand in cash. He was even more pissed off to see that Kelli had brought Mallory, Connie, and Patsy in tow.

"Just partyin', Nedley," Kelli explained. "Just having a good time. It's not like I have anything else to do around here anyway." The other women joined in her laughter as they sat heavily upon the couches. Kelli got up to get them drinks.

Although he knew he should say or do something, Ned was just too sore to get into it. Instead, he slunk away to the bedroom.

"You might wanna stay up," Patsy yelled after him. "Leo's coming over in a few minutes."

***

Mehelnechuk wore his best Armani suit as he accompanied Phil, Marvin Bouchard's lawyer, into jail. He knew that the only way to talk to Bouchard without anyone listening was to discuss it in front of a lawyer and claim attorney-client privilege. He had never met Bouchard's lawyer before, but he knew anyone who'd represent such a miserable fuck must know how to play ball.

There was some media presence outside the jail, but nobody took his picture. Mehelnechuk, careful to keep only the right side of his face toward the media, blended in with the other lawyers making their way in and out of the jail. To them, he was just a short-haired, clean-shaven white guy in a nice suit, not what they expected a criminal to look like. While the security guards did pat him down, Mehelnechuk was not required to show any identification, so he signed in as "Hugh G. Rection."

Inside, he saw Bouchard relaxing with a bunch of other prisoners waiting for their visitors. The moment he saw Mehelnechuk, Bouchard straightened up. Three guards took him into an interview room so he could speak with his lawyers in private. Bouchard and Mehelnechuk sat across the tattered old desk from one another. The lawyer sat on a couch behind them. Mehelnechuk stared at Bouchard for a long time before calmly asking: "Do you realize what a fuck-up you are?"

"Look, Ivan, you left me in charge of Martinsville . . ."

"Yeah, but I did not give you permission to risk everything I have spent years building up," Mehelnechuk's voice sounded threatening. "Why do you constantly have to be in the public eye—I read about you in newspapers, I see you on TV, every time I look around there's a picture of your stupid shit-eating grin."

"But that was the plan; everyone sees me so they don't see you."

"I know what you were trying to do," Mehelnechuk scolded. "But you pushed it too far. I wanted you to be well known among our people, not Public Enemy No. 1—you got that?"

"Yes."

"Okay, I took a look at your lawyer's notes and they actually don't have shit against you. Thank Christ you followed procedure. You're only here by reputation, so you'll get off on lack of evidence before there's even a trial if your lawyer is any good."

"I'm the best defense att . . ."

"Didn't ask you," Mehelnechuk snapped. "Anyway, we gotta take care of this mess."

"Yeah."

"So who was the triggerman—who actually shot Vanden Boom?"

"Stinky."

"Holy shit, I never realized he had it in him."

"Yeah, wanted to earn his stripe."

"Earned more than that, my friend," Mehelnechuk chuckled. "And who did he report to?"

"Shithead."

"Shithead Ingram? That fuckin' drunk? It's amazing they pulled it off at all."

"Yeah," Bouchard started laughing.

"Well, you know the drill—try to keep your fuckin' mouth shut for a change and we can get you outta this," Mehelnechuk said. "But you are gonna owe me big-time again, brother."

"Understood."

***

Ned was relieved to hear Leo was on his way. He hoped that, with his help, he could get the still-partying women under control.

He emerged from the bedroom when he heard Leo arrive and was surprised by what he saw. Leo looked like a bum; he was unshaven, unwashed, and smelled terrible. He looked nervous and out of balance. And he kept scratching himself all over.

"What the fuck happened to you?" asked Ned.

"I could ask you the same thing."

"I was jumped by some fuckin' Lawbreakers while you were out partying with these whores."

"We're not whores; we're strippers," Patsy said. "Oh wait, I *am* a whore." All the women laughed.

When Leo joined in, Ned couldn't take it anymore. "Get the fuck out! All of you, get the fuck out!"

Leo gathered up the women and led them out. "Come on girls," he said. "I know when I'm not wanted."

"Not wanted? I threw you the fuck out."

Kelli stopped at the door and looked beseechingly at Ned. "Me too?"

"Maybe just for a day or two."

* * *

Mario DeVolo sat at the head of a long table with a TV behind him. Assembled at the table were a number of other Martinsville bar owners and other drug distributors. Behind them, up against the walls, were what remained of the Martinsville Lawbreakers and a few other non-aligned or disillusioned drug dealers.

Satisfied they were all paying attention, DeVolo replayed a part of that night's news. It was biker expert Jake Levine expounding on the new landcape in Martinsville. "With Bouchard now effectively out of picture, the Martinsville Sons of Satan are basically powerless," he said. "He was not just their president, but essentially their heart and their soul—without him, there will be an organized crime power vacuum in Martinsville."

After he shut it off, DeVolo stood up and started walking around the room, doing his best imitation of Robert DeNiro as Al Capone. "You hear that? The big man is down and the Sons are on their knees," he said. "Those bastards who have been overcharging us and cutting off any alternatives no longer have the power—they have nothing."

Applause filled the room. "They are on their knees and now is the time for us to take control of our own destinies," he continued. "We can get product at the price we want, from whoever we want, and charge whatever the hell we want."

More applause. "What I am suggesting, gentlemen, is that we form our own alliance—secret at first," he said. "I am offering you all an opportunity to join a new organization, an organization of strength and freedom."

The response was unanimous. After about two hours of negotiation, a new organized crime entity—the High Rollers—was formed. Their objective was not just to make make money, but to retake much of the territory the Sons of Satan had taken. And, if necessary, eventually eliminate them.

* * *

As soon as they got back to Leo and Patsy's place, June passed out on the living room couch. Connie wanted to stay, but began to sense that it was getting too weird between Leo and Patsy, so she left for Steve's. She convinced Kelli, who was babbling and giggling, to come with her by telling her that Steve just got a new hot tub and they should try it out. The rain had stopped so they decided to walk.

And it did get weird between Leo and Patsy. All night, he had been accusing her of conspiring with an old boyfriend—a Lawbreaker—to kill him. At first he was subtle, joking around; by the time they'd gotten home, he was shouting at her. "I know you two are trying to get rid of me," he said.

"Don't be ridiculous," she snapped back.

"Then why did you buy the coke from him . . . and why haven't *you* had any?"

"First of all, I didn't buy the coke from him. I bought it from Amanda at the Strip, she probably got it from Steve."

"Don't lie to me. It's bad coke. It's fuckin' poison and you know it. I can feel it—it's makin' me crazy. If it's so fuckin' good, why don't you have some?"

"I haven't had any of this coke because you and I have been doing coke non-stop for about a week. I need a fuckin' rest from it."

Leo, blue-skinned and twitching, lunged at her. He wrestled the bag of coke out of her hands, spilling some, and ran upstairs with it. Realizing he was going to the bathroom to flush it, Patsy ran after him. When she caught up with him on the stairs, he turned around and kicked her. She broke her fall down the stairs and managed get back up and force her way into the bathroom just as he was hovering over the toilet with the bag.

"C'mon, baby, lover, you don't wanna do that," she pleaded.

"Yeah, I know, I was just being nuts." He handed her the bag.

"Yeah, yeah, I know," she offered. "Why don't you just go to bed, smoke a joint . . . you know that always calms you down."

"Okay, okay," he said. "You wanna grab me a joint and a light? I'll be in the bedroom."

As she walked down the stairs, a disturbed-looking June asked her what was happening.

"Nothing, really, Leo's been under a lot of stress lately," she answered, while getting Leo a beer and a joint. "And he's really ramped up the coke use. He'll get over it."

Just as she turned around, Leo flew down the stairs. He pointed a gun at June's face and shouted: "I know what you fuckin' skank bitches are up to!"

Patsy screamed. June, too terrified to run, said, "I have no idea what you are talking about, Leo."

Leo slapped her in the jaw and trained his gun on Patsy. "You and you and that fuckin' boyfriend of yours are trying to kill me. I know you are."

June was sobbing too hard to speak; Patsy rushed to her aid. She shouted at Leo: "Put that gun away, you stupid asshole; nobody's trying to kill you."

Leo punched her with his left hand, keeping the gun trained on her at the same time. "We'll see who's try to kill who . . . get in the fuckin' car."

Patsy and Leo had one of those townhouses with a sunken garage under the living room. He marched the pair through the door and into Patsy's old Mazda. He sat in the rear seat with his gun barrel pressed against the back of Patsy's neck. It was covered from potential witnesses by the headrest. June sat motionless and expressionless in the passenger seat, a huge red mark on the right side of her face and running mascara the only indications from the outside that anything was wrong. There was very little traffic as the sun had only risen a half-hour earlier.

He told Patsy to drive. She asked where. He told her she knew.

She guessed that he meant to go to her ex-boyfriend's house—perhaps he wanted to confront him, maybe kill him. He'd probably let her go after he realized there was nothing going on between them—if things were allowed to get that far.

In all likelihood, this trip would be suicidal for Leo. Jeff lived in a house with two other career criminals, including a gunrunner. All of them were bigger, stronger, and more aggressive than Leo. In fact, Patsy had left Jeff because of the beatings and routine humiliations he and his friends put her through. They were bad men, ones she never wanted to see again. And they were easily capable of taking care of a relative lightweight like Leo.

She was thinking of how she'd distract him, when June did it for her. As Patsy waited at a stoplight, June made a break for it. She unlocked and opened the door as stealthily as she could, and once the car came to a complete stop, she flung it open and leapt outside.

As she landed, her right high heel snapped and she went down hard. Leo rose in his seat and shot through the still-open door. The first two shots went through both of her thighs. The third shot—the one that killed her—went through the fingers of her left hand, then penetrated her left lung.

Patsy darted out her door and into traffic. Brakes screeched and horns blared as motorists tried not to hit her or each other as they slid on the wet pavement.

Leo screamed and went after her, firing as he ran. Over their four-block chase, he managed to hit her in the right shoulder and shoot off a tiny chunk of her left ear. She could tell he was gaining on her and became desperate for a place to hide. She ran to the closest house and began pounding on the door and screaming. An elderly man let her in and locked the door behind him. Leo, right behind her, began pounding on the door. Patsy collapsed from exhaustion and loss of blood once inside. The elderly man called 911, but dropped the phone and ran down to the basement when Leo started shooting through the door. He was trying to kick it down when a patrol car screeched to a halt at the curb.

Leo ran for it, but was exhausted and knew he couldn't keep running away from the bigger, healthier cop who took chase when he bolted. He also knew that his handgun would do little against a Kevlar vest. He was trying to think of an idea when he saw a mother crossing the street with a child. He turned and grabbed the kid. He stopped, put his arm around the boy's chest, and stuck the gun up to his temple.

The mother screamed. The cop stopped in his tracks.

"Unless you want this kid's fuckin' brains all over the fuckin' street, you're gonna put the gun down!"

The young cop, who had never seen anything like this before, froze.

"Just put down the gun, sir, we don't want anyone to get hurt." He kept his pistol trained on Leo's head.

"I said, put the fuckin' gun down!"

"That's not going to happen, sir. Please drop the weapon and release the child. Nobody has to get hurt here."

Police sirens were getting louder and louder.

Leo began to freak out, screaming unintelligibly with saliva flying out of his mouth. The little boy cried and struggled. The mother screamed and screamed. And the cop kept his gun pointed at Leo's head.

Finally, Leo screamed out "Fuck this! Fuck you all!" and pulled the trigger. Shocked by the sound of the hammer banging inside an empty chamber, Leo pulled the trigger again and again. Nothing. After the fourth try, he threw the gun at the cop and ran.

Immediately, the cop chased him. Before the end of the block, the young cop had Leo down and immobilized.

Seconds later, the rest of the cops showed up—some in full armor and with semi-automatic weapons—surrounded them, and took care of the mother and child.

Leo was still babbling incoherently when they put him in the back of the police car.

***

Ned didn't want to answer his cellphone, but he knew he had to when he saw it was Steve who was calling.

"Leo's gone nuts and wasted a couple of whores out in the suburbs," he told him. "You have my permission to get out of town and lay low."

"What? Leo? Is he alright?"

"Listen, I told our brothers in Martinsville to be expecting you. You can live in their clubhouse for as long as necessary."

"What? How will I . . ."

"Just go."

Ned went to the garage and drove to the townhouse he once shared with Leo. He still had a key, but the garage door was still open. He drove the SSR inside and closed the garage door behind him. He ran into Leo's house and went immediately for his caches of drugs and cash. Convinced he had found them all, he threw everything into the SSR's bed. Back inside, he searched his closets and drawers for anything that could connect Leo to Ned or to the Death Dealers. He took his jacket, some bullets, some greeting cards, some hand-drawn maps and notes, two collections of photographs, a PC, and a cellphone. He tossed them all into the bed of the SSR and drove to a self-storage unit out by the airport. He dumped all the incriminating stuff in the locker and drove to Martinsville.

***

Lara arrived just in time to see Patsy's ambulance leave. Immediately, she sought out Clegg. He explained what he'd been told had happened.

"Who are the victims?"

"Kids just an ordinary kid in the wrong place at the wrong time—mom and he were headed to a bus stop so they could catch an early train to grandma's."

"And . . .?" she asked expectantly.

"Well, the fatality . . ."

"Fatality?"

"Yeah, it hasn't been declared yet, but she's a goner. Didn't get a name but the guys said she was a stripper."

"And the other?"

"One. I knew her, Patsy Wiggan, a tough mama who used to run with the Lawbreakers . . . hadn't seen her in a while, looks like she'll pull through."

"And the killer?"

"Don't know him at all, total skel . . . this is obviously the work of drug-induced paranoia."

"Which drug?"

"A stimulant, seems to be a little too organized for meth and looking at this scumbag, I don't think he gets his hands on coke too often, so I'd have to go with crack—but you never know until the tests return."

"This is your brain on drugs."

"Yeah, a human brain can only take so much stimulation before it pops. This guy is gone for good."

"Whaddaya mean?"

"Looney tunes."

"How about the cop?"

"Oh yeah, Bartholomew."

"Something of a hero, isn't he?"

"I'm sure that's what your readers will want to hear ..."

"You don't think so?"

"Well, I'd have punched that piece of shit's ticket before he laid a hand on the kid."

***

Marissa Banting had only been rowing with the Hill Park high school team for two weeks. Actually, she wasn't rowing, but she was part of the team. She was the coxswain, the person who shouts out "row! row! row!" to keep the rowers in rhythm. She was picked because, at 102 pounds, she put very little weight on the shell and, because she was so good looking, it kept the boys focused. She was loving her role as center of attention until, on a Thursday practice, the shell hit something in the water. She assumed it was a log or a plank from one of the rotting old docks. That's what she was thinking as the collision threw her into the bay.

She grabbed the floating object to stay afloat. She was smiling at the guys in the shell when she saw the horrified looks on their faces. Instinctively, she looked at the object she was hanging onto. After she saw the face, she had to be rescued by three members of the team. The body was later identified at that of Charlie "Stinky" Schaefer.

On the following day, two garbagemen emptying the dumpsters behind the Highpoint Mall noticed something out of the ordinary. It was a human hand. As they combed through the bin, they found a thigh, a torso, and eventually a head. The remains were later identified as those of Brandon "Shithead" Ingram.

CHAPTER 10

"La Grange." The ZZ Top song praising a rural whorehouse. The song seeped into Ned's brain long before he realized it was the ringer on his cellphone. He leapt from the cot he was sleeping in and felt around in his jeans for the phone. By the time he'd found it, he'd missed the call. But he knew who it was without checking. So he called Steve.

"Good morning."

"Sorry Steve, late night last night," Ned croaked into the phone. "Ever since I've been living in the clubhouse, I haven't really gotten a hell of a lot of sleep."

"The boys like to party . . . and they do it in shifts . . . I should have warned you."

"Oh, it's cool . . . just don't expect too much from me."

Ned heard Steve sigh. "Bad attitude, young man," Steve said. "I expect a lot out of you today . . . you're going to be meeting with the big boss tonight."

"Bouchard? I thought he was in jail."

Steve laughed. "No, *his* boss."

As Ned was leaving, he was pushed aside by two Death Dealers prospects who were dragging a teenager into the bar by his arms. The kid was screaming, and obviously in pain.

Little John Rautins, the ranking member in the clubhouse,

was also rousted by the noise, "What the fuck's going on?" he yelled.

"We caught this little fuck spreading the word he was a Death Dealer, and he was getting the wrong kind of 'attention' if ya know what I mean," one of the prospects said. "And you know what that means."

The kid in question looked terrified. Rautins looked at him and shook his head. "My hands are tied; do what you have to."

Rautins then put his arm around Ned and led him out of the room. They could hear the prospects slapping the boy around as he cried out to be left alone. After what sounded like one particularly brutal hit, he went silent and Ned could hear the prospects hooting congratulations at one another.

Ned, disturbed, asked Rautins if that kind of brutality was really necessary.

Rautins laughed. "It's something we inherited from the Sons," he said. You gotta punish fakes. Otherwise, your name means nothing."

"Yeah, but it looked like they were gonna kill that kid."

"I'll be the first to admit that those two have a tendency to go too far," Rautins said. "But, in our particular business, they take a lot of the pressure off guys like you and me."

The two prospects put the bloodied kid in a blanket and carried him past Ned and Rautins.

"You didn't kill him, did you?"

"Nah, just taught him a lesson."

"What you gonna do with his ass now?"

"Dump him in the alley behind the Lawbreakers' clubhouse—then see what happens."

***

Ned had never been to such a fancy restaurant in his life—and he felt awkward about wearing jeans and a T-shirt. Steve, dressed almost exactly the same and covered in tattoos, didn't seem to care.

The hostess, waiting behind a lecturn, was clearly disturbed by their appearance. Again, Steve didn't seem to care. He walked up to her confidently and said to her: "Mehelnechuk party."

Immediately, her sneer turned to a welcoming, if manufactured, smile. "Oh, right this way, gentlemen," she said with a veneer of friendliness. "Mr. Mehelnechuk is expecting you."

She guided them to a large table where a lone man was seated, reading a newspaper. He was wearing a beautifully tailored suit and very expensive leather shoes. As he approached, Ned could see that he had a big gold watch and other obvious jewelry.

When Mehelnechuk put his newspaper down, Ned recognized him as the guy with the scar that he'd seen a couple of times before at the clubhouse. Ned was surprised this guy would be at a meeting with the boss.

"Hello, gentlemen," he said.

"Hey, Ivan," said Steve. "Looking good."

"Steven," Mehelnechuk nodded, then looked at Ned. "Great to have you here, Mr. Aiken. Order anything you want—tonight is your night."

"Uh . . . thank you, sir."

"Drop the formalities. I'm Ivan," Mehelnechuk said as he extended his hand. "It's very nice to finally meet you."

"Meet *me*? Why?"

"I've known about your work for quite some time now, and I have to admit that I'm more than a little impressed."

"Uh . . . thank you, thank you."

"Sit down, relax; you are among friends here . . . really."

They ate dinner together. Ivan ordered something in French for a confused Ned, who was happily surprised to get a steak, French fries, and green beans.

After they ate and exchanged pleasantries, Mehelnechuk got down to business. "Ned, the organization is grateful for what you did—how fast you thought and how quickly you acted—in the Babineau situation."

"What? Cleaning up after Leo? That just seemed like the right thing to do."

"Do you hear this kid, Steve? Seriously, you are one in a million—or at least a thousand. Most of our guys would just stay at home and wait it out, or run away. But you went in, beat the cops, and kept the rest of us out of trouble—your instincts are those of a future chapter executive."

Ned felt warm in the face. He didn't know what to say.

"Anyway," Mehelnechuk continued as the waiter brought them desserts and after-dinner drinks. "The organization is very grateful for what you did in the Babineau situation."

"What did I do?"

Mehelnechuk laughed, and Steve followed suit. "Don't worry, just keep it up," Mehelnechuk paused. "So . . . what's this thief giving you?"

"Sorry?"

"What's your deal with Steve?"

"Thirty percent."

"It's thirty-five now."

Steve blanched. "Don't worry, Steve, you'll both be happy to know that Ned's territory now includes Stoney Point and Rockston; the five percent you lost on this one distributor will be more than made up by his bigger area."

The three agreed it was an equitable deal, and Ned indicated that he was eager to get back to work. Ivan suggested they go outside to enjoy some cigars.

Outside on the sidewalk, the three men were smoking and chatting, telling jokes, and dissing enemies when Ivan suddenly handed something to Steve.

He, in turn, handed the plastic bag to Ned. Confused, Ned was looking in his hands when he heard the whoop of a police car that had stopped just in front of them. Without thinking, he threw the bag into a nearby hedge.

The cops piled out of the three cars that had arrived and arrested Mehelnechuk, Steve, and Ned.

Three hours later, Ned was in jail for possession of methamphetamine (there wasn't enough in the bag to warrant a trafficking charge), while Steve and Mehelnechuk were released due to lack of evidence.

* * *

Antonio McIntyre knew that when white people he didn't know approached him on the street, they were either cops or guys looking for drugs. And these guys—two scruffy-looking dudes who piled out of an old Chevy S-10 pickup—didn't look like cops. But in his line of business, Antonio knew that it was wise to treat 'em all like cops until you knew they weren't.

The bigger of the two walked out with his hand outstretched. "Tony," he said. "We're friends of Paul's."

Antonio didn't shake his hand. "Paul? What Paul? I know a lot of Pauls."

"C'mon, Tony, don't be like that—big fat Paul with the beard down to here," the man paused. Even though he knew which Paul they were talking about, Antonio offered no response. "He thinks we're cops," the man said. "Stan, why don't you show him we ain't cops?"

As instructed, Stan reached into his paper shopping bag and pulled out a sawed-off shotgun. He pumped one shot through Antonio's chest and another that took off most of his face.

* * *

Later that same day, another Martinsville street-level dealer—Don Queen, who distributed weed, hash, and meth at a local bowling alley—received a visit from three tough-looking guys who asked to speak with him in his office.

Unlike Antonio, who was afraid of getting arrested, Don was afraid of getting his ass kicked, so he did what they said. He recognized one of the young men as the younger brother of a guy he knew from high school—Ryan Knowles—and he knew that anyone from that family was too psycho to be a cop, let alone an undercover one.

Don led them into the windowless storage room behind a hand-written "employees only" sign, and sat down on a cardboard box full of toilet paper rolls. He asked what he could do for them.

Their obvious leader asked how much he was paying the Sons of Satan for product.

Rather than mess around with these guys, Don told them the truth without hesitation.

"Wow," said the tough guy. "Don't you think that's a bit high just for weed?"

"That's not for weed; that's for hash," said Don, hoping that they'd sympathize with him.

"Wow. What say we give you weed, hash, and meth for three-quarters of what you pay now? Better stuff even."

"I'd say I'd love it, but I don't want to get into any trouble with the Sons."

"Let us worry about the Sons."

Then the the younger Knowles brother laughed and said, "Maybe you should worry more about us than the Sons." Then he kicked Don's makeshift seat into shreds until Don was sitting on the floor. The Knowles kid was laughing like a maniac. Don tried to laugh along. He noticed that all of them had matching rings. On each of them were a pair of dice and the name "High Rollers."

***

On his first full day in jail, Ned was sitting in the exercise yard when he was approached by a handsome young man with glasses. He introduced himself as Sean Feeney. "Ivan wants you to know that he's very impressed with what you did at the restaurant, and wants you to know that you'll be taken care of both inside and after you get out," he said.

"Thanks," Ned replied, thinking the guy looked more like a car salesman than a biker. "I appreciate that."

"No, seriously—drugs, booze, smokes, porn, whatever— you just come to me."

"Well, a little weed wouldn't kill me."

"I heard that."

"It's a big relief to talk with you. I was afraid I'd get jumped in here."

"Don't worry about that, we totally run this fuckin' wing," Feeney assured him. "Even the warden is scared to piss us off. See those two fuckers?" He pointed at two huge men with shaved heads, long beards, and tattoos so thick they looked like patterned turtleneck sweaters under their prison shirts.

"They'll make sure nothing happens to you," Feeney told Ned. "They're ours. We own them." The two men acknowledged him with simultaneous nods.

"Great, because to tell you the truth, I was afraid I might run into someone who wants me to be his girlfriend, if you know what I mean."

"Are you trying to tell me you want a bitch?"

"You can get a woman in here?"

"No, no, no, a bitch—what are you, my grandmother?"

"Oh, oh, oh, not interested, don't go that way."

Feeney laughed. "Well, well, Mr. Macho, keep one thing in mind—it's not queer if you're on top."

***

After the tough guys left, Don Queen phoned his connection with the Sons of Satan. He was sketchy about details, but he told them about the High Rollers rings and the Knowles boy. Within three hours, the news of a rival gang pressuring dealers to sell their drugs had filtered up to Mehelnechuk. He called a meeting of his Martinsville members along with those of the Huns, a nearby puppet club, for that night. The only excuses for not attending, he insisted, were being in a jail cell, a hospital bed, or on a slab in the morgue.

***

Feeney kept his word and supplied Ned with enough weed to help him go to sleep every night he was in jail. And, much to Ned's surprise, neither the guards nor the prisoners in adjacent cells ever said a word about the smoke. As Kelli's visits became rarer, and her attention seemed to wane even when she did show up, Ned found himself hanging around Feeney more and more. They'd work out, play cards, or just shoot the shit for hours.

Ned was a little weirded out by Andreas, though. Andreas was a little Venezuelan guy who hung around and did everything Feeney told him to do. Andreas asked Ned to call him "Vanessa" (Feeney did), but he just couldn't bring himself to.

Andreas generally didn't interfere when Ned and Feeney were together, except when he occasionally brought them drinks or smokes. But on one occasion, he erupted into a crying jag, screaming something in Spanish and getting all red in the face. Quickly, Feeney excused himself from Ned by saying, "I gotta go handle this." He put his arm around Andreas' shoulders and led him out of the common room. They didn't come back until the next day.

After he started to be seen with Feeney more frequently, Ned was generally treated better by inmates and guards alike. The same guys who had called him "shithead" and "faggot" and had handled him with truly unnecessary roughness when he was being brought to jail, now called him Ned, or even Mr. Aiken.

Ned didn't smoke the night before his preliminary hearing, though, because he wanted to appear absolutely clean and sober before the judge. Instead, he stayed up all night—aware that, while drugs and friends could make prison tolerable, he'd do anything he could to spend as little time as possible there.

* * *

Many members of the Sons of Satan didn't like it when Mehelnechuk called a meeting. Normally, Sons of Satan meetings were rollicking parties with booze, drugs, and call girls; but when Mehelnechuk called one, it was always something important and it was best to arrive sober.

They filed into "church" somberly. Many were surprised to see Dave "Apache" Carter in full colors.

Less than a year earlier, Mehelnechuk had made an example out of him. Many in the organization thought that Carter was using way too much coke, and when he came to his brothers for help with a $46,000 debt he owed his Italian suppliers, Mehelnechuk was outraged. It was, he said, the responsibility of members to make money with drugs, not to lose it. He had already banned the use of cocaine and methamphetamines among club members and prospects. But the capper for Mehelnechuk was that Carter came into the clubhouse, begging like some junkie. The boss kicked him out of the club, took his bike, took his colors, and made him get his member's tattoo covered over. Where the smiling skull in the top hat once adorned his skinny bicep, there was now just a dark blue circle the size of a crabapple.

But he didn't kick Carter out entirely. In order to keep the peace and maintain cordial business relations, Mehelnechuk paid the Italians from the club's coffers. After deducting the $11,000 Carter's bike sold for, the disgraced former member still owed the Martinsville Sons of Satan $35,000. Mehelnechuk wanted him to work it off, so he reduced Carter's rank to hangaround, and said he'd make him perform a variety of tasks for the club until his debt was paid.

There was a problem with that plan. Carter only had one discernable talent. He killed people. Before the war with the Lawbreakers, Carter had proven to be a poor drug salesman, often snorting more than he sold. And at a skinny five-foot-seven, he had no value when it came to intimidating witnesses or debtors. Charmless, he failed as a pimp. He was too stupid to be a reliable arsonist and too disorganized to be a decent fence. But he was a remorseless bastard who could kill someone and forget about it the moment he was paid.

That talent had came in very handy during the war with the Lawbreakers. Of the twenty-one Lawbreakers and associates who had been killed, all but five were shot by Carter. And that didn't include the two guys he shot just because he thought they *looked* like Lawbreakers.

Killing, he said, was easy. Get a clean weapon from the club. Find the guy. Get him alone and shoot him. Drop the weapon. Walk away. Get paid.

As surprising as his presence in full colors was, it was even more startling for many to see him take a place at the table alongside Mehelnechuk and the empty seat reserved for Bouchard.

After some initial pleasantries, Mehelnechuk left the room.

His old friend, Mike "Sloppy" Rose, took over. A few months earlier, Rose had been an old-school biker—long hair, beard, body covered in tats, always in filthy jeans. But since Mehelnechuk had become president, Rose had cleaned up. The beard was gone, his hair was short and neat, and he often wore casual but clean clothes that covered most of his ink. He got to the point. "Gentlemen," he said. "We are at war."

Rose improvised from the script Mehelnechuk had written for him. An avid reader on the subject of war and strategy, Mehelnechuk was an admirer of Pope Urban II—who taught that the only way to get men to go to war was to make the war seem like a necessary cause against an evil enemy. They had to be convinced not only that they were in danger, but that the enemy was worthy of nothing less than extermination. Of course, psychos like Dave Carter needed no convincing.

"Our very existence as a club is at stake," Rose told them. "In the last few days, two of our associates have been murdered, and a bomb exploded in Peterson's Harley-Davidson."

There was an audible gasp in the room.

"Don't worry, nobody was hurt. But any of us could have been there—any one of us could have been dead."

Rose had their full attention now.

"There is a force out there," he continued. "It is a force that is hell bent on destroying us; on murdering you, you, you, you, and you." He pointed into the crowd. "They want us dead," he said. "And they will not rest until you . . . are . . . dead—all of you. . . . But we're not gonna let that happen!"

The crowd roared. Carter laughed.

Later on, they broke into smaller teams. The prices were circulated. Each member or prospect would be paid ten thousand for the murder of a High Rollers member, five thousand for a High Rollers prospect, and two thousand for a High Rollers associate.

***

Ned waited quietly and politely as the other hearings dragged on before his name was called. He was disturbed not to see Mehelnechuk, or Steve, or anyone else he knew in the courtroom, but his defense lawyer told him that everything would be cool.

The judge was a mean-looking old bastard who looked very much like he wanted to be somewhere else.

When Ned's case came up, the opposing lawyers informed the judge what had happened. Acting on an anonymous tip, a police task force had descended on Cowan's Fine Dining. There they saw Ivan Mehelnechuk, Steve Schultz, and another man they later identified as Edward Aiken standing on the sidewalk. One officer saw Aiken throw an object into the hedge, recovered it, and determined it was methamphetamine.

Before the prosecution could even speak, the judge interrupted. "This officer, Darrell Tucker, is he the same Darrell

Tucker who was indicted for planting evidence in the Vontae Williams case?"

"I'll have to check my notes," said the prosecutor, as he glanced through some papers. "Yes, yes he is."

"And he, Tucker, is the only person who saw the accused in possession of the controlled substance?"

"Yes."

"And he was acting on an anonymous tip?"

"Yes."

"Can you read to me exactly what his statement says?" the judge asked. "Just the part about when he saw the accused with the substance in question."

"Yes, here it is." The prosecutor then read from Tucker's statement: "... 'at that point, I exited the car and, as I approached Mr. Mehelnechuk, Mr. Schultz, and Mr. Aiken, Mr. Aiken then appeared to throw an object into the shrubbery' ..."

"And Tucker was the only witness to this act?"

"Yes."

"So you're telling me, Ms. Prosecutor, that the only person who 'appeared' to see Mr. Aiken throw the controlled substance is a police officer who has been indicted previously for planting evidence?"

"He was not convicted."

"As I recall, he plea bargained down to a lesser charge," the judge snapped. "And he was the only one who saw this, despite the fact that it allegedly happened on a Saturday night at one of the most popular restaurants in the city's entertainment district?"

"Yes."

"Well then, I just don't think you have enough evidence to bring this case to trial," the judge said. "The controlled substance could have been anyone's. Case dismissed."

Ned's defense attorney looked him in the face and grinned broadly. "See, I told you everything would be all right."

* * *

On their way to school, two twelve-year-old boys decided to take the long way to school. Seventh-graders new to New Aberdeen Middle School, they had already been targeted as nerds and subjected to a great deal of bullying. Security was pretty tight at the schoolyard, but they knew better than to take the obvious way home.

They walked through an alley they had walked through many times before, when Brian noticed a refrigerator box on its side. Of course, both boys said they were too old to play in a refrigerator box, but they just couldn't resist poking it.

Sunil, the bolder of the two, looked inside first. He fell to the ground and started gagging. Shaking, Brian peered into the box. Then he ran all the way home.

When he got home, he told his mom what he had seen and she didn't believe him. The police did. They eventually recovered the body of Daniel "Bamm Bamm" Johansson from the alley. It was nude, bound, and every inch of it except for the face was covered in burns the coroner later determined were inflicted by acetylene torches.

* * *

Lara called Clegg. She was working on one of those stories that she knew would be e-mailed around the country once it was published. Two kids tried to rob a warehouse, and they would have gotten away with it, but two other guys were trying to rob it the same night. The kids saw the older guys and fled. Their only means of escape was to climb an eight-foot fence with barbed wire. One made it over; the other didn't. The one who didn't—a sixteen-year-old named Rodney Morgason who had a number of prior arrests—managed to make it over the crest, but got his shoe caught in the wire on the top of the fence. Unable to extricate his foot from his high-top sneaker, he was still hanging there a half-hour later when the police arrived.

It was one of those stupid criminal stories people loved. She knew it would make its way around the world just minutes after it was published. Since she had grown quite fond of Clegg, Lara thought it would be nice to let him come up with some kind of witty quote that would make him—at least momentarily—world famous.

But he wasn't up to it.

One of the things Lara liked about Clegg was that he was always upbeat, always ready for a laugh. It didn't matter how horrifying, how heartbreaking the situation was, Clegg could always say something that would either make her laugh or at least want to. But he couldn't today, despite the fact she had served him up a situation that was just begging for a punchline.

"What's up, John?" she asked, suddenly realizing it was the first time she had ever called him anything other than his last name or "sergeant."

"Sorry, kid," he said. "Got a lot on my mind . . . with the bikers."

"What?" she asked, confused. "Bouchard's in jail. The bikers are over."

He sighed audibly. "It's the fact that he's in jail that makes me think there's gonna be a rain of shit over there in Martinsville and that Springfield is gonna get caught up in the storm."

CHAPTER 11

Bouchard was in a common room watching *Cops* on TV with some guys he knew. Those seated closest to him were members and prospects of the Sons of Satan and neighboring puppet gangs. The others in the room were hoping they soon would be.

Five heavily armed guards walked in. The oldest one—huge, bristly-haired, with a prominent moustache—barked out, "Bouchard, boss wants to see you."

"Can't you see I'm busy?" snapped Bouchard to general laughter in the room. "I'll get to him when I can."

"Uh uh, you have to go now," insisted the top guard. "In fact, you'll want to go."

***

After being released from jail, the first place Ned went was Steve's. When he got there, he found that Steve was delighted. But he wasn't excited about Ned's liberation—he'd predicted that would happen sooner or later; he really wanted to tell someone about his new house.

Steve lived in a pretty nice place in a quiet residential neighborhood, but he was very excited about moving up and out of it. One of his dealers—a former federal agent who'd changed allegiances to become a big-time importer and distributor—had gone down for twenty years, and his wife was desperate to sell their huge mansion. It was just out of town and it stood on its own grounds surrounded by a stone fence. The original part of the house was over one hundred and fifty years old and made of fieldstone, but it had been added onto so many times that the new, shiny, aluminum-clad part of the house increased the total floor area fourfold. It had six bedrooms, four fireplaces, a horizon pool, and two hot tubs (one indoor and one out). It was, for Steve, a dream come true.

It would be owned not by Steve himself, but by an escort company officially owned by his great-great aunt, who was ninety-four and lived in a nursing home back in New York. She had Alzheimer's and didn't speak much English, but Steve had managed to get her to sign a will that left all her possessions to him.

Steve explained all of this to Ned as they sat on the couch in his living room, then checked himself, remembering Ned's situation.

"Oh hey, man, you just got out, I'm sorry. I wasn't thinking," he apologized with what Ned took to be sincerity. "Deerhunter, go get Ned a beer—a real beer, none of that cheap shit I let you shitheads drink."

Ned noticed that Martin "Deerhunter" Krentz hadn't said a word since he arrived. Ned knew Krentz well because they were both Death Dealers prospects and they had run a few errands together. Nobody ever told him so, but Ned surmised that Krentz earned his nickname because of his slight resemblance to a young Christopher Walken. Ned was surprised that, when Krentz came back, he offered the Stella Artois to him wordlessly, like a prospect must to a full member, and went back to his seat by the window. Ned had always considered Krentz slightly ahead of him in the pecking order, but now, he assumed, things had changed.

After opening his beer and taking a long draw, Steve started enthusing even more about the house. He seemed most excited by one particular plan he had for it.

"I'm gonna make pornos!" he shouted.

Steve sent Krentz out to buy more beer so he could explain his plan to Ned. He told him about Joel Greene, a young man from Martinsville who wanted to be a filmmaker. Joel's dad paid for him to go to the best film school in the Midwest and bought him a lot of equipment, but refused to pay for his big project. He had planned on financing his son's film, until he found out what it was. Joel wanted to make a documentary about how big corporations and brand names were responsible for all of society's ills. Of course, since the old man made his money distributing top-dollar sneakers and sportswear—for a big corporation that depends on the sanctity of brand names— he cut the boy off.

Joel had a dream, training, equipment, and a ton of friends who would work for nothing, or next to it. All he needed was money. The banks wouldn't talk to him. In fact, nobody with any real money wanted to talk to him. He was about to give up on his plan when he found himself discussing the plan with Rico, the guy who sold him and his friends weed. Rico laughed at him, and told him that only stupid and lazy people couldn't find money. Joel took that as a job offer and refused, telling him he didn't want to do anything illegal. Rico laughed again and promised to introduce him to a good friend of his.

Eventually he did. This friend, another drug dealer, passed Joel onto the guy he got his drugs from. This happened a few times, until Joel found explaining his idea to Steve across a table at a medium-priced steak house. Joel, a vegetarian, had a salad, which Steve found hilarious. Steve told him he liked the idea and offered to front him the entire production costs up to

$250,000, but would not pay a penny for distribution and marketing. That, he said, was Joel's job. And, in the unlikely event that the production didn't make Steve his money back (along with a reasonable-sounding ten percent after one year), they would work something out later. "Nothing illegal, of course," Steve told him. Joel readily agreed, and left the meeting thinking of clever "guerilla marketing" ideas.

Steve was as good as his word. He paid for every part of production quickly and politely. He never complained and even insisted the crew be paid union rates, despite the fact that none of them belonged to any union. He'd sometimes drop by the sets to solve a problem with police or other regulators or to calm down one of Joel's creditors. And best of all, according to Joel, was the fact that neither Steve nor any of the men he sent down to help out ever gave an opinion as to what should be in the movie. They just let Joel and his friends make whatever they wanted.

After the film—*Branded for Life*—was done, Joel entered it into a few festivals, but drew few viewers. He rapidly lost money traveling to attend the premieres. After a long and exhausting search, he couldn't find a single theater within two hour's drive from Springfield to show his film. He eventually rented an old porn theater in Chinatown with the last of Steve's money and started showing *Branded for Life* four times a day until two bikers came to the theater and told him he had to see Steve.

They escorted him into Steve's office. After a personable exchange, Steve got to the point. "I need you to pay me my $275,000."

Joel shook his head as though he did not understand. "I don't have it," he stuttered. "The movie only grossed about seven thousand."

"Well, I guess you owe me a lot of money then . . ."

"Are you going to kill me?"

Steve laughed. "Don't be ridiculous; look, I just want my money back. I don't want to hurt anyone," he said.

Joel looked like he was going to drop.

"I know you don't have it," Steve eased up. "And we both know there's no way you can get it."

Joel didn't know what to say.

"Maybe we can work something out—something that helps both of us," Steve said.

Joel managed a weak smile.

"You know why you failed, Joel?" Steve said. "It was your movie. and you were wrong. You think the big corporations are to blame for everything in the world, when it's actually puffed-up little shits like you who run their mouths off without knowing shit."

For perhaps the first time in his life, Joel kept his opinion to himself.

"You blame your father for everything wrong in your life when all he did was pay for the right to have his son tell him he's an asshole," Steve said. "Just doesn't seem right to me."

The other bikers (two more had come into the room since Steve had started) laughed. One playfully punched Joel on the left bicep. Joel put his head in his hands.

"But you're pretty handy with the camera, you know your way around an editing machine, and you have lots of talented friends," Steve continued. "I'll tell you what—you can pay me back by working for me."

"Working for you?" he said. "What would I do?"

"You'll be doing what you love," Steve told him. "You'll be making movies."

Steve laughed again as he recounted the story to Ned.

"So now I've got the kid living in the guest house," Steve said, pointing out the window to what looked like a refurbished stable or garage. "We haven't made any movies yet, but I have a distribution deal in place with this guy in the San Fernando Valley."

"Wow," was all Ned could say.

"Yeah, it's a sweet business, you pay the girls about two thousand a scene—although I have lots of local girls who'll work for way less than that—and you can sell it for $85,000," he said enthusiastically. "Plus you can recut for compilations and Internet video and end up making a quick and easy six digits on a $10,000 investment—and the best part is that it's all totally legal and legit."

"What about all the other costs?"

"There really aren't any—Joel and his friends will work for free, I already own all the equipment left over from his stupid-ass movie, and we can use this place for the sets," Steve was beaming. "As for dudes, anyone who can keep it up will want to work for free—I know I'm going to be in as many as I can."

"Really? Steve Schultz the porn star?"

"Don't you laugh my friend. I can even pay myself a salary for fuckin' and there's nothing the cops or even the tax-man can do about it because there is a very well-defined line between paying for sex and paying for sex in front of a camera—it's sweet," He grinned. "But seriously, man, I can always use talent—what say you and I do a spit-roast on Melody? You always liked her."

Ned coughed, stumbling on his words. "Well, yeah, Melody is kind of good looking, but I don't think that kind of work is for me."

"Sometimes I just don't understand you, Ned," Steve said, smiling. "But you bring in a lot of money."

* * *

The normally unflappable Bouchard was in a state of shock. He was standing just outside the front door of the jail he'd been in with nothing but a paper bag full of the possessions he had on him when he was arrested. He would have called someone for a ride, but his cellphone was out of juice and he didn't have any quarters for the payphones.

Just a half-hour earlier, he was in an office with a low-level jail administrator who told him that the district attorney had decided to drop all charges against him due to a lack of evidence. He was free to go. Bouchard asked if he could use his telephone. The administrator told him that he was under strict orders not to allow that.

So Bouchard went through the discharge routine without anyone outside knowing. He correctly assumed that the assistant district attorney had handled it this way to avoid letting the media know he was getting out.

He thought about hailing a cab for home, but instead walked to the clubhouse. He needed a beer.

About halfway there, he was stopped by a woman with two children. "Are you 'Big Mother' Bouchard?" she asked.

"Yes, I am."

"Can I get a picture of you with my kids?"

"Sure," he said, and knelt down to put his arms around the two kids. He smiled broadly.

* * *

Ned arrived home. Kelli was fixing herself a sandwich. She ran out, hugged and kissed him, and told him, how happy she was that he was home. Since it was about 7:30 in the evening, he was surprised to find that she was nude under her robe.

They had just begun to talk about what jail had been like when Mallory came out of the bedroom. Ned was shocked. Kelli laughed. "Don't think I've gone all lesbonic on you, Ned; we were just getting dressed to go out," she said, then paused. "I just get lonely when you're not here and having Mal over just calms me down a little."

Ned said he understood. After Kelli got dressed, the three of them talked about jail and how rough it was. Ned told them about Feeney and how he'd made things easier for him in there. And he told them about Andreas/Vanessa, which made them laugh. They had a few drinks and talked for about forty-five minutes when the conversation dragged to a complete stop. Ned looked at Mallory, then at Kelli. Kelli looked at Ned, then at Mallory. Kelli cleared her throat.

"Oh, look at the time," Mallory said. "It's definitely time to go."

"Yeah," agreed Ned.

"Yeah, okay then; so Kelli, are you gonna come with me or will I see you later?"

"Uh . . . I think we're staying at home tonight."

"Oh, yeah, right. Ned's back. You two want to be alone."

* * *

Although Rose's speech had given the Sons of Satan a boost, they were still losing the war. In the two weeks that had passed since he had given the speech, three Sons of Satan-associated dealers had been killed in various nearby towns, a bar belonging to a retired member of the Sons of Satan was razed in a fire, and a bomb exploded on the patio of a Springfield bar known to be a Death Dealer's hangout. There were no fatalities, but an accountant who worked closely with the gang lost an arm.

In retaliation, two Death Dealers prospects built a bomb they intended to use to destroy a suburban Springfield bar at which the owner was no longer buying from them. As one of the would-be bombers was preparing to connect the blasting cap to the C4, the other knocked over a beer bottle. As they raced to pick up the blasting cap before it got wet, one of them knocked over the table with the C4. Richie "the Little Prince" Trelawney was blown to bits while "Deerhunter" Krentz lost both arms and the use of his right leg.

Mehelnechuk didn't like this war. He didn't want to bomb bars at all. Not only was there the chance of innocent people getting hurt, but killing dealers he could potentially lure back into the fold was bad for business.

So he called Bouchard—who had reassumed the role of general once he returned from jail—into his office. "Marv, we gotta do something about these *girls*," he said, using the Sons of Satan slang term for enemy or non-associated bikers.

I know, the men are ready, but we can't tell who they are. Should we shoot every man with a ring? Every bar owner who won't buy our product?"

"I'll bet you'd like that, you sick fuck." Mehelnechuk laughed. "But I have a better plan."

"I'm ready."

"Well, a cop friend of mine in Springfield tells me that the Lawbreakers over there aren't just wearing their colors; they're wearing High Rollers rings," he said. "So it's apparent that the Lawbreakers are either working for the so-called High Rollers or they are part of a larger group along with, I assume, the Italians, some bar owners, some rejects, and some wannabes."

"The Italians? They sell to us!"

"And they like to keep their options open."

"So why don't you get Steve to take care of it over there?" Bouchard asked.

"That bag of shit? All he's done since I sent him there is get richer and make a spectacle of himself—besides, he's way outnumbered."

"So what's the plan?"

"I want you to assign a few of your men—prospects, friends, cops, anyone—to keep an eye on the few remaining Martinsville Lawbreakers and find out where they are coming from and going to and who they are seeing."

"And what about Springfield?"

"I'll send Carter over there; that'll throw the fear of God into 'em."

* * *

After getting out of bed at one in the afternoon, Ned did nothing for the rest of the day. He knew he had a lot to take care of—Kelli, his business, his obligations to the club—but he didn't care. It was his first full day out of jail and he was gonna spend it his way.

And he did. Ned watched TV and drank beer until the phone rang at 5:30. It was Steve. He told him it was essential that they meet with the boys that night. Ned said that was cool.

He shouted out to Kelli. "Hey, babe, I gotta meet Steve tonight."

"Where you meeting him?"

"His house."

"Not the Strip?"

"Nope, his place."

"Are you sure?"

"Yeah, he wants to talk about some calling-card scam."

After Ned left, Kelli put together her dancing costume, called Mallory for a ride, and did a couple of hits of meth.

CHAPTER 12

The pain was unbearable. Ever since he killed Tyler, Ned simply couldn't relax. What sleep he had was fleeting and fear-filled. He couldn't sit and he couldn't stop. And his bones ached from all the physical work he had done with Dario. It was like the worst hangover he could imagine. All he wanted to do was lie down.

But Ned had a lot to think about. Kelli appeared to be gone for good this time, but—in retrospect—he realized he should have seen it coming.

Ned also realized that he was a criminal. He was a real, full-time drug dealer. He'd been to jail and now, at least technically, he was a murderer. Ned was surprised how little guilt he felt about the death of that loudmouth at the Strip. He hadn't intended to kill the guy, just beat him up. It was a freak accident.

On the plus side, he'd gotten away with it. After seeing how easily, confidently, almost professionally Steve and his boys handled the body, the witnesses, and the scene, his fear of getting caught dissipated very quickly. He was more embarrassed than afraid. And he had earned his patch. Ned hadn't gone into business with André intending to be a biker, but he had to admit that the Death Dealers had treated him right. He even liked riding the Harley.

Steve had assigned two other prospects to take over his business while he was in jail. They had done so quietly and without incident. Better yet, Steve had forced them to put thirty percent of their gross aside for Ned. So after his release, he found a nice payday waiting for him and two employees who did his job and paid him. It was less money than he was used to—but not by much. His replacements had expanded his distribution territories by a large margin with their home neighborhoods—and he hadn't done anything to earn it.

His greatest threat at this point was actually boredom. He called Steve. "You need something to do?" He laughed. "You're a full member now; you have people to do things for you."

"Yeah, so I just get money for sitting on my ass?"

"Essentially, although it's likely the club will have some duties for you. Of course, there are always ways to make more money. . . . What you should do is set up a legitimate business so that you can pay taxes, maybe get a mortgage, or whatever—keep you out of jail."

"Makes sense, but I only know one business."

Steve laughed again. "You can do anything. You don't even have to be involved, just hire some kid with skills. But stay away from escorts and strippers—they are mine and mine alone."

"I could do something connected to that, something that helps us both—what about Internet porn?"

"You could, I suppose, but nobody's making any money on it anymore, too many people giving it away for free—besides, the feds are all over that shit. One wrong step and it's just too much liability."

"Yeah."

"I know what you could do, though. You could start a dating website."

"I don't know anything about the Internet."

"You don't have to. One of Joel's friends is a web designer; he knows all that shit. I can give him to you."

"Sounds cool."

"Yeah, and we could put a couple of my girls up there looking for 'dates'... that should get the ball rolling; come by the clubhouse and we'll set you up."

* * *

Ray "Toots" Vandersloot walked into Mehelnechuk's office. The boss was inside talking with Bouchard. Normally, he knew better than to disturb them, but this was a time of war and he thought they would welcome any news. "You hear they burned down Matt's?" he asked.

Matt's was actually Madd Dogg's Tattoos and Body Piercing, a downtown shop owned by Sons of Satan associate Matt Ireson, and frequented by many bikers.

"Anybody hurt?" asked Mehelnechuk.

"No, but the place is totally gone, and I'm not sure what kind of insurance he had."

"Shit, y'know what? I'm getting pretty fuckin' sick of this. It's only a matter of time until somebody important gets killed."

"So what's your plan?" asked Bouchard.

"Stay in here for this, man," Mehelnechuk said to Vandersloot. "I want you and everyone else to know that I am putting Bouchard in charge of rooting out these *girls*—these so-called High Rollers—from our midst, and if a few innocent drug dealers get hurt along the way, that's just too fuckin'bad."

"I thought you were all about bringing other clubs into our organization."

"This is no ordinary club," Mehelnechuk told him. "These

guys were put together to go to war with us; so we have no choice but to go to war with them."

* * *

It was Ned's first time alone with Lessard, and he didn't like it at all. Of all the Death Dealers he knew, Lessard was the only one who actually scared him. Ned intellectually acknowledged that any of them could be violent if provoked, but only Lessard seemed like he could go off at anyone at any time. And he had a reputation for being hard on prospects. Ned wanted to leave, but couldn't. He had a meeting with Steve, and knew better than to miss it. It was supposed to have happened by now, but Steve's door remained closed. Ned could feel his hands and arms get light, just on the verge of trembling when he heard Lessard bellow.

"Prospect!" he shouted. "Get me another god-damned beer!"

Ned got up from his seat at the bar, went into the fridge, and grabbed a bottle for Lessard. He opened it, and brought it to his table. Lessard stared at him in the eyes unblinkingly, but his mood seemed to soften a little. He laughed without mirth. "I guess I shouldn't call you 'prospect' any more, now you're a member," he said. "What should I call you?"

"Well, my name is Ned, and Steve calls me 'Crash' for some reason."

"Why don't I call you what you really are . . . cop?"

"What?"

Lessard stood up. "I know you're a fuckin' cop," he said. "Look at you, you walk in here all clean . . . no tats until Steve forced you to get one, no piercings . . . nobody knows you but André, nobody deals with you but André . . . then we find out André's been talking to the cops to save his own worthless ass."

By this time he had backed Ned up against the bar.

"I'm not a cop, I swear it," Ned said. He could hear his voice shake.

"How do I know that? You never buy meth from me. Everyone buys meth from me. Only a cop wouldn't buy meth from me—I got the best meth."

"I buy from Steve; he'd get pissed off if I bought from you too."

"Steve doesn't have to know."

Ned regained some courage and slipped out from between Lessard and the bar. "Is that what this is about?" He said. "You're calling me a cop so I'll buy from you? Pretty fuckin' lame sales pitch."

"What? Are you doubting me?" Lessard's eyes were totally out of focus now. Ned could tell he was losing control, and he genuinely feared for his life.

Lessard backed him up again, this time against a wall. Then he put his beefy forearm under his chin and pressed against his throat. "If you want to leave this room alive, you'll prove to me you're no cop," he shouted inches away from Ned's face, showering it in saliva. "Sit down."

Ned sat in the chair Lessard indicated. Lessard pulled out his gun and placed it on a chair beside his own. Then he pulled out a bag full of methamphetamine crystals and a hunting knife with a blade as long as his hand. He dumped a few of the transparent shards onto the table and started grinding them down into a white powder with his knife.

"An undercover cop can do a lot of things, a lot of illegal things even," Lessard, much calmer since he sat down, said to Ned. "But he can't take meth—not only are they forbidden by their bosses to take meth because they say it's so damn addictive, but any testimony they give after they have taken meth ain't worth shit . . ."

Ned watched as Lessard expertly ground the meth.

". . . so if you are a cop, you won't take the meth and I'll have to kill you, or you could be a cop, you take the meth and then your word ain't worth shit in court; or you aren't a cop and you just take the fuckin' hit and we are square—no matter what happens, I win."

"I suppose I have no choice."

"You have no choice," Lessard said as he arranged the meth in a tidy line on Ned's side of the table. He also handed Ned a straw.

Ned took a deep breath and leaned over the table. He was putting the straw into his right nostril when Steve's door opened. Everyone paused.

Steve got an angry look on his face, and shouted: "Fuck, Ned! I told you to stay off the shit!"

Gagliano, who had been in the office with Steve, started laughing.

"But, but, but . . ." Ned stammered.

"But-but-but, you sound like a fuckin' motorboat, just get that fuckin' straw outta your nose and get in my office," he ordered. "And if I catch you playing around with that shit again, I will personally see to it that you will work as a jizzmopper at the skankiest strip joint in the whole fuckin' Midwest for the rest of your useless life."

Ned smiled and got up from the table. His eyes caught Lessard's. "This is not over," the big man told him.

"Yes it is, you stupid fuck," Steve yelled. "Put your gun away, put your knife away, put your drugs away, and do your fuckin' job."

Lessard sullenly packed up his stuff.

"Hey," Gagliano piped in. "How come the Lizard can do meth, and me and Crash can't?"

"Because he was a total fuck-up even before I inherited him," Schultz shot back. "You two have futures."

Lessard angrily kicked a chair over as Gagliano grabbed himself a beer, and Ned followed Steve into his office.

Once the door was closed, Steve told Ned: "Don't worry about him; he's all noise."

"I'm not so sure," Ned said with an involuntary shudder. "He thought I was a cop."

"Well, he is nuts, but who can blame him?" Steve said. "You don't look like a biker and nobody knew fuck all about you before I grabbed you."

"And he said something about André going to the cops."

"Meth makes people paranoid," Steve assured him. "That was his paranoia talking—he sees a cop behind every tree and Lawbreakers under his bed when he isn't seeing imaginary bugs crawling on his skin."

"So André wasn't killed for being a rat?"

Steve laughed derisively. "No way. André had no reason to go to the cops. His business—as you now know first hand—was booming," he said. "André was killed by the Lawbreakers, our enemies, the ones who want to take over our territory, our business."

Ned sighed.

"Now that's out of the way, we can get to business," Steve said. "Now that you're a full-patch member, you're going to have to be introduced around to prevent people from thinking the wrong things about you—think of it as a coming-out party."

"What do I have to do?"

"Well, you have to dress like a biker for a change; fly the

colors, wear your Death Dealers jacket and try to look the part," he said. "Then get on the Harley I gave you and ride with us up to Burgessville."

"Then what?"

"You're so suspicious you sound like that gorilla outside. Jesus, Ned, calm down," Steve said. "It's a party—all you do is have fun, meet a few people—it'll be great, a chance to blow off some steam."

"What about Lessard? Will he be there?"

Steve laughed.

"Don't you worry about him," he said with a smile. "He's getting a new assignment; he might not be able to make the party."

When he saw Steve stand up, Ned followed suit. When Steve opened the door, Ned walked out and over to where Gagliano was sitting at the bar. He tried not to look at Lessard.

"Lessard, get your sorry ass in here!" Steve shouted.

As Lessard got up and started walking to the office, Ned stared at him. He marveled at how malevolent he looked even while just walking away.

"Boo!" Gagliano shouted, and Ned jumped, dropping his beer bottle. Gagliano laughed like a teenager.

***

Dave "Apache" Carter arrived at the Death Dealers' clubhouse and presented himself to Steve. "Hi," he said. "Mike Rose sent me down from Martinsville to take care of your little problem."

"So you're the exterminator?"

"Yup."

"Sloppy told me all about you," Steve smiled. "Welcome to Springfield. I'll set you up."

They sat in the bar and drank and talked. Steve had one of the prospects go out for Chinese food. Before it arrived, Ned did.

"Ned 'Crash' Aiken, just the man I wanted to see," Steve said. "My friend Dave here is new in town and will need to crash at your place until we get him a decent place to stay."

Ned didn't like the idea, but agreed anyway. The three of them sat and ate the Chinese food and discussed sports, the weather, and everything but business. After about an hour and a half, Steve told the other two he had to go.

"But what about my idea?"

"What idea?"

"The dating site."

"Yeah, sure, sounds great. I'll send Joel's pal over to your place tomorrow."

"Great."

Ned was not at all happy that he had to take this scruffy little dude home and let him sleep in the guestroom. But it was a direct order from Steve; there was no room for negotiation.

* * *

Lara was feeling a little envious. It's not like she wanted to see all the shootings, arsons, and bombings that had occurred in Martinsville happen in Springfield; she just wanted something interesting to report on. For the past few weeks, it had been nothing more than drunk driving, kids stealing each other's iPods, and one poor bastard who was caught on video stealing the donations box for a children's hospital off the counter of a convenience store. So she called biker expert Jake Levine to talk about what was happening in Martinsville.

"Looks like you have a war going on up there," she said.

"Really? A few drug dealers die and a few bars happen to catch fire and that's a war?" he said, condescendingly. "Drug dealers die; that's an occupational hazard. Fires happen when people want insurance money."

"But my sources say that all of the deaths were dealers associated with the Sons of Satan," she persevered, "and all of the businesses targeted were also associated with the Sons. Don't you think that's just a bit too coincidental?"

"Not at all. The Sons run organized crime in this city," he replied. "I think it would be hard to find a dealer or a bar that did not have some association with them."

"But there must be other criminals out there," Lara pressed on, "the Italians, the rest of the Lawbreakers, dealers who don't want to play ball with the Sons, bikers they rejected for membership or they kicked out. My sources tell me . . ."

"Your sources? You're the crime reporter in Springfield, and you're trying to tell me what's happening in Martinsville?" Levine spouted back. "I'm sure you are trying very hard, but Martinsville is a big city, much more complicated than Springfield . . ."

"So you're saying there's no crime organization fighting against the Sons of Satan in Martinsville?"

"Exactly, there just isn't anyone left to fight them . . . nobody who matters anyway."

"Interesting," she said. "One last thing, what can you tell me about Ivan Mehelnechuk?"

"Yeah, isn't he the little wee guy with the funny face?" he said. "From Springfield, I think."

"Yeah."

"Small-timer, has a lot of patches on his jacket, but never been arrested, never been seen with any of the big guys," he answered. "It seems that whenever anything big goes down, he's never around."

"Like Clark Kent."

"Oh, I think your hometown pride is running away with you on that one; Mehelnechuk is little more than an errand boy who's managed to gain membership by keeping his mouth shut and staying out of trouble."

"I see."

After a few moments of awkward silence, Levine asked, "Whatever happened to Delvecchio? I liked him; he always asked me the right questions."

"Oh, Johnny, he's moved up in the world," she said cheerfully. "No more crime. He's our religion reporter now."

Levine laughed. "That sounds about right for him."

* * *

Ned didn't want to talk, but he could tell his passenger did. Carter was nervous, playing with every knob and switch in the SSR, adjusting the fan speed and temperature no fewer than two dozen times in the first mile. Assuming that conversation would help calm him down, Ned asked him what he was doing in Springfield.

"So you don't know who I am then?"

"Well, I know your name."

"You don't know me."

"Okay, I don't."

"You should, I am the best at what I do."

Ned chuckled. "Oh yeah, what's that?"

"I'm a killer."

"Oh yeah?"

"Do you remember when the Sons were getting rid of the Lawbreakers in Martinsville?"

"You did that, did you?"

"Most of it."

"You'll have to forgive me, but I just don't think you look like a killer."

Carter laughed. "I get that a lot," he said. "But I only have one talent and I gotta keep a roof over my head."

"I see, survival of the fittest, is that it?"

Carter laughed and slapped his knee. "Survival of the fittest my ass!" he shouted. "Look at me, I'm tiny, I'm a drug addict, I'm old, I'm in awful shape; look, I have the arms of a nine-year-old girl. It is not survival of the fittest, my friend; but survival of the baddest, the meanest, the craziest," he continued. "You don't need muscles to kill someone, just a reason . . . and one of these."

As he looked over to see Carter's rather cheap and workmanlike gun, he noticed he had a "Dirty Dog" patch on his jacket. The Sons of Satan and affiliated clubs only give those to members who have killed for the club. Steve halfheartedly offered one to Ned after the Tyler incident, but Ned refused it on the grounds that it was an accident and it hadn't helped the club at all.

"Yeah," Ned said. "I'd be lost without mine."

Carter snickered. "You're no killer," he said.

***

Bouchard was having a few beers with Vandersloot at a Martinsville strip joint they operated when Lawrence "Picasso" Parisi came running in. He was excited and out of breath. Bouchard and Vandersloot took him into the office and sat him down.

"Big news," he began as soon as he could. "Two *girls*—Denton and Watson—were seen with Spangler downtown."

Spangler, he had no need to remind them, was a former Sons of Satan prospect who was a good earner, but was kicked out for stealing from the club. He later formed his own gang, the Lone Wolves, with a couple of high school buddies, but they disbanded after one of them ran into some Lawbreakers at a bar and had his jaw broken.

"They were all wearing jackets with the name 'High Rollers' on the back," Parisi reported.

"Excellent work, my friend," Bouchard said. "Please give this man five hundred dollars, Toots. Where did you see them?"

"Coming out of the Wentworth," he said. That made perfect sense to Bouchard. Mario DeVolo had operated Martinsville's Italian mafia out of the Wentworth for years. He'd been a major drug supplier for the Sons for as long as Bouchard could remember and he had also hired the club's members and prospects to pressure debtors and intimidate witnesses. One of Bouchard's first jobs—breaking the knees of a recalcitrant gambler who owed one of DeVolo's sons twelve thousand bucks—was conducted in a back room at the Wentworth.

But in recent years, starting at about the time Mehelnechuk had taken over and instituted his new rules, DeVolo had been growing increasingly prone to complaints. He didn't like the stranglehold the Sons had on what appeared to be every market. He didn't like how much they charged when he compared it to what they paid. And he definitely didn't like their willingness to go elsewhere for drugs if the price was right.

Bouchard agreed with Mehelnechuk's suspicion that DeVolo was at the head of—or at least involved with—these High Rollers, and that they were made up of Lawbreakers, non-affiliated bikers, and rejects like Spangler—basically every criminal in Martinsville who wasn't wearing Sons of Satan colors.

"Where did they go?"

"I lost them, they were on Harleys and I was in my pickup. They went through an alley. I couldn't keep up."

"Too bad, you could have made another five hundred dollars," Bouchard laughed. "But good job anyway. Why don't you go out front and tell the ladies to show you a good time. Toots, take him outside."

Parisi grinned as Vandersloot escorted him out. Bouchard called Mehelnechuk on a cellphone he'd bought that day (he'd discard it in a couple of weeks to avoid having his calls intercepted by the cops—a trick the bikers had learned from Al-Qaeda).

"Well, I know who the problem is," he reported. "It's DeVolo and all the *girls* in town, probably some from out of town as well."

"Makes sense," Mehelnechuk concurred. "Our garlic-eating friend probably wants to have an alternative market for his products so that he can play us off one another, allowing him to dictate the rules—I'm surprised it took him this long to put a team together."

"We can't take him out at the Wentworth or at home, but he's pretty vulnerable when he goes to his horse farm."

"We're not taking him out at all; we're not fighting the Italians."

"Why not?"

"We'd lose."

"Is that so?"

"Yeah, you want some crazy-ass godfathers and Guidos coming from New York and New Jersey? I've seen what they're capable of—and they are everywhere—they would all kill a hundred of ours to avenge the death of just one of their own. Besides, he's our top supplier. Where do you think we'd get product?"

"Scott Kreig?"

Mehelnechuk laughed. "Scott's a good guy and everything, but he can't get us a tenth of what the Italians can."

"So what do we do, just let him get away with killing our guys?"

"No, we kill his guys," Mehelnechuk said. "We make it so difficult, so costly for him to do business with anyone other than us, that he'll give up—but you leave him, his family, and his own men alone. Spread the word: anyone so much as looks like a High Roller or whatever they call themselves is a dead man. Any dealer who refuses to do business with us is dead."

"You're not against me bringing in some reinforcements, are you?"

"Not as such, what did you have in mind?"

"Just gonna grab some of the more psychotic elements from some chapters and puppets."

"Fine, just leave Carter in Springfield; he's got a job to do there."

CHAPTER 13

Ned really wanted Carter out of his house. Not only was he filthy, but he stayed up all night trying to talk. And when Ned didn't want to talk, Carter would wander around and talk with himself. It disturbed Ned to have a self-proclaimed serial killer walking around his house at night, even if they were officially on the same side. So he was relieved to hear that Steve had called both of them in for a meeting at the Strip.

Ned was surprised to see two other guys in Steve's office. One was Sean Feeney, who had helped Ned out in jail. The other was Mike "Bandit" Sharpe, who Ned knew from around the clubhouse. He was a big guy, not as stupid as most, but with something of a mean streak. He was prospecting for Steve, and Ned knew he'd been in a few scrapes and come out on the better side.

After some hellos and introductions, Ned and Carter sat down. Steve spoke to Carter first. "You're all set up, man," he said, and handed him a knapsack. "Take this, it has some clothes, some cash, and some tools; go see Daria—the one with glasses—outside. She'll take you to your new apartment."

"Thanks, Steve."

"Good luck."

"I don't need luck," Carter said, and left.

Steve then turned his attention to Ned. "I know I said I'd

set you up on that website, but so much has come up, I've had to delay," he said. "But I have another job for you.

You know Buster's Tavern out in Hamner?"

Ned said he'd heard of it. That he knew it was a strip joint that did pretty good business.

"Glad to hear it," Steve said. "It's one of mine. But things have changed a little with the unpleasantness up in Martinsville. The head office needs some manpower from us, and I had to send some of our best men up there."

"Does this have anything to do with Carter?"

Steve laughed. "Kind of . . . think of it as an exchange program."

"And how do I fit in?"

"How would you like to make lots of money?"

"What would I be doing?"

"Taking care of my investment," Steve said. "Buster's is one of my favorite places. Not only do I have a great distribution center there, but it makes a shitload of money from the cover charge and beer sales. You would manage the place. Oversee the daily operations both of the bar and the distribution center, make sure nobody's stealing from me, make sure the girls are fresh and giving plenty of mileage. Of course, you'll still be earning from your existing businesses as well."

"Sounds easy, when would I start?"

"Well, you'll need an assistant, so he's going with you," Steve said, pointing to Sharpe. "Go to Buster's tomorrow and talk to the head bartender—some Russian chick, I forget her name—and tell her who you are, and she'll set everything up."

"Sounds pretty fuckin' sweet," said Sharpe.

"Oh, and by the way, Ned, keep an eye on this motherfucker," Steve gestured at Sharpe. "He'll take everything he can get his fuckin' hands on. Don't look at me like that," he said to Ned's prospective assistant, "you know you do—and make sure you get the lakefront house on Water Street, and he gets the apartment above the laundromat on Main."

"Will do," Ned replied. He looked over at Sharpe, who was hanging his head. At first he thought Sharpe was ashamed, but then he heard him laughing.

"Seriously, keep an eye on him, or he'll rob you blind."

After Ned left with Sharpe, Steve and Feeney started to talk about the dating website Joel's friend had hooked up for him.

* * *

What surprised Ned was all the women hanging out and the scores of children running around. Some of them belonged to the members and the prospects of the Death Dealers who were headed out to Burgessville, but most were just from the neighborhood. He had heard that some kids idolized bikers, but he didn't believe it until he saw it. Parents were getting pictures of their sons on Harleys and with their daughters hugging bikers. Some were even getting the bikers to sign red and black bandannas and T-shirts that supported the Sons of Satan, but which did not actually reproduce their name or logo. The gang was careful with its corporate ID, and these weren't family—they were fans.

The Death Dealers looked pretty impressive. They all had black leather jackets with the top-hatted skull logo on them. The full members (like Ned himself) had two rockers—one on top that said "Death Dealers" and one on the bottom that said "Springfield." The prospects looked pretty much the same, but didn't have the bottom rocker. The other riders—the hangarounds, the friends, and some other business associates—tried to blend in as best as possible. They all wore patchless black leather jackets and tried to look tough. All of them had Harley-Davidsons with varying degrees of customization. Mixed among them were the women, friends, and associates who didn't ride. They dressed as closely as they could to the biker style, and milled around in the parking lot, occasionally bringing food and drinks to the bikers.

Steve—whose jacket was adorned not just with the patches on the back, but dozens more on the front and all down the sleeves like military decorations—was surrounded by a crowd, mostly women.

They took off towards Burgessville with Steve in the front. Ned noticed that the prospects worked very hard not to pass him, no matter how fast or slow he went. Order, he thought to himself, meant everything to bikers. When they arrived in the great muddy field at Burgessville, many hundreds of bikers were already there. Ned saw dozens of different patches, but all of them were getting along like old friends. Here and there, he saw bikers drinking, smoking, eating, wrestling, and just having a good time. There were lots of locals mixed in among them.

Ned saw Bouchard, who he knew from the news, talking to crowds, while serious-looking bikers waited in line to go into a tent behind him. Ned didn't know it, but Mehelnechuk was inside, interviewing the presidents and important members of other clubs who were vying to become Sons of Satan chapters or puppets.

Ned decided to take the weekend off. He decided not to worry. So he started drinking and smoking with the guys as soon as he got there. By the time Steve came to get him for that night's show, Ned was too drunk to be much good to anyone. He attended the festivities, but didn't really remember anything that happened.

***

As Bouchard had ordered, the Martinsville Sons of Satan began to fire back at a largely unidentifiable enemy. One of the first targets was Moe Gannon. He was in prison for most of the Sons of Satan's earlier war against the Lawbreakers, so he had remained unscathed. But when he came out, he was disheartened by what he came back to. The Martinsville Lawbreakers had been reduced to six full members afraid to wear their colors in public, three prospects of varying abilities, no associates of note, two semi-independent prostitutes, and a few dealers the Sons found too small-time or too crazy to do business with. He did his best to keep them together and encouraged them to get back in the game. And it was he who approached DeVolo with the idea that later became the High Rollers.

Bouchard knew he was out and figured that he was probably involved with the Rollers, so he sent two guys, Harry "Hardcore" Rollins and Karl "Pop" Warner, to take care of him. When they got to the address they'd been given, they saw a black BMW 750iL in the driveway out front. Protected by a hedge on the driver's side and concealed by almost total darkness, the two men planted an explosive device that would be triggered by the car's ignition.

It worked. The following morning, the car's owner was obliterated in a storm of molten metal, plastic, and leather. But the problem was that Gannon had sold the house almost immediately after getting out of prison and had moved into a downtown condo. The Sons had instead killed real estate investor and financial advisor Khaled Raja. The newspapers speculated that elements back in Raja's native country of Pakistan wanted him dead for reasons they did not disclose.

The Sons of Satan's aim was true on their next target.

Warner, hoping to make amends for the botched assassination attempt on Gannon, tracked down Fred Longo—a failed Sons of Satan prospect whom he heard was fencing. Warner saw him walk into a bar they both used to frequent, and followed him in. There was nobody else in the bar but the bartender, who knew them both. Longo turned around to see his old friend, smiled, and started to say hello, but froze when he saw Warner's gun. Warner stared at Longo's High Rollers ring.

"Jesus, Pop, not in here," whined Al the bartender.

Longo just stood there, trying to assess the situation when Warner shot him three times in the face. Al shouted his complaints about the mess as Warner dropped the gun and fled.

***

While the first blows against the High Rollers in Martinsville were largely insignificant, the same was not true for Springfield. Carter, dressed in old jeans and a hooded sweatshirt, moved silently around the streets of Springfield. On his first day downtown, he spotted a Lawbreaker in full colors. He noticed that the rocker (bottom patch) that normally said "Springfield" had been replaced with one that read "High Rollers." He was with two other tough-looking guys, and they were on foot.

So Carter followed them discreetly. When they went into a run-down little diner called the Eggs O'Lent, he stayed outside. As they were being seated, he went into the tiny convenience store next door and bought a pack of cigarets. When he came back out, he went into the diner. He spotted the Lawbreaker, a big fellow, maybe three hundred pounds with a shaved head, red beard, and no mustache. Probably forty. His two younger friends were skinny and both had long hair. One had a scraggly mustache. A fourth man had joined them.

Smaller, more nervous, he was dressed in a teal golf shirt and green cargo pants.

Carter took a seat in the booth opposite them. He ordered a coffee and a ham-and-cheese sandwich. He rummaged around in his knapsack, finally pulling out a newspaper.

The waitress delivered his coffee and sandwich. He called her back. "Hey, this coffee's cold. Could you bring me a hot one?"

She nodded and turned. Then Carter stood up with a .357 Magnum.

His first shot went into the Lawbreaker's face. The second missed. The third and fourth went into moustache-man's chest. The fifth went into the other tough guy's temple and the sixth into his neck. The nervous man slumped under the table. Carter pulled another, smaller handgun out of his knapsack and shot him four times.

He then dropped the guns and left. The waitress and the other customers had hit the floor.

Carter walked about a block and caught a bus back to his apartment.

***

Ned didn't really like Sharpe all that much. On the drive to Hamner, he wouldn't shut up. Mostly, he aired his opinions on whatever subject he liked, and Ned found it annoying that he'd talk at length about one tiny aspect of a subject without any context. He took about ten minutes to explain how he could never drive a hatchback or SUV for fear that if it was rear-ended, the stuff in his trunk would fly up and hit him in the back of the head. Ned tried to explain that things don't really work that way, and that cargo covers and headrests wouldn't really let it happen anyway, but Sharpe answered everything he said with a smug "You'll see."

Once that subject was laid to rest, the twenty-seven-year-old Sharpe launched into a lengthy soliloquy about his fifty-one-year-old wife and their unlikely sex life. Ned couldn't wait for the drive to end.

When it did, the two men walked into Buster's together—Ned annoyed and frustrated, Sharpe jubilant that he had made a new friend. It was an old building, much more tasteful than the slab-sided Strip. The windows of the nineteenth-century building had been blacked out and were covered over with posters of barely dressed women to give passersby an idea of what went on inside. Above the main entrance, there was a sign that read, "Liquor in the front, poker in the rear." Ned smiled, realizing Steve had hung it there; it was typical of his sense of humor.

The bar wasn't open for business yet, so Sharpe banged on the door. A cleaning woman let them in. Inside were two women talking to each other in a foreign language. The older of them was dressed in jeans and a Harley-Davidson T-shirt, while the younger one appeared to be wearing a rather stylized form of underwear. As the younger one was chattering away, the older one nodded from time to time, and gave occasional single-syllable responses. Ned could see that she was busy with some paperwork, but couldn't tell exactly what it was.

"Hi, I'm Ned Aiken," Ned addressed the older one. "Steve sent me to run this place."

The older one sighed, stood up, and shook his hand. "I am Daniela Eminescu."

Ned liked Daniela's face. He could see her native intelligence. She had high cheekbones, a big nose, and green eyes. Although the light in Buster's was poor, he could tell she was almost beautiful. She looked kind of like the models in magazines that had pictures of women with their clothes on. "I guess you actually run this place," he laughed.

She smiled and nodded. "Last managers Steve sends know nothing about business, just want to drink and fight; so I learn how to run the bar," she said. "And now we are making lots of money."

"Looks like the best thing I could do would be to stay out of your way," he said.

Sharpe cleared his throat.

"Oh, yeah," Ned said. "This is Mike Sharpe; he's here to help me."

"Hello, Mike," Daniela said as she went back to her work. She motioned at the younger girl. "This, boys, is Liliya."

Liliya rose from her chair and greeted Ned. She was strange looking. No more than five feet tall, she was very thin with enormous breasts. She wore a ton of makeup on her long, thin face and had dyed her hair a very pale pink. Ned was wondering if it was a wig when she asked him: "You vant ploe chob?"

"What?"

Daniela looked at Ned like he was an idiot, and told him with obvious frustration: "She wants to know if you want a blow job."

Ned was flustered. "Uh, uh, no—uh, thank you—not right now."

Liliya shrugged and turned to Sharpe, who was grinning. "Don't mind my friend," he told her. "He's just feeling a little queer since he left jail."

"I *know* zis vun vants ploe chob," Liliya said, as she grabbed Sharpe by the hand and led him into a back room.

After they left, Ned felt very self-conscious. "Friendly little thing, isn't she?" he said.

"It's all she knows," Daniela replied. "I hate to admit it, but I'm actually glad to get a few minutes peace from her constant talk-talk-talk."

"Yeah, I could tell. What was that you guys were speaking, anyway, Russian?"

Daniela sighed again. "No, we are from a country you have never heard of."

"Try me."

"Moldova."

"You made that up."

Daniela laughed. "No, is real; Moldova is tiny country squished between Romania and Ukraine," she told him. "You would like it; it has beaches, mountains, lots of pretty girls, and everyone sounds like Dracula, even babies."

"If it's so nice, what are you doing here?"

"There is no money in Moldova and men there—especially army and police—can be very cruel," she said. "Many Moldavan women leave for better life; every once in a while a man in fancy car comes through town and tells all the girls they can get jobs as models and actresses in America, or Canada, or Australia. The younger ones believe them; the older ones go anyway."

"Maybe that's why Moldovan men are cruel, all the decent-looking women have left."

"Don't flirt with me, is bad for business."

Ned laughed. "So tell me about the business."

"Okay, men pay five bucks to come in after seven (before that is free), they buy cheap beer for high prices, also have terrible food for much money," she said. "This is accomplished by naked girls dancing on stage and in back room."

"Sounds simple."

"But there are complications. Entry to VIP room costs bottle of cheap champagne we charge $100 for."

"What happens in the VIP room?"

"Usually nothing, it depends on the girl—most of them are what you people call 'escorts,' you know?" She stuck her tongue in her left cheek and moved her right hand in a pantomime of oral sex.

"Like Liliya?"

Daniela sighed again. "Yes, poor Liliya. She has been doing nothing else since she was thirteen, no high school, no nothing."

"Boy, things sure must be tough in Moldova."

"In Moldova?" Daniela gave him a sharp look. "In Moldova, she was good girl, but her parents gave her to a man who took her to Montreal to teach her how be stripper and prostitute."

"At thirteen?"

"Yes, such papers are very easy to obtain there—Montreal is like Bangkok, they say—and once she is legal in Canada, that makes her legal here, in U.S.A.—it has long been this way."

"So how old is she now?"

"She says seventeen; her papers say twenty-three," Daniela paused as Sharpe and Liliya came back into the room. "But what is really important is that I get bookkeeping done." And she went back to her work.

Sharpe grabbed himself a beer and sat down at the bar. "You ever dance, Daniela?"

"You could not afford it, big boy."

* * *

Lara arrived at the Eggs O'Lent diner and was stopped by a pair of big cops. Clegg waved her through, but the cops made her photographer stay outside.

The bodies had been removed, but Clegg had Lara wait in the doorway so that they wouldn't contaminate any evidence. "They told me a biker had been shot," she said.

"One full-patch Lawbreaker and two hangarounds," he said. "And another victim: all dead."

"Wow! Who was the other guy?"

"Mario Espinosa, runs a sporting goods shop in the Dover Mall," he told her. "Don't put this in that paper, but he had a severe gambling problem."

"Is that why he's dead?"

"Quite the opposite. Nobody ever kills a debtor: you might break his legs, but you don't kill him. If you do, how do you get your money?"

"Makes sense."

"Besides, you see that briefcase there? It has what I estimate to be about fifteen thousand in cash in it."

"So, Espinosa was paying his debt."

"It would appear that he was paying it or part of it, yes."

"So the killer didn't want that to happen."

"Not so fast ... maybe the killer didn't know it was happening. Your sharp reporter's mind noticed that the money is still here, right?"

"Right, so someone just wanted to kill some Lawbreakers—and this guy just happened to be with them."

Clegg didn't say anything, but touched his right index finger to his nose. Then he took her outside, away from the other cops. "One other thing you may be interested in knowing—y'know the bottom rocker?"

"The patch on the jacket that says which chapter the biker is from?"

"Yeah, this guy's didn't say Springfield."

"So he was from out of town?"

"There you go jumping to conclusions again, I didn't say that."

"So what did it say?"

"High Rollers."

"What are the High Rollers?"

"Everybody's got a theory, Mason—our organized crime guy—says the Italians are recruiting Lawbreakers and other miscreants to fight the Sons and their puppet gangs."

"So who's the killer? One of the Death Dealers?"

"You tell me."

Lara was about to ask another question when Monica Grillo, the reporter from the local TV station showed up. Clegg greeted her and told Lara: "Think about what I said, and I'll have my press person e-mail you all the details about names and ages of the victims and all that."

"Any witnesses I can talk to?"

"All the material witnesses have been taken to the shop to be debriefed. The only one left is that guy; he didn't see the shooting, but he did see the alleged killer exit the building—you can have him, we're done with him." Clegg put his index finger to his right temple and pulled an imaginary trigger.

Lara rushed up to the short, bald man who was chattering to the two cops who were trying to keep onlookers back. She introduced herself as the crime reporter from the *Silhouette*, and he stopped bothering the cops and started talking non-stop to her. He began talking about all kinds of things, not much of it related to the shootings. Finally, she stopped him and asked if he could describe the man he saw leave the restaurant.

"Oh yeah, oh yeah, no problem," he said. "As soon as I heard the shots—they went pop, pop, pop, like firecrackers—I ran over, and I saw the guy come out just as plain as day and walk around the corner."

"Did you follow him?"

"No, I started to look inside the diner and, to tell you the truth, I couldn't move. I was just too stunned."

"What happened next?"

"Well, somebody must have called 9-1-1, because the cops got here first, then the ambulance guys—I told them the same thing I told you."

"So you saw the man who left; could you describe him?"

"He was a white guy, maybe forty, skinny, short with short, dark hair."

"What was he wearing?

"Jeans, one of those hooded sweatshirts the kids all wear—dark blue or black—but there were no pictures or writing on it, just plain."

"The victims were associated with a local motorcycle gang . . ."

"Oh, no, no, no, this guy was no biker, he was real small—like five-foot-four and skinny—and he had short hair, no beard, no moustache, no leather jacket."

"Okay, okay, can you tell me anything else about him?"

"Yeah, yeah, he just kinda looked . . . looked like a nobody."

CHAPTER 14

Feeney looked at the man he'd just had sex with and sighed. He knew how handsome he was. And with his money, he was pretty sure he could have any gay man and most of the straight women in Springfield. But Ronnie was a big, hairy blob. He had bad teeth, and sometimes he even smelled bad. Feeney wasn't the smartest guy in the world, but even he was surprised at how stupid, how unworldly, how happy not to pursue knowledge Ronnie was. But he couldn't help but be totally attracted to the big man. There was something indefinable about him. Feeney left it at that. A more intellectually curious man may have delved deeper into the cause of the attraction, but Feeney didn't want to know. Instead, he looked at the rolls of fat on his stomach, his sweaty, sagging bitch tits and listened to his loud, arrhythmic open-mouth snoring and wanted to have sex with him again.

They met through *letsgettogether.com*, the dating website Steve set up for Feeney to help launder his drug money. When Joel's friend Paul showed up to set up the site, Feeney made sure he set up a gay page on the site because "that's where the money is."

And that's how he met Ronnie. The first person to reply to Feeney's own ad, Ronnie possessed a number of liabilities when it came to starting a relationship. Not only was he obese, but he was also a part-time criminal who lived with his mother. Ronnie worked nights as a motel concierge, and he was leafing through a lot of gay porn on the motel's PC until he came across an ad for *letsgettogether.com*. Two days later, he was rolling around in bed with Feeney.

When Ronnie finally woke up, Feeney took him out for breakfast.

At the diner, Ronnie asked: "How long you been in the Sons?"

"What makes you say that?"

Ronnie laughed. "I knew a guy who pretended he was in the Sons, then they caught up with him—and he still can't walk right. I seen your tats—they wouldn't let anyone get away with those—you're the real thing."

"So, what are you, a cop?"

Ronnie looked startled, then sheepishly answered. "Actually, I tried to be, but I had some trouble with my record and the written exams. I grew up wanting to be a cop, but it didn't work out."

"So what do you do now?"

"My real job is as a night desk man at the Shangri-La. Of course, I sell a little weed there and take a few bucks from the whores for looking the other way."

"Oh, so you're an outlaw, are you?" Feeney laughed. "Who do you work with?"

"A variety of people."

"I'm getting the feeling you pay retail for weed and sell it for about the same."

Ronnie hung his head and giggled. "Yeah, and I'd like that to change."

Feeney put his head in his hands and sighed. He knew he was in deep now. If Ronnie told anyone about their tryst, the results could be harsh, even fatal. Having a prison bitch is one thing, but having a boyfriend outside was another entirely.

That meant he had to get rid of Ronnie—or keep him happy.

* * *

Ned was sitting in his office at Buster's watching Daniela work when Liliya, unasked, brought him a beer and a plate of french fries. She smiled shyly and hurried out of the office. Ned had tried to get Liliya off the stage by teaching her how to be a waitress, but Daniela convinced him it would be bad for business.

"She likes you," Daniela said without looking at him.

"I think she likes everybody."

"No, she likes almost nobody; but she does like you, really."

"Wonderful, maybe we can adopt her."

Daniela laughed. "You should be nice to her; she makes us a lot of money."

"I'll tell you what would make us a lot of money," he said. "Putting you up on that stage and letting you shake that thing—every guy who comes in here asks me why you aren't up on stage."

"It's not going to happen," she said. She couldn't tell from his face where the conversation was going. So she sighed and told him the story. "I used to dance, but my visa ran out, and I was denied another one," she told him.

"So you're an illegal immigrant?"

"Yes, I am," she said. "And that limits what I can do."

"Officially, you can't do anything."

"Officially, yes, but when the immigration people come, they check every dancer very carefully, but they don't bother with the employees who have their clothes on," she said. "I'm just another bartender. I look like American girl, I work for cash, I stay off books, I walk free."

"And they check Liliya?"

"Every time, but she has papers—they are totally inaccurate, but they are official."

There were a few moments of awkward silence as Ned contemplated what she had said. "I have a feeling this is a situation you find suits you," he said. "That maybe you kind of forgot to renew your visa, so that this exact situation might just come around."

Daniela did her best to look innocent. "I'm not that smart," she said.

They both laughed.

Realizing that she'd better change the subject, she said; "Your friend, Mr. Mike, you know he just sits in the bar and takes beers from the fridge all day."

"Good," he said. "Better he sits here getting drunk all day than he gets busy trying to help run our business."

Daniela grinned. "We have a saying back in Moldova— today he steals beer, tomorrow he steals money."

"No you don't."

"We should."

***

Bouchard was extremely happy to see Mike Rose. "What's up, Sloppy? Tough day at the office?"

"A good day, my friend, we got two girls down."

"Members?"

"One prospect, one hangaround."

"How do you know?"

"Well, before everything went black, these two decided to talk, you know, negotiate for a better deal."

"Isn't that nice; what did they say?"

"Pretty much what you said they would: The High Rollers started out with Gannon's Lawbreakers and DeVolo, then added some bar owners, all the unattached girls in the state and a rogue's gallery of other weirdoes and oddballs."

"So who were these girls?"

"You remember the Black Vipers?"

"Yeah," Bouchard laughed. "Frank Lotti's gang—used to meet in his mom's basement and specialized in boosting kids' Nintendos from minivans ... they must be scraping the bottom of the barrel for manpower."

"Maybe, but it doesn't take much manpower to kill," Rose reminded him. "Just before it all went down, the hangaround decided to try to make things a little better for himself by telling us a little bit more about the prospect—including the fact that he was the one responsible for the unpleasantness at the baseball game."

"Casey?" Bouchard was referring to Casey Setterstrom, who ran a very successful independent drug distribution center from his comic book shop, and had been killed at a baseball game only three weeks after forming an alliance with the Sons. Setterstrom had just finished watching his son play a little league game and was headed for the restroom a few steps from the field, when a gunman shot him twice and ran into a van which promptly sped away from the scene.

"Yep," said Rose.

"Did they say anything else?"

"Nah, mostly just crying."

Bouchard laughed as he went to the safe to get Rose's money. "How many people are you sharing this with?"

"One member and two prospects, who will be paid accordingly."

After dismissing Rose, Bouchard called Feeney into his office. "I have an assignment befitting someone of your talents," he said. "You heard of Freddie McAfee?"

"Sure," Feeney responded, "isn't he with the Springfield Lawbreakers? Big dude, maybe three hundred pounds, dangerous."

"That's the man, but he's not in Springfield right now. A friend of ours told me he's gone to Webster's Falls to recruit the local bikers there to come over to the High Rollers."

"Webster's Falls? That's at least six hundred miles away," Feeney said. "Don't we have some kind of presence there?"

"We did, and all six of them are inside because they leaned on one of their whores too hard."

"What?"

"Yeah, one of them told her his cut of her gross went from twenty percent to forty percent, so she went to the cops," Bouchard said. "After she finished talking, they all wound up inside—we sent some guys down there, but we can't spare 'em anymore because of the current unpleasantness, so now we just have a few prospects trying to keep it alive."

"So McAfee's down there stirring up shit?"

"Uh-huh. The local girls—they call themselves the Devil's Own—have been on the fence for a while," Bouchard said. "Ivan's been there a couple of times to wine and dine their president, but he got sent up, so we're not even sure who's in charge there anymore."

"So why doesn't Ivan go back down?"

Bouchard glared at him. "You don't question what Ivan does," he snapped. "Besides, with God knows who in charge of the Devil's Own, we thought it would better to get rid of the High Rollers option than to compete with them."

"So that's where I come in . . ."

"Yep, do it whatever way you want—it should be easy, nobody knows you down there—but you better get started right away, before McAfee convinces them to join."

"Can I fly?"

"Better to drive."

"Can I bring a friend?"

"None of my guys, we need them all."

"No, no."

"Don't bring a woman."

"No, just a friend."

***

The little guy had been sitting in the back of the bar since noon. He was on his second beer four hours later, and the waitress was getting more than a little frustrated with him. Her mood changed when she saw the bikers come in.

There were two distinct rules of thought about bikers at Chauncey's. Two of the older waitresses refused to serve them because they were lousy, ass-pinching outlaws; the rest of them loved them because they ordered big and they tipped big. In the worst end of a town that had almost no money, the bikers were a much-desired source of income.

Maura Swiminer was one of them. She didn't mind a few slaps on the butt in exchange for what the bikers gave her. Besides, it was dead that night. The only other customers were the old couple who sipped coffee, read newspapers, and always left a few quarters for a tip, and the little weird guy who had taken a couple of hours to finish two draft beers. Even at an outrageous-for-Springfield twenty percent, his tip would be less than two bucks.

So she rushed to the bikers. She took their order. One of

them smacked her ass—business as usual. She returned to their table with a mess of wings and fries and beer. Just as they were digging in, the little guy in the back stood up. At first, it looked like he was getting ready to go. But then he approached the bikers' table, as though he had something to say. They looked at him, confused. The stranger pulled a sawed-off pump-action shotgun from his coat and killed two of the three of them. The other one, the only full patch, grabbed Maura by the neck and by the thighs and held her in front of him like a shield.

Carter kept shooting. He tried to miss Maura, but knew he couldn't. He didn't have any reason to hurt her, but he had a job to do. He pumped three shells into the pair of them. He killed the full-patch High Roller. Maura lay on top of the corpse screaming in pain from the pellets in her face and thigh.

After the kills, Carter went to Steve's office. "There is a war here in Springfield and I have done my part: I have killed eleven people, and the rest of you have killed none."

"That's true," said Steve. "But this is a Martinsville war, not a Springfield war, and you were sent here by Bouchard or Rose or one of them—we didn't even want you here—so if you want something, you should get it from them."

Carter laughed. "Nope, I am cleaning up Springfield and you are the boss of Springfield. You know it, I know it," he said. "The Martinsville boys pay me, but now you must pay me, or I will go home."

"Okay, okay, okay, I will admit that having you here has been good for business," Steve grinned. "But I'm kinda short on cash right now, can I pay you in product?"

"By product, you mean . . ."

"You know, meth . . . coke . . ."

"I thought Ivan said those things were illegal."

"Ivan's in Martinsville, I'm the boss here."

* * *

As they drove to Webster's Falls, Feeney could tell Ronnie was excited. This fat, failed cop would do just about anything to be a real outlaw. And if Feeney could get him hangaround status, maybe he'd get the idea he could become a prospect or even a member. If he had that kind of status to protect, maybe he'd keep his mouth shut. Otherwise, things could get difficult. Ronnie, Feeney realized, was in love with him—or at least as close to love as someone like Ronnie could be. If Feeney tried to get rid of him, things could get ugly. A petulant, immature man even by biker standards, Ronnie was likely to break Feeney's secret even if it cost him his own pointless life. Feeney's plan, then, was to provide Ronnie a point in life—which would allow him to move on voluntarily.

Feeney stopped the car about a block from the Webster's Falls clubhouse, opened the trunk and took out his colors. Sons of Satan rarely wear their colors on trips because it attracts cops as well as other bikers. But Feeney didn't know any of the guys inside the clubhouse and thought the safest thing to do was to let them know right away who and what he was.

It was a sad little clubhouse. A former dry cleaning store, the Sons had put metal curtains over the windows, and never pulled them up. There was an eight-foot fence topped with barbed wire no more than four feet from the façade. The door, metal and windowless, was painted black with the letters "S.O.S.M.C.W.F." at eye level. The single video camera mounted above the front door looked like it wasn't working. And Feeney had to park on the street.

He hit the buzzer and sensed Ronnie pacing nervously behind him. The door opened, and a young man welcomed him in. Inside, the clubouse was cramped. There was the usual graffiti, old furniture, and beer fridges, but it looked like a truckload of stuff in a trunk's worth of room. The three prospects inside seemed oblivious to their claustrophobic surroundings and were sipping beer and lying on the furniture. When they saw Feeney in his colors, they jumped to their feet, as though an officer had just entered their barracks. Feeney grinned. Ronnie beamed.

"Fallen on a bit of hard times, I see," Feeney said.

"Yeah, there was this whore . . ." one of them began.

"I know the story," Feeney interrupted. "I'm here to do a job—where can I find McAfee?'

"Murphy, get this man a beer, one for his friend too," said the biker who had let them in. "He's operating out of the Sta-A-Nite, just outside of town on Route 6."

"Is he alone?"

"He parties—gets real drunk, occasionally brings back a whore."

"Not playing it real safe, is he?" Feeney said. The locals laughed. "Well, if you guys were any kind of threat, maybe he would." They stopped laughing.

Feeney took a couple of handguns from his hosts and left. He took Ronnie to dinner and checked into another motel, just down the road from the Sta-A-Nite. They watched TV and drank beer until midnight. Then they went to the car and waited.

About two hours later, they were awakened by the rumbling of a Harley. A big man in a leather jacket got off the bike. He had a woman with him. She stumbled when she got off the bike; they both laughed.

Feeney handed Ronnie a gun. "You gotta do this." Feeney had decided that if Ronnie had committed a murder, he would have something to hold over him in case he ever decided he wanted to talk to anyone about their relationship. Ronnie, however, mistook the gesture as a gift. He thought Feeney was allowing him to be the triggerman so that he could prove himself worthy, perhaps even worthy enough to become a Son of Satan.

Eager to show Feeney that he'd made the right decision, Ronnie grabbed the gun and swung the door open. He turned back, told Feeney he loved him, and leapt out the door.

The girl saw Ronnie first and screamed. She ducked and ran as Ronnie's first shot hit McAfee in the leg. The next bullet took out his left elbow. Screaming in pain, McAfee took four more bullets before he went silent.

"Jesus, Ronnie," Feeney shouted after Ronnie had gotten back in the car. "Throw the fuckin' gun away!"

"I can't; the cops have my prints on file!"

Ronnie took off his jacket and wiped the gun down. Feeney had already started driving out of the Sta-A-Nite's parking lot, so Ronnie threw the gun into a roadside ditch full of leaves.

"Is he dead?"

"Yeah."

"You sure?"

"I emptied the gun into him."

"What about the whore?"

"I don't know. I guess she ran."

"You guess? You guess? Man, this is some fucked up."

"It was my first time."

* * *

Bouchard and a prospect named Harris were driving with their girlfriends from Martinsville to Bouchard's country home in St. Pierre. He'd bought it originally for skiing, but soon realized he liked it just as much in the summer. The four of them were back on the road after stopping for lunch when a state trooper lit up and sounded his siren behind them.

After they stopped, Bouchard handed his license, insurance card, and registration through the window, and asked, "What's the problem, officer?"

The cop was polite, but gave Bouchard no information. Bouchard shrugged to his passengers as the young cop went back to his car with the documents. Within about ten minutes, three Martinsville police cars showed up at the scene. The cops conferred with the state trooper for a few moments. Then two of them pulled their guns and aimed them at Bouchard's car. Another two cops walked over to the car. One of them asked Bouchard to step out. As he did, the other cop instructed him to put his hands behind his head and frisked him.

The first cop said: "Mr. Marvin Bouchard, you are under arrest for felony, sexual assault . . ."

"This is bullshit."

". . . you have the right to remain silent . . ."

"I know my fuckin' rights."

The cop read them anyway.

The cops also took in Harris, who had an unregistered handgun. Neither of the two girls had a valid driver's license, so the cops called a tow truck and gave the girls the number of a taxi company that serviced the area.

* * *

Back in Martinsville, Feeney and Ronnie were having a few beers before going to meet Rose. They were feeling pretty loose, not just because the newspapers had reported McAfee as dead, but because, with Bouchard in jail, they wouldn't have to deal with the man himself. Instead, they would get paid by

Rose; who was far less prone to ask questions. And, because the weapon hadn't yet been found, the cops and media were speculating that the hit was not a professional job.

Soon after they sat down, they were greeted by a couple of prospects Feeney knew only as Boner and Bad News who came to sit with them. After a few pleasantries and another round of beer, Boner asked Feeney what he'd been up to.

Ronnie interjected before Feeney could speak. "We just got back from Webster's Falls," he said excitedly. "We're the guys who offed McAfee!"

Boner glared at Feeney. Feeney shouted: "Yeah, we totally killed McAfee in softball," he said. "Our company team beat theirs twenty-three to two."

Ronnie was oblivious. "No, no, no. I shot him, I shot him in the motel parking lot," he continued animatedly. "His head exploded like a melon—pow!"

Boner and Bad News got up and left without a word.

Feeney stood Ronnie up and took him to the men's room. He made sure nobody was in either of the stalls and then held the door shut. He spoke quietly. "You fucking idiot, you just confessed to a murder in a public place, a place the cops know we hang out at and could have been bugged—anyone could have heard you."

"I didn't know . . ."

"And worst of all, you implicated me."

"I didn't know . . ."

"If the wrong person heard you, you could get twenty-five years for not knowing, and I would get almost as much."

"I'm sorry," Ronnie said as he exploded into tears and started to hug Feeney.

Feeney patted him on the back and told him everything would be okay, because there was no way the owner would let the cops bug the place, and the other people in the bar were not the kind to go report things to the police. "Half of them probably got outstanding warrants of their own."

Feeney stood there, one hand holding Ronnie as he blubbered and the other still holding the door shut. And as he did, he came to a conclusion—there's only one cure for stupid, and it's a bullet in the head.

* * *

Clegg couldn't believe his luck. A couple of uniforms brought in a guy for tearing up his girlfriend's apartment, and he just happened to have a big bag of meth on him. Even better, the skel was Eddie Aarhus, whom Clegg happened to know had some association with the Death Dealers.

He actually caught himself whistling a happy tune on the way to the interrogation room. "Hey, Eddie," he said as he got into the chair across from the prisoner. "I knew I'd see you again, just not this soon. Stupid move on your part."

"I ain't telling you shit."

"Oh, c'mon, Ed, neither of us believes that's true," Clegg said. "You've already ratted twice on your pals to stay outta jail. Why not make it an even three?"

Aarhus couldn't help but laugh. "It's different this time."

"Really? Because I have enough here to pretty much guarantee eight years."

"It's different."

"I know why it's different—because you're moving product for the Death Dealers now; the Lawbreakers found out it was you who sent Alfredsson to prison, and you're running out of options . . ."

"No."

"...and the Death Dealers are a more violent bunch anyway. You think that if they found out you were a rat, you wouldn't just be out of business—you'd be dead."

Eddie just sighed.

"It's okay, Ed. You're right—they would kill you if they found out..."

Ed looked at Clegg. A tear welled up in his right eye.

"...so you don't have to tell me who your dealer is."

Ed smiled.

"You're gonna have to face B and E and willful destruction charges for your girlfriend's place, but I'll forget about the meth if you do me a favor."

"What kind of favor?"

"I have a friend who's a reporter. You tell her what I want you to tell her and I'll forget I ever saw any meth."

"Will she use my name?"

"Nope. And your B and E charge will keep your friends from thinking you talked to get off."

"Okay then."

Clegg left to call Lara, then returned to the interrogation room to coach Aarhus on what to say. By the time she arrived, he was pretty comfortable. After a few preliminary questions that indicated he was a local drug dealer with close ties to the Death Dealers, Lara asked him about the war.

"Yeah, there's a war going on, everybody knows it, but nobody wants to talk about it. The Lawbreakers and the Death Dealers—who everybody knows are run by the Sons of Satan—are fighting it out on the streets of not just Springfield, but a bunch of cities for the right to sell drugs on the street."

"Who's winning?"

"It was the Lawbreakers for a long time, but now it's the Death Dealers."

"Is that because of the recent assassinations?"

"Yeah."

"And the Death Dealers are behind them?"

"Yeah, you might not believe me, but all the murders were done by one man—a professional assassin the Death Dealers brought in from Martinsville."

"Will you tell me his name?"

"I can't."

"When will the war stop?"

"When the Death Dealers run the town."

"Then what happens? The assassin gets sent to another town?"

"No, they plan to kill him."

"What?"

"After he's done in Springfield, they're gonna kill him because he's getting too wild, won't follow orders anymore. He's just too dangerous, even for them."

"How do you know all this?"

Aarhus looked at Clegg, who nodded.

"I'm done. I got nothing more to say."

Acting under Clegg's orders, a uniform took Aarhus back to his cell. Clegg grinned at Lara. "Don't say I never gave you anything."

She beamed.

* * *

Feeney had actually killed a guy before. His brother was a bouncer at Hurlihy's before Steve took it over, and he had to kick this one drunken tough guy out because he was grabbing all the dancers. The guy came back a half hour later with a shotgun. Feeney jumped him before he could get to his brother and the two of them beat him up. The guy later died in hospital from loss of blood. After some aggressive plea bargaining, Feeney's brother, Mikey, got three years and Feeney himself got eighteen months.

But this was totally different. Feeney had to go out with the intention of killing a man. A man whom, only days ago, he had considered his boyfriend. He didn't have time for sentiment. Besides, he could find another Ronnie in half an hour. He packed a gun and headed for the motel where Ronnie worked nights. The plan was to walk in when he saw Ronnie alone, shoot him in the head, and then grab some valuable stuff to make it look like a robbery. Easy in, easy out.

He brought two guns. A shotgun and a handgun. He drove to the motel but parked across the road. He planned to wait until he could tell there were no customers in the lobby, for when Ronnie was alone.

He sat in his car for about twenty minutes. But there was one old woman who sat in the couch opposite Ronnie's desk and talked and talked with him. Feeney wondered if he could get away with murdering Ronnie in front of her or if he would have to kill her too.

He was pondering that decision when he was awoken from his thoughts by sirens. Within seconds of each other, three cop cars showed up, sirens blaring. The cops got out, guns drawn, and hustled into the motel's office. A few minutes later, they emerged with Ronnie. His hands were cuffed behind his head, but he was smiling and chatting with the cops. Feeney didn't want to wait around; he drove away—quietly, obeying all street signs and speed limits—and went home.

***

Ned didn't want to go to Steve's, but he didn't have a choice. When the big man calls, you go. Steve wouldn't tell him why he wanted him, but he made sure Ned knew it was mandatory.

When he showed up at the mansion, Ned was surprised to see a bunch of cars there. Something was going on. But it wasn't something gangster, because most of the cars were pretty shitty. It was all Mazda 3s, Honda Civics, and stuff like that, not the usual Cadillacs, Lexuses, and big SUVs.

Once inside, he could tell what was going on. There were lights and wires everywhere. People were walking around with coffee and walkie-talkies. Steve was making one of his movies. Because the house was so large, it took a while to find him. Finally, he asked one of the guys who was milling about, and he told him Steve was in the 'Green Room.' When Ned looked at him, confused, the guy pointed.

Ned opened the door and saw Steve and a thin, curly haired woman sitting in what appeared to be matching barber chairs. They were both wearing white bathrobes. The room was full of lights and mirrors. An effeminate young man was spraying the woman's hair, while a small, older woman was applying makeup to Steve's face. His eyes were closed.

Ned cleared his throat. Steve opened his eyes and grinned broadly. "Crash Aiken!" He said. "So glad you could come."

"You called me down."

Steve dismissed the other people in the room. "Isn't this exciting?" he said. "Bet you've never been on a movie set before."

"No, no, you got me there."

"Let me show you around."

"Maybe we should get business out of the way first."

Steve's face dropped. "Yeah, maybe you're right. How are things going in Hamner?"

"Great—making lots of money, no problems with the police."

"Yeah, what about the Bandit?"

"Well, I'd like to tell you he's helping, but it'd be more accurate to say he's not hurting us that much."

"What do you mean?"

"Well, he doesn't do any work—other than act as something of a deterrent to any wannabe tough guys because he's so big and ugly—and he steals beer and harasses the dancers, but mostly he just hangs around all day."

"Acting funny at all?"

"If stupid is funny, then yes."

"Well, you don't have to worry about him anymore."

"Why?"

"A friend of mine who just happens to work for the Hamner PD told me that our mutual friend has been talking to the Springfield PD."

"What? He knows everything about me!"

"Don't worry. If they wanted you, you'd be behind bars right now," Steve said. "They want me. I hate to be the one to tell you this, but you're pretty small-time."

"Aren't you worried?"

"Do I look worried?" Steve laughed. "Listen, I just need you to tell him he's been sent back to Springfield—that I have a job for him. He'll believe you."

"What if he doesn't?"

"Then you've got a job to do." Steve paused, then laughed. "You always worry, Ned—he'll believe you. Don't be such a pussy."

"Okay."

"Do you know Adam Stockton?"

"Yeah, he was a year behind me in school. Big guy. Why?"

"Because I'm sending him to Hamner to help you out."

"He's one of us?"

Steve nodded, then clapped his hands. "Okay, now that business is over, we can get down to pleasure—which is also my business now."

Ned paused. "Uh, no thanks, watching other people have sex isn't really my thing."

"I thought you'd say that, so I'm offering you a starring role, well, co-starring—I'm the star," Steve smiled. "I could always use a tag-team partner."

"I don't think so. I told you that before."

"But I have something that might change your mind."

Steve led Ned into a bedroom, where he fully expected to see Melody or some other attractive girl. Instead, he was shocked to see Kelli. A little thinner, a lot more worn-down looking and with her hair dyed black. They looked at each other for a full minute before anybody said anything.

It was Steve who spoke. "Why don't I leave you two alone for a few minutes. I'm sure you have plenty to catch up on."

Kelli got up and hugged Ned. Then she let out a nervous giggle. "Hey, baby, it's so good to see you," she said with a smile. "How have you been?"

Ned stammered at first, but finally managed: "Good, good, good, real good—and you?"

She giggled again. It was something she had never really done before, and it annoyed him. "I'm doing great. I share a place with Mal," she paused. "And I work for Steve now." Another giggle.

"Dancing?"

"This and that."

A long pause. "I'm up in Hamner now, managing a bar," he said. "It's good, really good."

"You got a girlfriend?" She giggled.

"Yeah, yeah I do."

"I'm so glad to hear that," she hugged him again.

Steve walked in. "Time to go to work, Kelli," he said.

She kissed Ned on the nose and left the room.

Steve looked at Ned. "Are you sure I can't get you to do a scene or two?" Steve asked. "A quick and dirty thousand bucks."

"No. I'm cool."

"You are cool, right? Not upset, I mean."

"Oh yeah, yeah, I'm fine. That stuff's all behind me now, right? That was our deal."

"Yeah, I want you to know this wasn't a test—but if it was, you would have passed."

* * *

Feeney knew it was gonna happen, but he was surprised at how quickly it all went down. He was sitting on the couch, drinking a beer and watching *The Usual Suspects* when the police knocked on his door. An hour later, he was in an interrogation room with two FBI agents. They both wore cheap suits, but the older one, Quayle, had the gravity to pull it off. The other was a total musclehead, so his clothes had awkward tight spots and he tended to twitch and play with his earring when he wasn't talking. Feeney could smell his cologne in the small, harshly lit room.

"Okay, so we get a tip this skel at the hotel has two unregistered handguns, and we send a couple of units to pick him up," Detective-Lieutenant Robert Quayle said with a look of studied and utterly fake astonishment. "And, without any offers or anything from us—really, he didn't get anything—he offers to tell us all about how he murdered this dude in Webster's Falls with his—get this—gay lover who just happens to be a full-patch Son of Satan."

"I don't know what you're talking about."

"Yes you do," Quayle's partner, Dave Novello, said with a smug grin. "We've got times, places, dates, everything—I even know what all of your fuckin' tattoos look like."

"So I changed in front of some faggot at the health club; that doesn't make me a murderer."

"Oh don't worry, we know you didn't shoot anyone—Ronnie's copped to all that—as long as the ballistics back up what he says, we know he pulled the trigger," said Quayle. "But we do have you as the driver, and even if you get off, a lot of embarrassing stuff will come out that could, let's say, endanger your standing in the club."

Feeney sighed. He knew they had him. "So what do you want?"

"We'll drop the charges against you and keep your name out of Ronnie's trial," said Novello, "if you'll agree to wear a recording device."

It was exactly what Feeney had feared the most. But he knew he had no choice.

Novello dropped the tiny recorder on the table.

Feeney looked at it. "What's that there?" he asked. He pointed at a few spots of caked blood on some of the white tape that was stuck to the recorder.

Quayle sighed. "Jesus, Dave, you could have cleaned it off before you brought it out."

* * *

About a week after he was released from jail, Bouchard threw a small party. He had lots to celebrate. His accuser, a former part-time stripper he met through Steve, decided against pressing charges. She didn't give her lawyer a reason why. Bouchard was released that day. Three of Vandersloot's men followed her around for a while. One of them saw her riding on the back of Moe Gannon's Harley. Two days later, her nude body was found bound and gagged in a trash receptacle behind a supermarket in the city's north end.

Two days after that, one of Mehelnechuk's most carefully thought-out plans went into effect. He paid dearly to bring in two members of the Sons of Satan from a chapter in Oregon. He specifically wanted them because he recalled meeting them at a party and they struck him as looking less like bikers than they did officer workers. He also hired Darryl, the guy who looked after Mehelnechuk's cars, because he knew the Lawbreakers believed the Sons of Satan never did business with black people.

Their job was to deliver a big-screen TV to the Lawbreakers' clubhouse in Springfield. Two of Steve's men had stolen a van from a local electronics retailer and had a pair of uniforms made up for Darryl and the guys from Oregon. When they got to the clubhouse, they told the prospect at the door that the TV was a gift from the main office to reward the Springfield chapter for standing up to the Sons of Satan. Since there were no full members in the clubhouse, the prospect checked the papers. The names and addresses matched, so he told the guys to bring it in.

The three workers placed it where the prospect wanted it. He told them to take it out of the box and set it up. The two guys from Oregon looked at each other. One of them said: "No way, man; we get paid to drive, not to assemble."

The prospect offered them fifty dollars. They declined. Darryl said he'd do it for fifty dollars. Peter, one of the guys from Oregon remembered that Darryl hadn't been let in on the plan. As far as he knew, he was just delivering a TV. He didn't even know that Mehelnechuk or Bouchard were bikers.

Peter put his hand on Darryl's shoulder. "You can't do it, man, union rules."

"Fuck that? Who's gonna know?"

Peter walked over to the Lawbreakers prospect in charge and put his arm around him. He whispered into his ear. "I didn't want to have to tell you this, but Darryl has a learning disability," he said. "If you want your TV all fucked up, by all means, let him assemble it."

The prospect told Peter he understood and turned to Darryl. "Thanks, but no thanks, man. I have some people here who can handle it."

Darryl looked over at Peter. "Fuck you, you racist bastard."

"Yeah, yeah," Peter said. "Tell me all about it on the ride home."

"Don't worry, I will."

The three of them left the clubhouse, and got into the van. Peter stomped on the gas, and Darryl, who was riding in the back, tumbled all the way back to the rear doors. "What the fuck?" he yelled.

Then they heard the blast. It was so huge that the windows on buildings three blocks away shattered. Smoke billowed from the Lawbreakers' clubhouse. As soon as the prospect and a hangaround lifted the screen from the box, it triggered the roughly nine pounds of C4 plastic explosive inside. Four men within viewing distance of the TV were obliterated. Two others died from flying debris. Another lost an arm. No full-patch members were present, but the Lawbreakers' farm team had taken a huge hit, and the clubhouse was rendered useless.

Inside the van, Darryl patted Peter on the back and thanked him.

* * *

Things were very different at Buster's once Sharpe was gone. Adam Stockton, the new guy Steve sent down, was completely different from his predecessor. Not only was he a friendly, amiable guy, but he worked. Stockton hauled beer, chased away troublemakers, and even took a few shifts behind the bar. He kept his hands off the dancers, helped Ned negotiate deals, and kept everyone who worked at the bar loose.

Things were so much better that Ned found himself incredibly relaxed. But he couldn't say the same for Daniela, who was working as hard and as many hours as she had before. She had softened her tone towards Ned, and he had grown quite fond of her. He'd been attracted to her looks and natural grace from the moment he'd met her, but now he'd come to appreciate—even anticipate—her witty comments.

He found himself wanting to make her happy. So while they were sitting together in his office, he interrupted her story about how stupid the beer delivery guy was to suggest she take a break.

"You've been working so hard, why don't you take a few days off—just go enjoy yourself."

She was suspicious. "Why? What have I done?" she asked.

"I'm not punishing you, Dani," Ned said. "I'm rewarding you . . . take a vacation."

She folded her arms in front of her chest. She liked that he called her Dani. It was the first time she'd been called that by anyone in years. "Bar would fall apart, crumble to pieces without me here."

"Look, I understand that you have trust issues and all that, but we can struggle by for two or three days. Believe it or not, Adam is actually competent. I can help more than usual and Liliya has been talking about how much she wants to be a bouncer—we'll be fine."

"I'll think about it."

* * *

Carter knew that being high all the time was making him reckless, but Steve kept giving him more and more coke—and it certainly made doing his job easier. Since the Eggs O'Lent diner incident, Carter had shot six more men associated with the High Rollers, killing five of them.

He'd even joined in the crowd of onlookers after one of his murders, and nobody recognized him. Although he knew better than to get too cocky, he was feeling pretty close to invincible. And that's why he was thinking big. He was tired of offing drug dealers in their shitty apartments or run-down bars. He wanted to make a real score. Not for the money, but for the prestige.

He decided on a target on his own. Declan Allenson was considered an up-and-comer in Springfield. He'd been a Death Dealers prospect (and a good friend of André's), but he couldn't take the disorganization and leadership failings and changed allegiances to the Lawbreakers. He was not only a powerful drug dealer, but he was also running a very lucrative car theft business in which stolen luxury cars were reduced to parts that were then shipped to China for reassembly.

Carter knew that Allenson owned a legit used car lot and spent a lot of time there. But he was never alone—he employed some pretty tough characters and had a pair of Rottweilers roaming around the place. When he arrived at Dexy's Used Cars, Carter walked by both growling dogs and a mean-looking guy who was trying to shine up an old Buick. He went into the trailer that served as an office, and walked right up to Allenson. "I'm interested in that old Audi A4 you've got out there," Carter said. He was holding an ad Allenson had put in a local paper. "Does it really have just 54,000 miles on it?"

Allenson smiled broadly. "Would I lie?"

"I don't know," Carter said. "You *are* a used-car salesman."

"Get a load of the balls on this guy," Allenson laughed. The other two salesmen in the trailer laughed along with him

"Lemme take this guy," one of them offered.

Allenson shook his head. "No, he amuses me. Besides, I have a feeling we can get this guy to pay full price and then grab his address and get the car back by morning."

His employee laughed.

"Okay, okay, why don't we go take a look at the car then?" Allenson said to Carter.

"Great."

"Just lemme see your driver's license first," Allenson looked the document over. "Thank you, Mr. Marino; hey, are you related to the Marinos who live on Queenston Road?"

"No, I'm not from here," said Carter.

Inside the Audi, they talked about the car's features and how well it handled in the snow. Carter asked if he could take it on the highway. Allenson said it was okay, as long as they got back to the dealership soon. But Carter missed the on-ramp and went down a country road instead. "Just to test it out," he said. "If it can handle these dirt roads, I'll know it can handle anything."

"Just don't get it dirty," Allenson laughed.

Carter stopped the car and looked out the passenger window past Allenson. "Hey," he said. "Is that girl naked?"

Allenson turned to look. "Where?" he said.

Carter took a .44 Magnum out of his jacket and shot Allenson in the back of the head. The bullet came out his mouth and shattered the passenger window.

"Aw, shit," Carter said, and put his head in his hands laughing. He reached over Allenson's body and opened the passenger door. He put his back against his own door and kicked Allenson's body out. It wasn't easy. Allenson weighed about a hundred pounds more than Carter. When the body was finally out of the car, Carter wiped the gun down, threw it away in a field, and drove back to the city.

CHAPTER 15

Feeney didn't like where they put the recorder. Not only was it uncomfortable on his sternum, he thought it stood out. He thought that it was obvious, and that he'd be killed the second he showed up at the clubhouse. So he took the long way there, along the lake, just to clear his head.

He knew what the Sons did to snitches. He was there when they caught one. A cop who owed Vandersloot some money told him that Sam Cain had been collaborating with the ATF on an investigation that involved Bouchard. That night, Vandersloot invited Cain to dinner. Cain got in his car and started driving for Vandersloot's place in the country. About halfway there, a minivan blocked his way. It wouldn't move. Then a pickup truck pulled up behind him. Cain started to turn into the oncoming lane to get around the minivan, but the pickup truck rammed his car. Three masked men with guns leapt out of the minivan. The first opened Cain's passenger-side door and said in a familiar voice, "Give us all your money and nobody gets hurt."

A police bug caught the hijacking on tape to just after Cain blurted out, "What the fuck, Petey, why are you ..." The last sounds on the tape were four gunshots, some laughing, and the squeal of tires.

Feeney was there and he had heard the story a number of times. Not only did the guys involved like to tell the story, but the ranking members encouraged its retelling to remind the prospects what happens to snitches.

Of course, Feeney thought to himself that this was all Ronnie's fault. Asshole wannabe-cop-turned-wannabe-gangster proved too stupid to do either job. It infuriated Feeney that Ronnie gave him up to the cops so easily. And that he was too stupid to even get himself off for it. They wouldn't have even known about the McAfee job unless he blabbed. The cops thought it was hilarious. They brought the fat fuck in for a misdemeanor and, with no urging, he admits to a murder and sells out a full-patch Son of Satan who, the cops are delighted to learn, is also his homo boyfriend.

The problem was that Ronnie wanted to be a big shot. He'd tell anyone what they wanted to hear, even if it meant prison time. He just wanted the cops to like him, to listen to him; he didn't think about the consequences.

If only he had been a few minutes earlier, Feeney thought to himself. The cops would be investigating an armed robbery gone wrong. Ronnie would have been silenced forever.

But it didn't go down that way. And now the cops owned him. They wanted him to record conversations with Bouchard, Rose, Vandersloot, or any other big guy. It wouldn't be too hard. Guys talked about deals with him all the time. They trusted him. He'd done his time in the club—and in prison. They knew he'd never be a rat.

Feeney thought about how much Ronnie'd say before they finally killed him—there was no way he'd last very long in prison. And Feeney thought about his daughters Sydney and Britny, whom he'd had with his high school girlfriend Josie before he became a biker. He slowed his car down and eventually stopped at the beach. There was nobody there because it was too cold, and the waves were big because of the wind. He walked out onto the sand, then onto an old concrete pier. He unbuttoned his shirt, took off the recorder, and threw it as far as he could into the water. He laughed. Then he sat down on the pier, pulled his gun out, put the barrel in his mouth, and gently pulled the trigger.

* * *

An off-duty cop passed Carter on the highway. The cop wondered what a high-end car with dealer plates was doing on a road miles from a dealership, the sale price still scrawled across the windscreen, it's passenger window open on a chilly day like this. Instinctively, he reached for his cellphone.

Five miles down the road, Carter saw the flashing lights in his rearview mirror. He put on his right turn signal and slowed down by the side of the road. The cops followed him. Just as the Audi was almost stopped, he floored it. The troopers turned on their siren and pursued him. They called for help.

Carter kept accelerating, but misjudged the distance between him and a semi. The right front bumper of the Audi just touched the back of the trailer, but it was enough to send the car spinning. It came to rest in a low part of the median strip.

Carter managed to get out of the car and run a few steps before one of the troopers tackled him.

* * *

Bouchard always felt self-conscious about eating with Mehelnechuk. He just seemed so critical of his eating and drinking habits, and it made Bouchard feel uncouth, like some kind of barbarian compared to the genteel boss. Mehelnechuk never really said anything, but Bouchard could tell from his face and actions. The worst part was that he tended to finish his meal long before Mehelnechuk had even made a dent in his. It made Bouchard feel awkward.

But this was business. It was a victory dinner of sorts. Ever since Bouchard's men had bombed the Lawbreakers' Springfield headquarters, they had been absolutely silent. No shootings, no fires, no threats, no nothing. Mehelnechuk could tell things were working from the little signs as well. More and more often, Sons of Satan were wearing their colors in public, and Bouchard had even stopped wearing his body armor when he was out in public. And at least two recalcitrant dealers that he knew of had returned to the fold on a no-questions-asked basis.

Mehelnechuk was just getting into his veal chop and Bouchard was starting on his first post-dinner beer when a prospect who had been waiting outside approached the table. He spoke to Bouchard. "There's a fellow outside who says he needs to talk with you."

Bouchard laughed. "Do you know him?"

"No, little guy, looks like a nobody," said the prospect. "But he says he has a message for you from Mr. Wentworth and that you would know what that means."

Bouchard looked at Mehelnechuk. Mehelnechuk nodded almost imperceptibly.

"Okay, pat him down and bring him to the table," Bouchard said. "And make sure he knows you are beside him at all times."

The prospect brought the young man to the table and stood beside him as he sat next to Bouchard. Bouchard recognized him from the wedding of DeVolo's niece. He nodded at Mehelnechuk.

"What can I do for you, young man?"

"My boss, he wants to meet you."

"Mr. Wentworth?"

"Yeah, at the usual spot."

"When?"

"Tomorrow night, about seven—there will be dinner."

"Well, you better make a lot of spaghetti and meatballs because I'm coming with a lot of my friends."

"That was expected."

"Tell him we'll be there. Now let me eat my dinner in peace."

After the prospect escorted the little man out, Mehelnechuk couldn't help but smile. Bouchard laughed out loud.

***

Clegg wasn't the sort of cop who'd play hunches very often, but he thought he'd try a little something out on the prisoner that the uniforms had brought in. He'd been in the interrogation room with Carter for about forty-five minutes, and was getting nowhere. Clegg could tell the little guy was still tweaking. He was heavily addicted to cocaine or methamphetamine and had been away from it for the three days he was in jail. He shook and twitched and yammered on and on. But still he kept a cap on his mouth when it came to anything valuable, telling Clegg next to nothing.

So Clegg took out his wild card. He showed Carter Lara's newspaper article that quoted the unidentified biker about the war. Carter's lips moved as he read it, then he started laughing mirthlessly about half way through. He looked Clegg in the eye and said: "How do you like that? After everything I've done for them, they're going to kill me."

Clegg tried very hard not to look astonished. "Yeah, that's how it goes sometimes," he said. "Tough bunch of boys in a rough business."

"Tell me about it," Carter said. "And if that's how they want to play it, they can go fuck themselves—what kind of deal will you give me?"

"Depends on what you have, and what you've done."

"I've got it all, and I've done it all," Carter grinned broadly but without any detectable emotion. "I got people you never heard of doing shit you don't know about."

"Lemme get the prosecutor on the phone," Clegg told him. "I think we can work something out."

***

Ned was driving back to Hamner when his phone rang. It was Mehelnechuk. "Is this a fresh phone?" he asked. Ned assured him it was. "Okay, then pull over. We need to talk."

Ned did as he was told.

"How do you like it there in Hamner?"

Ned told him he liked it a lot, especially since Stockton had shown up.

"Good," he answered. "How would you like to stay there?"

"Of course," he said. "But I don't know what Steve needs from me."

He could hear Mehelnechuk laugh. "Steve? Remember, he works for me ... actually, he works for somebody who works for somebody who works for me. I'll take care of him."

Ned laughed. "So what did you have in mind?"

"Well, I'm thinking about setting up another club up there in Hamner, just clean-cut guys like you—short hair, no beards, no jackets, no patches, no tats, just a bunch of normal-looking guys," Mehelnechuk said. "You'd do the same sort of thing that you're doing now, just attract a whole lot less attention to your-selves—hell, you could even give up the Harley—and you'd be my top guy."

Now Ned was smiling. "That sounds exactly like something I'd really like."

"Yeah, I thought so," said Mehelnechuk. "Let's get together later this week and we'll talk—I come in to Springfield most Sundays to take my folks to church. Maybe we can hook up afterwards?"

"I'll be there."

After he hung up, Ned raced back to Hamner. When he arrived, he hugged and kissed Daniela. Liliya giggled. Daniela found herself laughing. She said something in their native language and Liliya nodded and left the room.

"What's gotten into you?" she asked Ned. "This is not how you usually greet employees."

He smiled broadly. "Well, everything has changed," he said. "I don't work for Steve anymore and I'm about to get very rich. How does that sound?"

"It sounds great." Daniela was still confused.

"It's better than great. Look, why don't you and I go out to dinner tonight to celebrate?" he said.

She turned her head but kept looking at him. "Sure."

At dinner that night, Ned explained to her about Kelli, about how Mehelnechuk wanted him to be president of a new kind of club. They talked, they ate, they drank, and they flirted. He brought up her vacation again and suggested they go to North Beach for a few days. By the time she woke up in Ned's house, they had already decided she'd move in. It was, she thought to herself, perhaps the happiest she had ever been.

***

Ever since she had taken the crime reporter job, Lara's parents had been reminding her constantly to be careful. They'd call her, e-mail her, text her, and even write her letters telling her to be careful. At first, she thought it was sweet, but then it really got on her nerves. It wasn't that she didn't think they had faith in her, just that they never got more specific than "be careful."

She was actually very careful and never had felt that her job put her in any danger. Most of the lowlifes she dealt with were more stupid than frightening, and she almost always ended up talking to them after they'd been caught. Sitting in a cell or an interrogation room, they tended to drop their tough-guy personas and look to her for understanding to tell their side of the story. None of them were guilty in their stories, just great guys who were tricked, made a mistake, or were bedeviled by mistaken identity or someone out to get them.

It helped to have Clegg around too. Not only was he the biggest guy around, he was plenty tough. All he had to do was show up and things quieted down. Over the time they had been working together, they had developed not just a trust, but a friendship. She felt a lot safer with him in town.

But things had changed over the last couple of days. Just after Clegg had left to take part in a joint-district task force project in Martinsville, Lara started working on a story about Mehelnechuk. She went around to all his old haunts—his high school, the fast-food restaurant he had worked at for two weeks, his friends, his lawyer, and the businesses she had heard that he owned—and nobody wanted to talk. It was like there was an invisible wall of silence that emerged whenever she mentioned his name.

She also noticed that a certain type of man always seemed to be around, staring at her, no matter where she went. Because she was so pretty, Lara was used to being stared at, but not in this way. These men weren't hoping to meet her. They were keeping an eye on her.

Four days after she started the research on the Mehelnechuk

story, Lara was driving home from the paper when she noticed a Jeep trailing her. She turned towards the highway, he turned with her. She turned back into town. He followed. At a stoplight, she studied his face. He was a big guy with long hair. He was wearing sunglasses and had a Fu Manchu style moustache. Just before she parked at her condo, she memorized the license plate.

When she got out of the car, she was surprised to find herself running for the door. Once inside, she was shocked to find her laptop missing. Nothing else was wrong with the place, but the laptop was gone.

She called the police and asked for Clegg, even though she knew he was in Martinsville.

* * *

The sound was thunderous. Bouchard had collected twenty-five of the meanest-looking bikers he could, put them in full colors, and rode them down Hartford Street, Martinsville's main drag. In open defiance of the law, not one of them was wearing a helmet.

They stopped in front of the Wentworth Hotel, dismounted, and walked in the front door. Bouchard was in the lead. They went into the grand ballroom. DeVolo and his men had already taken their places on one side of the table. Suits, ties, gold, and hairspray faced off against leather, denim, patches, and beards.

But the atmosphere was cordial. DeVolo stood up and shook hands with Bouchard. If the press were invited, that would have been the money shot, the one that made the front pages. But of course they weren't. This was business: the business of organized crime.

Over the evening, many topics were discussed. The

Italians would supply the Sons and their vassals, and nobody else. The High Rollers would be disbanded. The Sons would have their pick of the best of them. The others would be run off. Both sides agreed that coke must be sold at $50,000 a kilo. The penalty for selling for less would be death. The Sons would continue to supply labor to the Italians for jobs like debt collection, witness intimidation, and protection rackets. The Sons would buy drugs from no other suppliers. And Scott Kreig would die.

Bouchard had a problem with the last item on the agenda. He knew Kreig was an old high school friend of Mehelnechuk's, and that he had stood by the Sons when the Italians and their Lawbreaker stooges were at war with them. Bouchard excused himself from the table.

"This is most unprecedented," said DeVolo.

"Calm down, Mario," said Bouchard. "I just gotta take a leak." He headed toward the men's room. Two bikers started to come with him, but he waved them off.

When he finally got into the men's room, he checked to see that it was clear. It was. He dialed Mehelnechuk.

"Yeah?" was his answer.

"It's going exactly as you said it would, except for one thing," Bouchard said. Then he paused. "They want us to kill Scott."

"Yeah? That's not too surprising. He is their biggest competition in town."

"But isn't he your friend?"

"Aren't the Lawbreakers their friends?"

Bouchard laughed. "Okay, cool, I was just checking."

"Just do what I told you."

***

Ned sat through Ukrainian Orthodox mass with Mehelnechuk and his octogenarian mother and father. It was mostly in Ukrainian, so he just tried to mimic what everyone else did. Afterwards, they went back to Mehelnechuk's mom's place for cabbage rolls and coffee. She spoke about Ivan's success as a plumbing supply salesman (which was his official job), and how proud she was of him. And before she would allow them to go, she made Ivan promise to take care of his young friend and keep him out of trouble.

As they drove up to Johnny Reb's in Mehelnechuk's black Jaguar, Ned asked him why he went to Martinsville, why he just didn't set up shop in Springfield, or move his operation back there once he was successful. Mehelnechuk just smiled and tersely said, "You don't shit where you live." Ned suspected the real answer was more complex.

When they got into the bar, they walked straight into the office. There were already five young men inside it. They were all clean-cut, with short hair and no obvious tattoos or jewelry. They wore clean jeans or khakis with collared shirts or sweaters. Ned noticed one held a Nike baseball cap in his right hand. He was presumably polite enough to know to take his hat off indoors.

"This is your team, Ned," Mehelenechuk said as he waved his arm at the young men. "These are the Managers."

"The Managers?"

"Yeah, here's how it's going to go down: you get rid of all the biker gear, dress like an ordinary businessman, do your taxes, buy a house, all that shit," he said. "You run things in Hamner exactly as you have been, but never get your hands dirty. Someone needs a beating—call a biker. Someone wants drugs or a hooker—call a biker. They work for you now."

"Kind of like how a prospect works for a member?"

"No, the bikers aren't your slaves. They are your employees. It's gonna work more like how, say, the Death Dealers represent the Sons' interests in Springfield," Mehelnechuk corrected him. "I expect you will treat them with the respect they deserve, and that means money as well."

"I get it."

"And be smart about who you ask to do what," he said. "And you only take orders from me or one of my closest associates."

"Like who?"

"Bouchard, Vandersloot, Rose, those kinds of guys."

"Okay."

"And one other thing, you kick up to me now, not Steve."

"Thirty percent?"

"Yup."

"Does Steve know?"

"I have a feeling you'd like to tell him."

Ned laughed. "And these guys?"

"They do what you do, but in other cities," Mehelnechuk told him. "Peter here runs Ransberry. Dominic runs Clarksborough. You get the picture—work the details out among yourselves."

"Can I keep Stockton?"

"I expected you would. He fits the mold."

"Why are we doing this? I mean, I'm not saying I don't like it. But why are we adding yet another gang?"

"What we are adding is another layer," Mehelnechuk spoke as though he was talking to a five-year-old. "Suppose I need a job done. I tell Rose, he tells you, you tell one of Steve's men who hires some skel."

"I see, the skel gets caught and he can only rat on Steve's guy. If Steve's guy rats, he can only nail me . . ."

"And you were specifically chosen not just because you are a good earner and because you clean up well, but because you know that the wages of exposing your superiors to prosecution is death."

Ned laughed weakly.

* * *

Clegg had been called up to Martinsville for a reason. According to at least a few informants, the Martinsville Sons of Satan were planning something huge. Clegg had been assigned to the group of officers from various forces who were watching the Sons of Satan clubhouse.

It was mostly boring, sitting in cars or on the curb watching the clubhouse. Now and then, another cop Clegg knew would come and talk with him, but they didn't have much new to say. Once, a prospect he arrested a year ago in Springfield dropped by to say "hi," but wouldn't say anything of value. He basically just wanted to show Clegg that he was back on the streets and in good standing with the club.

Clegg was tired and bored, actually yawning, when he first heard it. All the officers fell silent and looked at one another. It was a low rumbling, not unlike what you'd expect a tsunami or coming storm to sound like. And it got louder, and louder, and louder.

When the first of the bikers finally turned the corner, Clegg could make out some of the Sons' biggest brass. There was Bouchard, Vandersloot, and Rose. He was surprised to see Mehelnechuk in the very front—a spot the bikers usually only allow the most high-ranking member to ride—and he made a mental note to talk to Lara when he got back to Springfield.

Behind the bosses rode the lesser Sons members. Some

were from Springfield and other cities. Next came the prospects and members from puppet clubs like the Death Dealers. Behind them were members of clubs that Clegg knew the Sons had been actively recruiting. He saw patches for the Devil's Own, the Black Diamonds, the Huns, the One-Eyed Jacks, and several others. And then, at the very end, Clegg saw something he never could have predicted. Behind the flotsam and jetsam of the biker world were no less than three dozen Lawbreakers, some of whom he recognized from Springfield. At the front of them was Moe Gannon.

While most of the bikers were jubilant, the Lawbreakers—especially the ones from Springfield—filed into the Sons of Satan clubhouse pretending it was no big deal. One wide-eyed young cop bumped Clegg on the arm and said, "There must be every biker for a thousand miles in there." All Clegg could do was nod.

For about forty-five minutes, the dozen or so cops and the few reporters who showed up buzzed with anticipation. The consensus was that this was a giant biker summit that would at best establish a peace among them and at worst align them against the Italians.

None was actually prepared for what came next. First, it was a couple of the Devil's Own. They walked out of the clubhouse, turned around, held their hands above their heads, and upstretched their middle fingers. Their jackets now bore the smiling skull emblem. The rockers read "Sons of Satan" and "New Hamburg." After them, a deluge of newly minted Sons of Satan came pouring onto the streets.

The last of them were the former Lawbreakers. Their jackets now read "Sons of Satan" and "Springfield West." The Death Dealers had already been christened "Springfield East." As the former Lawbreakers joined in the festivities with their new brothers, one of the cops yelled, "So much for Lawbreaker pride." But it was an impotent volley. As far as the bikers were concerned, the Lawbreakers were extinct in Springfield, in Martinsville, and everywhere else within a day's ride. And those outside the new arrangement were enemies, former brothers or not.

* * *

Lara was running late from yoga at the rec center. She had a meeting at one o'clock to discuss (actually, she thought, to defend) how much time she was spending on the Mehelnechuk project. She knew she had to look professional, so she took her time getting ready in the change room.

Satisfied she looked the part, Lara bounded from the rec center and into the parking lot. The first thing she saw was the Jeep that the big man who was following her drove. It was parked—illegally—right in front of the door. She stared at it, transfixed. Because of the deeply tinted windows, she couldn't tell if there was anyone inside. She was about to go back into the rec center (meeting be damned!), when she felt a searing pain in her arm. Then another in her left ear. Then she felt very dizzy and fell face first onto the pavement and lost consciousness. She didn't see the masked gunman behind her throw his handgun down and run behind the rec center into a waiting car. She didn't see the Jeep speed away. She didn't see anything.

* * *

Curt Steele, an assistant district attorney, was exhausted after a two-hour meeting with Carter. He was shocked at how many people Carter had killed, but was even more astonished by what a horrible little shit he was. Steele had dealt with psychopaths and sociopaths before, but had never seen anyone like this. Nobody, he had thought until he met Carter, could be absolutely devoid of empathy.

Carter told him all about his job as an assassin in Martinsville and now Springfield. He talked about it in the same way an ordinary person might talk about their job. He bragged about the pay and fringe benefits, and he complained about the hours, his bosses, and all the traveling. Carter droned on about killing as though it were some far more mundane task. He felt no guilt, no empathy for his victims. He clearly knew what he was doing was against the law and that he'd been caught—but Steele could detect no indication that Carter believed what he was doing was actually wrong. He looked at murder as another person might look at data entry or trash collection.

But Steele knew that offering him a deal wouldn't anger too many people, no matter how egregious the man was or how many people he'd killed. The murders Carter committed rid the streets of killers, drug dealers, and thieves, and the information he had could give Steele the ability to arrest two hundred, maybe three hundred, other criminals, and put a serious dent in both the bikers and the Italian mafia. Besides, a good defense attorney could even make an insanity plea stick if Carter ever went to trial, which would defeat the purpose of prosecuting him anyway.

If he pulled this off, Steele would be a shoo-in for district attorney, and—if he played his cards right—he could eventually be Springfield's first black mayor.

He thought about it all the way back to his office. He made a few phone calls to find out about Carter's priors and his reputation. He cross-referenced Carter's admissions with the case files he had Clegg fax over. He came out of his office four-and-a-half hours later convinced he could not only bring down the bikers in Springfield and maybe Martinsville, but he could also make a dent in the local Italian mafia. All it would cost is a deal with a mass murderer, who'd probably end up in a mental home anyway.

He phoned his wife and told her to call the babysitter. They were going to Le Perigourdine, her favorite restaurant. They had something to celebrate.

Steele climbed into his Lexus, and pushed the start button. He appreciated the hum of the engine more than usual. After fighting with city traffic, he relaxed a little more on the highway. Very few people in the tidy little town of Herman's Ford worked in the city, so traffic on the road there was always light. That's why he was so surprised that an old pickup with two men was tailgating him. Must be some farmers, he thought; they always drive like nuts. His first thought was to step on the accelerator and blow them away, but he didn't want any moving violations on his record. Unbecoming for a future mayor. Instead, he memorized the license plate. Wouldn't they be surprised, he laughed to himself, when they realized who they were dealing with.

So he patiently waited for them to pass. Just after they both took the off-ramp onto deserted Westcott Road, they did start to pass. As they drew even with him, the young man in the passenger seat rolled down his window as though he had something to say. Steele ignored them. He wasn't looking when the man pulled out the shotgun. He pumped two shots into Steele's driver's side window.

The Lexus spun out. The pickup stopped and reversed, almost ramming the Lexus. The shooter got out of the truck. He tried the car's door, but it was locked. He could see Steele inside, still moving. He sent two more volleys of hot metal into Steele's head. He stopped moving.

The gunman wiped the shotgun down with his shirt, threw it in the Lexus's window, and raced back to the pickup. It made a U-turn and sped away, back toward the city.

CHAPTER 16

"Please tell me it wasn't you," Mehelnechuk said to Bouchard. He was calm, but Bouchard could hear the anger seething out of every syllable.

"My hands were tied," he responded.

"What?"

"My cop told me that Carter had spilled everything to the ADA," Bouchard said. "It was either kill him, or we'd all go to prison."

"We'd all go to prison," Mehelnechuk mocked him in a sing-song voice. "Is that so?"

"Yeah, Carter was prepared to tell them everything."

"Carter, right, Carter," Mehelnechuk said. "The drug-addicted mass murderer who no jury in the world would ever believe."

"But he knew everything."

"Everything? Really? Who did you tell Carter to kill? Who did I tell Carter to kill?"

"Well, our men did . . ."

"Yeah, and they keep their mouths shut and take their punishment or they die," Mehelnechuk scolded. "That's the plan, that's always been the plan, it's the only way that works."

"But Carter wasn't keeping his mouth shut, and the cops had him under special security."

"We could always get to him," Mehelnechuk commented and paused. "Let me get this straight. Do you really think the way to silence Carter was to kill the one listening to him?"

"Well, if you kill anyone who listens, people won't be lining up to listen anymore," Bouchard said. "Remember, two people can keep a secret if one of them is dead."

That answer enraged Mehelnechuk, who was now shouting. "You stupid fuck! What do you think this is—Colombia?" he screamed. "There are gangs we are not prepared to take on and one of them is the U.S. government."

"But we do that all the time."

"No, no we don't." Mehelnechuk shook his head and spoke much more softly. "We break the laws and the cops chase us around. It's an equilibrium. We stay ahead of them and we stay safe—they arrest some of our small fry, it makes them feel good about themselves, and then we recruit more small fry. That's the way it works—business as usual."

He paused, then continued. "But you have upset that equilibrium," he continued. "You just declared war on the wrong people."

"I really don't think so."

"Then you are fucked, and I won't let you take me with you."

"We'll just wait and see what happens."

"Yeah," Mehelnechuk's tone lightened. "But I gotta hand it to you with how you handled the Italians. It all went according to plan."

"Well, that was mostly your doing."

"Thanks, you are too kind," Mehelnechuk smiled. "Which reminds me, did you take care of the other thing?"

"I sent a team out."

* * *

Scott Kreig had always considered himself a man of unusually good fortune. He was nice looking and popular. He was a good friend of Mehelnechuk's in high school and even rode around with him for a while, but quit before either of them got too serious. Instead, he took over his father's real estate business when the old man retired. Kreig was adept at the business, and became a millionaire before he was twenty-five.

He met an older South American man who wanted to buy a house in Springfield for his niece. The older man, Santiago Barajas, introduced Kreig not just to his niece, Yolanda Martinez, but to cocaine. The girl he liked right away and he eventually married her. Things were different with cocaine. He tried it a couple of times and enjoyed the high, but couldn't stand the hangover. But he did realize he could make a lot more money selling cocaine than he could selling houses. Barajas agreed.

And Kreig had it much easier than most. He had one trustworthy supplier—hell, he was family—and one reliable client. He never sold directly to Mehelnechuk, but always to somebody in the Sons, who he knew worked for him. Right now, his contact was Rose.

Kreig didn't even have to keep the books; that was Yolanda's job. In fact, Kreig did little other than look good and collect money. He had a kid who picked up a package at the airport once a month, another kid who gave it to Rose, and a third who brought a knapsack full of cash back to the house. And as long as he kept the real estate business running, nobody suspected a thing. Tall, blond, and given to wearing impeccable, but utterly conservative suits, he certainly didn't look like a drug dealer. He even drove a Volvo.

And it was in that Volvo that he decided to take Yolanda on a surprise trip. She'd been working hard lately, so Scott decided to treat her with a long weekend at Cambridge Hall, a spa resort just outside Springfield.

After dinner, they were returning to their suite when they saw the housekeeper's pushcart in front of their door. Yolanda said something angrily in Spanish, and the housekeeper apologized and pushed her cart out of the way. Still a little bit drunk, the Kreigs stepped into the suite. As soon as Scott shut the door behind them, two men in ski masks emerged from the suite's bathroom and attacked them. The first grabbed Yolanda, threw her to the ground, held her down, and prevented her from screaming. The other man knocked Scott to the ground and pumped six shots from a silenced handgun into his chest. As soon as he threw the gun to the ground, they both ran.

Yolanda, shocked, crawled over to Scott on her hands and knees. He was dead.

***

Ordinarily, Clegg would be irritated by a trip to the hospital. The antiseptic smell, the groans of the elderly, and stink of the food were a part of his job he could do without. But he was there to see Lara, so things were different. The overwhelming feeling he had was concern. He didn't want to betray any emotion as he sat in the chair beside Lara's hospital bed. But he couldn't help himself. "You know this wouldn't have happened if I was here," he said. "And I'll catch the bastard who did this."

"I know you will," Lara said softly. "And it's not because you're a good cop."

"What?"

"It's because I'm a good reporter," she said. "The license plate number is TAC 820."

He laughed and wrote it down.

It didn't take that long to track down Lara's shooter. Clegg visited the owner of the Jeep registered to the TAC 820 license plate, who said it had been stolen and had a copy of the police report to prove it. He told Clegg who he thought had stolen it—a neighbor who lived down the road and had always admired the Jeep. He ran with a tough crowd, might even have been a biker. Clegg asked for a more thorough description. The description matched what Lara had told him, so he called some of the cops he trusted the most and told them there was someone dangerous he absolutely had to take down.

Thirty minutes later, eight cops had surrounded 4915 Walmer Road. It was a run-down little shack just out of town. It had boarded-up windows and the remains of a chain-link fence. There was an old washing machine rusting away in the back yard. And there was a stolen Jeep parked in the doorless garage. Clegg figured the man inside was bold but not very smart. He considered that a dangerous combination.

He sent Detective Jimmy Lewis to go look into the front window. Lewis signaled that the man was inside and he trained his gun on him. Clegg kicked the door down, and he and another cop came rushing in with their guns drawn.

The man inside, Preston Wilhite, ran for the back door. Two cops had already come bursting through it. Preston put his hands up. Clegg grabbed them and put them in cuffs. He read him his rights as he led him to the car.

Back in the interrogation room, it didn't take Wilhite long to crack. Once presented with a charge of first-degree murder, he quickly admitted that he was involved, but was not the triggerman. After very little convincing, he gave up the name Pat Duncan.

He didn't know his address, but it didn't matter. Clegg was well aware of who Duncan was. A former Lawbreaker, he changed sides after he saw how quickly the Sons of Satan routed the Lawbreakers in Martinsville and how his fellow Springfield Lawbreakers brothers did nothing to help their brothers in the big city.

Many considered Duncan something of an up-and-comer in the organization, but it was clear that the Death Dealers were forcing him to go through a period of hazing, perhaps penance, before they would allow him any real responsibility. It made sense to Clegg that Duncan would have to kill for the club to gain membership—and that a high-profile daytime job would definitely cement the deal.

Clegg left Wilhite to chill in his cell, and collected some of his friends to bring down Duncan. They arrived at his innocuous but valuable suburban house in unmarked cars. After it was established that he wasn't home, they waited in their cars. When a silver Honda pulled up in front of the house, Lewis ran the plates. It was registered to a sixty-two-year-old woman named Deborah Duncan. "It's him," Lewis said.

Just as Duncan was getting out of his car, the cops stormed him with weapons drawn, laser sights converging in a red spot on his chest. He dropped his briefcase and put his hands in the air. When they got to the car, Lewis arrested Duncan, and Clegg grabbed the briefcase.

Back at the station, they couldn't get Duncan to talk. But it didn't matter too much because Wilhite had already ratted him out. The best he could hope for would be a plea bargain down to aggravated assault. And Wilhite wasn't smart enough to ask for a deal, so he was going down for a few years at least as well.

But what puzzled Clegg was Duncan's briefcase. Inside, it was stuffed with spreadsheets. Pages and pages of spreadsheets, no less than two-and-half inches thick. Each of them had sets of numbers set against names. It was obvious that it listed dates against amounts and dollars. He didn't know exactly what he had, but he knew he had to keep it.

***

Clegg didn't like Steele's replacement as district attorney, Murray Hamilton. He knew him from when he was in private practice and considered him something of a soulless ambulance chaser. That he was appointed to take Steele's place after the murder was a great disappointment. Steele could be a bit of a pain with his ego and pomposity, but he put bad guys behind bars. He was thorough and fearless. Clegg didn't think that Hamilton would have quite the same ethical discipline.

Although it was unorthodox, Clegg asked Hamilton to meet him in the interrogation room. He sat in the small, windowless, pea-green cell. He wasn't bothered by its harsh fluorescent lights and their prominent hiss. He had grown too used to them to notice.

Hamilton arrived with a few associates, but they stayed outside the interrogation room. Clegg closed the door.

"Nice place you got here," Hamilton began. "A few plants, some drapes, could be something."

"C'mon, man," Clegg laughed. "You're a prosecutor now, Murray; you're not on the criminals' side any more."

"Oh, I forgot, I'm dealing with Mike Clegg—judge, jury, and from what I hear, executioner, of Springfield's east side," Hamilton said. "Why don't we just get down to business?"

"Fine with me," Clegg answered. "With this Carter asshole, we got them all dead to rights."

"Uhhhhh, about that John . . . ." Hamilton said. "I can't do it, old buddy."

Clegg exploded. "Whaddaya mean, you can't do it?" he shouted at him. "We have an assassin—*the* assassin—who is ready to give up everybody in the Sons and half the Italian mafia and you're telling him 'no thank you?'"

"But that's exactly the problem, John," Hamilton responded calmly. "You have to think about what he'll look like in court—what we have is an admitted serial murderer who is also a lifelong drug addict and petty thief. He's not exactly the type juries identify with."

"You're really saying no, you don't want his testimony to bring down most, if not all of the organized crime in this city?"

"Nobody will believe him, John. They just won't and you know it—and we don't want to be seen as letting him get away with murder."

Clegg sighed and ran his hand over his short, bristly hair. "They've gotten to you Murray."

Hamilton grinned. "What do you mean, John?"

"What I mean is that they have gotten to you," Clegg said monotonously, without looking at Hamilton. "Either they have paid you off, or they've told you that you'll end up like Steele—who was twice the man you'll ever be."

"Those are some pretty severe accusations," Hamilton said. "You're lucky nobody else is in here to hear them or I'd have your ass."

"That's why we're in here," Clegg told him. "I was afraid something like this would happen."

***

There were no cars around Steve's mansion when Ned drove up this time. No buzz of activity in the air. Ned correctly assumed it wasn't a filming day. After he got out of the car he was greeted by a couple of guys he knew to be prospects. They didn't recognize him, but the guy at the door did. He laughed at the outfit he was wearing. Ned had forgotten to take off his new work clothes, and suddenly felt foreign and strange in his khakis and pressed, blue, button-down shirt. "I'm working undercover," Ned told him, and they both laughed.

Steve was sitting on his couch in his now-familiar white bathrobe and staring blankly at the TV. *SpongeBob* was on, but the sound was off. Steve didn't seem to be watching anyway, just staring. He looked awful. Big bags were under his eyes, his skin was a pale yellow, and his lips were dry and cracked. He looked gaunt, as though he had lost at least twenty pounds.

He brightened up a little when he saw Ned, but Ned had a feeling it was contrived—a form of bravado. "Hey, you old son of a whore," Steve said, smiling. "How's it going?"

"Great, and you?"

"Good, good," Steve nodded. "Got a great new product . . . yeah . . . it's Viagra—I get a guy in Thailand to make it for me; then he ships it over in bags of candy. All I have to do is hire some girl to pick the purple ones out. It really works too."

"Sounds great; what do you think of the new setup?"

"Well, I don't like sharing the town with the fuckin' Lawbreakers, but I guess I always kind of did anyway."

"Hey, we're all brothers now, right? At least they're not shooting at us anymore."

"Always the company man, Aiken," said Steve. "What's with the getup, anyway?"

"So Ivan didn't tell you?" Ned said. "I mean, he said he wouldn't, but I wasn't sure whether or not to believe him."

"Tell me what?"

"I'm not with you anymore."

"They call you up to Martinsville? Getting a chance in the bigs?"

"No, I'm running a new group out of Hamner."

"Hamner? From my bar?"

"Ivan says it's not your bar anymore."

"I guess it's yours?"

"Yeah."

Steve put on a brave face, but Ned could tell he was crestfallen. "That's cool. I never got out there anyway. Besides, my focus should be here in Springfield."

"Yeah." Ned didn't have the heart to tell him that under the new deal, he was now essentially Steve's boss. He figured that he'd find out soon enough.

"So if you're not with the Death Dealers—oh, sorry, Sons of Satan Springfield East—anymore, you're gonna have to give back all the stuff I gave you."

"Well, I haven't lived in the house for a while, and I never used the vehicles," Ned said. "Except the Harley. I rode it here. I can leave it if you can get me a ride back to Hamner."

"Sure, sure thing, ask one of the assholes outside."

"Thanks."

Steve grinned. "Why're you is such a hurry? Why don't we have a little fun for old time's sake?"

Ned instantly wondered what would happen if Steve were to die. Would Mehelnechuk give him Springfield? Would he be boss of the city, or at least half of it? There's no fuckin' way he'd hand over his own hometown to the former Lawbreakers. Would the man who killed Steve get punished or rewarded? What if they never found out who it was?

Steve could tell Ned was deep in thought, so he snapped

his fingers in front of his face. "Hate to wake you up there, buddy. You gotta stay out of the product," Steve said. "I thought you might want to have a little party with old Steve-O."

Ned just looked at him without speaking. He was alone in his thoughts and wondering what his old boss could tell from the look on his face.

"Yeah, yeah, I could call up Kelli—she goes by the name Courtnee now, workin' outta Heaven's Angels—I'm sure she'd be happy to see you," Steve said. "And I got plenty of Viagra, so we could go all day and all night."

Ned laughed. "That's okay, Steve. I'm pretty sure I don't need either of them." He said good-bye, turned, and left.

* * *

Clegg was sitting at his desk listening to Jimmy Lewis's theory about bikers. It differed from his own philosophy that bikers were basically guys who either couldn't or didn't want to participate in what most considered to be mainstream society. Lewis disagreed. He explained that he had been talking to Kaz, a psychoanalyst friend of his, who said that—aside from psychopaths and sociopaths—when people commit crimes, it was a form of self-sabotage. He explained it at length, but in essence, he believed that bikers and other criminals were people who wanted to get caught. They were people who deep down felt that they needed to be punished.

Clegg was just about to tell him what he thought of psychoanalysts when a uniform said someone wanted to see him. That it was important.

Neither he nor Lewis had to be told who Yolanda Kreig was. She and Scott were known throughout the region for their wealth, style and philanthropy. Since his murder, she had gone into semi-seclusion, but her face had been all over the newspapers and local television.

The two cops introduced themselves. Yolanda didn't waste any time. "I have some very valuable information about organized crime in Martinsville, Springfield, and other places," she told them. "But I will not share any of it, unless I am guaranteed full and unconditional immunity."

Clegg was stunned. When he finally summoned the wherewithal to answer, he said, "I can't make you any promises, but I think you can rest assured you'll be okay if you talk. We'll need the DA's office to sign off. Don't you want a lawyer? Shouldn't you be talking to the authorities in Martinsville?"

"My lawyer is a crook. I can make my own deals," she snorted. "And I don't trust the Martinsville police. I've seen my husband and his associates deal with them too many times—that's why I came here. The men I know, the gangsters, they hate you, Clegg. So you must be honest."

Clegg thanked her and asked Lewis to make her comfortable. Back at his desk, Clegg was halfway through dialing Hamilton's number when he hung up. Instead of Hamilton, he called his boss—District Attorney Maria Tsafaras. It was not the way things were normally done, but he couldn't risk losing another one like he had Carter. It would be harder for Hamilton to find a way to turn down a deal with Yolanda—after all, she wasn't a murderer or, from the look of her, an addict—but if his life or livelihood was in danger, he couldn't be trusted.

Clegg did not know Tsafaras well, but hoped she could help. He explained the situation and took a personal risk by telling her what he thought was going on with Hamilton. Reluctant at first, she eventually agreed to meet with him and Yolanda.

Yolanda was surprised when the cops asked her not to

speak. They wanted her to wait until Tsafaras arrived. Lewis asked Clegg if perhaps they were risking her changing her mind, but Clegg disagreed. He insisted that this was a big decision for her, that she had weighed all the options, and that there was no going back for her. Instead, he instructed Lewis to get her coffee and anything else she wanted. He sent a uniform out to get her a crossword puzzle and a pen.

Upon her arrival, Tsafaras—short, dark-haired, and dressed in a well-tailored suit—strode up to Clegg and said, "This had better be worth it."

"If you're talking about me," Yolanda said from where she was waiting, "it will be."

Inside the interrogation room, Yolanda sat behind the desk and waited politely until Clegg turned on the video camera. Over the next thirty minutes, Yolanda confessed to everything she knew about her husband's business (but avoided mentioning her uncle). She gave names, places, and dates.

After she was done, Tsafaras asked her if she had any documentation, if she had kept a diary, or had any other written record of what she described.

"I did have," she said. "I had all the papers—I was the bookkeeper—but they broke in and stole everything the night Scott was killed."

Tsafaras took Clegg out of the interrogation room. "I dunno," she said. "It'll be her word against theirs."

"It'll give us a chance to bring 'em all in," he countered. "One of them will slip up."

"And what if none of them do?" she said. "Then we look like idiots—hell, Bouchard's gotten off so many raps he looks like a god to these assholes. I'm not sure we can risk it at this point."

"Hang on." Clegg went back to his desk. He pulled out the papers he had gotten from Duncan. He walked into the interrogation room and motioned for Tsafaras to follow him. He turned the video camera back on. He handed them to Yolanda and asked her if she recognized them.

"Of course I do," she said, surprised. "These are my records."

"And what does 'Honey' here mean," Clegg asked, pointing at one of the listings.

"Oh, that's Vandersloot," she smiled. "I called him that because that's what he always called me."

"What about 'Dirty'?"

"That's Bouchard, he always struck me as a dirty fellow—and that's Rose, and that's O'Donnell."

"What about this big one here, the one named 'Buttercup?'"

"That's Ivan ... Ivan Mehelnechuk."

CHAPTER 17

Every cop involved had been waiting months for this. They planned for the confrontation with the bikers the way the Cold War military prepared for a nuclear attack. The Joint Task Force was made up of officers from thirteen different municipal police forces, along with state troopers, FBI, and ATF agents. Two officers from both the Royal Canadian Mounted Police and the Mexican Federales were invited to observe. They had been training and waiting for months. And it was Yolanda's confession and subsequent deal with Tsafaras that made it happen.

It started with a conference call. The FBI had put Clegg in charge of all the local cops, and he chaired the meeting. He assured them everything would go down as they had practiced, and that they had been faxed all the names and addresses of the men they were after and the charges against them.

Dubbed "Operation Clean Sweep," the raid involved more than six hundred officers arresting two hundred and twelve bikers and their associates. Images of police breaking down doors and leading bikers out of their houses, apartments, offices, clubhouses, and bars flooded regional TV screens. The suspects ranged from an eighty-two-year-old accountant who was roused from bed and allowed to attach his oxygen tank and nasal canula before performing the "perp walk" for TV cameras to a fifteen-year-old drug runner who was taken from her math class by plainclothes officers.

Most went easily. There were a few struggles, but no shots fired. Bouchard mugged for the cameras and told the throngs of reporters who watched him that he'd done nothing wrong and expected "to have this all cleared up in an hour or so."

There were no reporters at Mehelnechuk's. He surrendered wordlessly to the three officers assigned to him. The only sound he made was an affirmative grunt after they asked if he understood when he was read the Miranda warning, advising him of his rights.

***

Ned and Daniela woke up late. The hotel bed was just so comfortable, so welcoming that neither of them wanted to leave it. When they finally did start getting dressed for brunch, Ned's phone began to beep. He chose to ignore it.

"You should answer your phone," Daniela said. "It might be important."

"It's just a text, probably spam."

"Who is Spam?"

Ned chuckled. "Nobody," he said. "Look, we're having a great time here; why ruin it with business?"

"Because good business is how we can afford such good times," she said. "Answer your phone, or it will bother us both all week."

He sighed and told her: "I will, but if this isn't important, I'm shutting my phone off until we get back to the bar."

She smiled in agreement.

Ned looked at the text: "Mass arrests, evrybdy dwn, cps lkng 4 U, get outta dodge." It was from Stockton's phone.

"Get some clothes and some cash," he told Daniela soberly.

She started packing without asking why. She didn't need to be told what was going on; she knew her days at the bar were over.

Once packed, they took the stairs down to the first floor and outside. Ned took Daniela to a car rental franchise about a block away. Fearing the bright yellow SSR was too obvious, he rented a silver Toyota Corolla—"just for the day."

He parked Daniela and the car outside an ATM. Inside he got the maximum cash advance he could from all six of his credit cards. He left his gun and all the drugs he had had taken from the hotel room and the SSR and put them in the bank's garbage can.

Obeying all traffic signs and speed limits, he got the Corolla onto the Interstate as quickly as he could. He was just passing the North Beach city limits when a trooper went past him in the other direction. Ned looked into his mirror and saw the dark blue Crown Victoria U-turn behind him. The cop was clearly following him, but his lights and siren were off.

Ned noticed that the cop stayed about a hundred yards or so behind him, neither gaining nor losing ground, and that he changed lanes whenever Ned did. Taking a risk, Ned took the off-ramp to the next town. Not far from the highway, he spotted a McDonald's.

He parked as close to the door as he could. Daniela, who had been silent since Ned asked her to pack, asked him why they were stopping.

"Don't pretend you don't know what's going on," he said. "Look, they're after me, they don't even know who you are—get lost, enjoy your life."

Daniela sighed. Then she smiled. "Okay, I will run. That's

a smart idea. I will run to McDonald's and save myself. Good-bye, Ned."

She didn't budge. After a few moments, Ned said, "You're not moving."

"Of course I'm not moving. I was joking," Daniela shot back. "Where would I go? Since I have been very young, you are the only man I have met who has acted like a man; I'm stuck with you whether I like it or not—where else would I go?"

Ned sighed, and smiled. "Last chance," he said.

"Even if the cops don't get me, there is no life for me on this side," she said. "Let's go. I don't like McDonald's any-way—too greasy."

Ned shifted the Corolla into drive and got back onto the interstate. The trooper was still behind him. At the next on-ramp, he was joined by another trooper and, a few minutes later, two local cop cars. After they had all collected, the first trooper put his lights and siren on.

Ned knew what he had to do. He floored it. He was just a few miles away from Ondasheeken. If he could make it onto the reservation, the cops would stop chasing him. They couldn't go onto the reservation. Willie told him that. It was like another country.

And once he was on the reservation, Willie could sneak him into Canada. He could get him papers. Willie owed him $21,000. That and the cash he had should be more than enough to take care of things and set them up on the other side of the border.

Ned could see the cops gaining on him. The Corolla was no match for the V8-powered Crown Victorias the cops were driving. But he knew something they didn't. He knew where he was going. There was a little dirt road off the highway that led to Ondasheeken. Generations of moonshiners, rumrunners, and other gangsters had used it for decades. He slammed on the car's brakes and it slid to a ninety-degree angle where the road met the interstate. The first cop car sped right past him. The others slammed on their brakes and spun around the Corolla.

Ned stomped on the accelerator. He sped down the deeply rutted road, leaving a huge cloud of dust behind him until it hit a stone that had been exposed after a recent storm. The right front wheel of the Corolla leapt into the air and the car rolled over, sliding to a stop no more than a football field away from the reservation.

Ned's head hit the car's doorframe as it slid, but he managed to regain his senses and crawl through the shattered window. He could hear the cops screaming at him, telling him to stop or they would shoot. But he could see Willie's house. He got up and kept running until he was tackled from behind. Flat on his stomach, his face in the gravel, a cop's knee in his back, he was cuffed, then hauled to his feet.

CHAPTER 18

The first six hours were pretty easy. Ned called his lawyer three times, but didn't get anything but an answering machine. It was pretty obvious to him that the lawyer was busy with bigger fish. He regretted not taking Mehelnechuk's advice about getting his own lawyer instead of relying on Steve's.

But he was already on his third shift of interrogators and hadn't given up a thing. All three sets tried the same tack.

"What if we told you we knew you were a drug dealer?"

"I'd say you were wrong."

"How do you know Steve Schultz?"

"He was a friend of my aunt's boyfriend. I met him once."

"How long have you been a Death Dealer?"

"What's a Death Dealer?"

"What do you do for a living?"

"I run a bar."

"Why did you flee when the police attempted to apprehend you?"

"I was once assaulted by a police officer and have since developed trust issues."

Ned stuck by his plan: defer, delay, and deny. It was something Mehelnechuk had taught him, and it was working. He could see the frustration on the cops' faces and hear it in their voices. They had hundreds of guys to question, Ned figured. The dumb guys, the weak guys, the addicted guys—that's who'd crack. All he had to do was stay strong, keep it together, and he'd be fine.

They offered him coffee. He said no. Something about the idea of a stimulant made him nervous. Instead he drank water. They gave him a vending machine sandwich for dinner. He ate it and later wished he hadn't.

The latest set of cops—an angry and stupid bald guy named Mayer and a fat guy named Chung—gave him another round of questions. The questions were the same, but he could tell these guys were much less familiar with the goings-on of organized crime in the area than the previous set of cops. Mayer played the tough guy, and Chung pretended to be his friend. Half of the time, Ned had to work hard not to laugh. It was especially amusing when they came to the part about the deal.

All three sets of cops assured him that if he cooperated with their investigation, they would go easy on him. But they didn't have much. So far, he had only been charged with resisting arrest and traffic violations. Since he'd gotten off the meth rap, he wouldn't be looking at any serious jail time. So what did he have to lose? They assured him that they knew he was trafficking for the Sons through Buster's. They told him they had informants.

"How can someone tell on me when I have done nothing wrong?"

"Listen, smart guy," said Mayer. "You know that we know who you are, and what you do. Make it easy on yourself and cooperate."

"You don't understand; I am cooperating. Gee, officer, I'd love to help you catch the bad guys, but I just haven't seen any."

"Laugh now, funny man," said Mayer. "But you will slip up, or one of your so-called brothers will deliver us your ass to save themselves."

Ned didn't believe it. Anyone higher up the food chain couldn't make a deal by giving him up, and anyone lower than him didn't really have anything that could stick to him. Besides, he hadn't really done much the cops could get him for. He had overseen plenty of operations, but his name was nowhere, he'd never signed anything and had never dealt with anyone who wasn't just as guilty as he was. Even if they got him for trafficking, he'd be out in a couple of years. Besides, he'd have plenty of friends in prison. It wouldn't be ideal, but it wouldn't be hell on Earth either if it didn't last too long.

And it certainly beat the alternative. He'd seen what happened to informants. It didn't take long for Ned to decide he'd rather spend a few years behind bars than get a bullet in the back of his head. He actually snickered to himself when he realized the decision was a "no-brainer."

He asked to call his lawyer again. Voicemail. Ned was even more determined not to talk until he could have a lawyer present.

But they went on for another hour, trying to coax him into talking, the cops asking him the same old questions, hoping he'd crack. Ned giving the same old answers, barely awake, but still in control of what he was saying.

Frustrated, the cops gave up on him. The two of them stood Ned up and brought him to the uniforms who would take him back to his cell. Chung assured Ned that he would be there for him if anything changed.

On his way back to his cell, Ned looked at the other men that he'd been grouped with. They were all lowlifes, nobody important. Just a bunch of junkies and small-timers. It actually made him feel good. Although these guys were the most likely to want to cut a deal with the cops, they were also the least likely to have any decent information. If the cops had lumped him in with them, it really did mean they didn't have shit on him.

Ned smiled, yawned, and stretched. All he wanted now was to get back to his cell and get some sleep. As he passed by the next set of waste cases waiting to be interviewed, he thought about how desperate they must be—not just in fear for their freedom, but being held away from their addiction. You could easily get weed in prison if you're a somebody, but meth and coke—that's a different story. It was harder to find, cost a ton, and supplies were never guaranteed. And half the time, he'd heard, you were paying your last dollar for powdered baby formula or ground-up laxatives.

There'd be no Feeney inside to help these losers, so they were going to the toughest rehab in the world. Ned knew what addicts were like first hand. It wasn't just Leo. He'd seen them come and go. He'd seen dozens of guys who'd sell out their mother for just one more hit. And he knew any of these guys would sell his ass for just one more day out of jail.

It was at that moment that Ned was overcome with the shock of recognition. It was slight at first, and then adrenaline coursed coldly through his body like a drug. One of the losers sitting there was an old friend. He was barely recognizable— maybe forty pounds lighter, heavily lined, covered in scabs and balding—but it was him: Dario Gagliano. He had been Steve's right-hand man, but seemed to have fallen off the map. Ned had assumed he'd been killed or maimed in the war, or had been given an out-of-town assignment. Now here he was: rounded up like everyone else and waiting to be interviewed.

It was sad, really. Despite his brutishness, Dario had something about him that Ned genuinely liked. He remembered when he first met Dario, how he showed him the ropes, how he . . .

Ned swallowed, then said, "Hey, Dare."

Dario looked up at him. Little registered in his sunken, bloodshot eyes at first, but then he focused and his face softened into a broad, toothless grin. "Hey," was all he said.

Ned rubbed his face with his hand and got the cops' attention. "I gotta go back in there," he whispered. "There's something I forgot to say."

The cops led him back into the interrogation room. Mayer looked at him. "Whaddaya want?" he asked.

"I want to know what you'll do for me if I give them all up?"

CHAPTER 19

"Eric! Eric, you lazy fuck!"

Ned had dozed off. And when he woke up, it took a moment to register that he was actually Eric.

It was Neil, his boss and a total bastard. One of those short little overachievers Ned had grown to hate, Neil was bald before he was thirty and seemed to have a need to take out all his frustrations on the rest of the world. He had the perfect position for it—he was office manager for a credit records keeping company. That gave him plenty of low-level employees to boss around.

And one of them was Ned, whom Neil knew as Eric Steadman. It was all part of the witness relocation program deal Ned had made with the FBI. They gave him a new name, a new job, and a little house by the highway just outside a medium-size East Coast city about twelve hundred miles away from Springfield. The FBI owned the house, and he was required to pay rent. The deal was that he'd get a new identity and lifelong FBI protection in exchange for his testimony against the top dogs in the Sons of Satan on the condition that he admitted and acknowledged every crime he had committed up to that point. They also gave him ten thousand dollars to get him on his feet. If anything came out after that meeting, he would be liable to prosecution and could go to prison with the very men he had told on.

So he spilled. Even he was surprised at how many laws he had broken when he was done telling the story. The FBI agents were surprised when he admitted the murder and disposal of Tyler Heath's corpse, but it fell under the letter deal they had signed, so they had to excuse it.

And it was just in time too. As Ned had anticipated, Dario also told the authorities everything he knew. Because of their testimony and that of the other eight bikers who turned State's witness, Steve got thirty to life. Mehelnechuck, Bouchard, and Vandersloot got twenty-five years apiece. Rose was one of the many who got only two years, which many others interpreted as evidence of his cooperation with police either before or after the raids. Of the two hundred and twelve arrested, forty-one were released right away due to lack of evidence or irregularities with their arrests. Through plea bargains, another sixty-two were back on the streets within eighteen months.

Although the top of the Sons of Satan hierarchy had been cut off, the body remained alive as many of the systems Mehelnechuk had put in place didn't require all that much brain power or finesse to manage. There were lots of people out there who still wanted drugs, steroids, and prostitutes, and there wasn't really anyone else who could supply them in any real numbers. So the freed Sons of Satan reformed, recruited new members, and did their best to reclaim their territories.

Ned was trying to reclaim something too. He guessed that being the guy who pushed a little cart around in a giant office delivering mail to morose people who spent their days staring at numbers on computer screens and never acknowledged him was better than being in prison. It was certainly better, much better, than a bullet in the back of the head.

Ned usually ate lunch alone because most of the mailroom

guys didn't speak that much English. But one day—about three weeks after he started working at the credit records company—a couple of dark-haired guys from the loading dock came to sit with him. One on either side.

They introduced themselves as Bob and Chuck and talked about work. They were pleasant enough, and Ned noticed that their accents were kind of like Daniela's, but not exactly. He asked if they were from Moldova.

"Moldova?" asked Bob, the older one. "No. We are from Serbia."

"'Bob' and 'Chuck' from Serbia?"

"You could not pronounce our real names. It would hurt our ears if you tried."

"I know Serbia," replied Ned. "Didn't we bomb your asses for having death squads and all that?"

"Yeah, yeah. Clinton is too afraid to face us, so he bombs our women and children," said Bob. "And what for? We are only fighting Muslims who knock down your trade towers and Croats who are on Nazi side in World War II—America is stupid sometimes at recognizing who friends and enemies really are."

Ned laughed. "I guess you have a point there."

"We were hoping you could help us," said Chuck, the younger one. "We have business proposition."

"No thanks. I don't do that sort of thing," Ned replied.

"Of course you don't!" Bob smiled. "But we ask ourselves, why is this man named Eric doing a job too boring even for Mexicans?"

Ned laughed.

". . . and why does this Eric have Texas biker tattoo?"

Ned stopped laughing.

"It's okay, Eric," Bob said. "I have been in American prison.

I know what all tattoos mean—and you are, I think, a very bad man—or perhaps a good man who has done some bad things."

"Okay, okay, you got me," he said. "I did used to run with a bad crowd, but now I'm getting my life back together."

"And you mentioned Moldova," Bob continued, his eyes burrowing into Ned's. "That means you have handled strippers or whores."

Ned stayed quiet.

"Our assumption is that someone wants to kill you, and that you are not wanting to be seen, hoping they will not catch you," Bob said.

Ned figured out these guys were not hired by the Sons of Satan. If they were, he would have been dead. And he surmised they didn't know he was being protected by the FBI. Otherwise, they would not have given him so much information. So he nodded.

"It's okay; we can help you," Bob put his arm around him.

"Yeah?"

"We are looking for someone like you—white American with no accent—to work for us," he said. "Just have to take package every once in a while from here to friends in Detroit—we will even buy you a car."

Ned thought about it. He could probably get to Detroit and back in a weekend. He only had to report to his FBI contact once a month, and that was on a weekday. He smiled at Bob. "Sure."

ACKNOWLEDGMENTS

Biker isn't a typical novel. While it is a work of fiction, I didn't make very much of it up. There's very little in *Biker* that didn't actually happen at one time or another.

Much of it comes from the research I did for my first book, *Fallen Angel*. While collecting the material necessary for that book, I had some great stories that just didn't fit because they didn't fit with the primary theme of Walter Stadnick's rise to power, couldn't be substantiated in time, or put me at risk of libel.

And since *Fallen Angel* was published, I have met dozens of other people—including bikers, their friends, their girl-friends, cops, lawyers, and others—who have told me more and more about their world. So *Biker* is as much a collabora-tive effort as any non-fiction book I could write. And I'd like to thank all of my collaborators here.

My thanks has to start with John Wiley & Sons' Rob-ert Harris, who believed in this crazy hybrid idea right from the start and is ultimately responsible for its existence. And, of course, the great Don Loney, the only editor any author would ever want, deserves just as much thanks. I'm grateful to the fantastic team at HarperCollins Canada for their work on this edition. Thanks also go to my agent B.G. Dilworth. I must also mention Leta Potter here.

And I am grateful to the people who talked with me. Most of them would prefer not to be mentioned by name, but there's no way I can leave out the incredibly informative Sergeant John Harris of Hamilton Police Services.

And I have to thank my wife and children, whose patience and creativity made writing *Biker* not only possible but enjoyable.